# SHACKLED

A DARK BRATVA ENEMIES-TO-LOVERS ROMANCE

WICKED VOWS
BOOK 5

JANE HENRY

# SYNOPSIS

In the dark shadows of the Bratva Underworld, where my family reigns, there are no rules — only power.

My life is black and white. Every choice designed to protect my family and crush our enemies.

Trust is a luxury I can't afford.

Then *she* comes—Isabella Morales, disguised as a boy, burning with defiance and danger.

*Forbidden fruit,* the daughter of rival cartel, she holds secrets that could unravel everything I've fought for. Letting her live could be my demise.

*But now she's mine.*

When she tries to run, I catch her. I vow I'll punish her for what she's done and teach her there's no escape. But Isabella is no ordinary captive. Half crazed, fearless, and seductive, the line between captor and captive quickly blurs.

In a world where loyalty is bought with blood and fear, Isabella is the one weakness I can't afford. But as our enemies close in, we're forced to navigate the deadly game of power and deceit.

I'll bind her to *me* and make her mine in a battle where surrender is the ultimate sin.

# CHAPTER ONE



I GRIN into the chilly autumn night, nearly skipping with glee.

This disguise is *so fucking awesome*. Literally, no one would ever suspect who I really am.

This was no last-minute disguise. Hell, I've been practicing wearing this all day.

First, the fake mustache because even the best disguise won't fully cover my Latina roots. Colombian men wear their beards like a badge of honor, their "five o'clock shadows" creeping in by noon. I have to blend in seamlessly. With a swift, practiced hand, I applied foundation to rough up my complexion. I'm aiming for *rugged* and *badass*. Contour sharpened my jawline and an eyebrow pencil added the perfect amount of stubble.

I refuse to cut my hair, so that was a tiny bit of a challenge.

It's slicked back and wound around my head, tucked under a black cap. Bulky, but no one will be paying attention.

I needed a masculine silhouette, so I had to wear a chest binder to flatten my breasts, thanks to my mama's generous genes. At least she gave me *something*. The clothing was kind of fun—a dark hoodie that conceals my figure and baggy pants with multiple pockets to give me some heft and a rugged appearance, paired with combat boots. I needed something masculine and practical for moving silently and blending in.

To mimic male body language, I adopted a slouched posture and broader stance, my walk more deliberate and heavy footed. Even if they saw me, they'd never suspect who I really am. Sadly, I have to mask the sexy hip sway. I have to do this consciously, since it's part of my whole persona to attract the eye and attention of any man within a fifty-yard radius. A girl must use every gift she's got.

This is only temporary, though. And fucking *necessary*.

And when I was ready to go, I took myself into The Cove— the prowling ground of our enemies—just to test it all out.

Not gonna lie, I had a damn good time for myself. I spoke in a deeper voice when I needed to—ordered coffee and asked for directions just to make sure I passed the test.

Not only did no one give me so much as a strange look, I caught a few girls making eyes at me.

*"Hola, beautiful," I said in my guy voice to a slender blonde near Starbucks. She blushed but didn't respond, then whispered to her friend behind me, who I winked at. Heh.*

Truth is, I wouldn't want to be a man for all the money in the world. I fucking love being a woman. But damn, it was fun to play for a little while.

And now, I'm ready. Now, it's go time.

I steel myself and clench my jaw. Now I take the next step.

If the Romanovs see me now, I'm still fucked, but at least they won't suspect who I really am. I'll get away—I always do—and *they'll* be none the wiser.

I intercepted communication between Aleksandr Romanov, one of the high-ranking officials in the Romanov Bratva, and his wife, Harper. They have small children and long, sleepless nights, so I figured eventually they'd get sloppy, and I wasn't wrong.

I mean, anyone else might've totally missed the little tip-off, but when Aleksandr told his wife *got another late night*, and she responded, *please be careful, it's so dark there, and I don't trust you're safe*, I knew exactly where they were going.

*Who's going?* she asked.

My heart took a giant leap at his response: *All of us.*

It's rare that *all* of the Romanov men are together.

Some of their wives work for them—I have it on good authority that Viktor's new wife Lydia actually *set fire to her ex*. Nevertheless, the Romanovs are still in the Dark Ages. They'd deny it. Hell, their wives draw a salary, but I'm not impressed. Show me a Bratva group with a woman in actual fucking *power. Authority. Leadership.*

Now *that* would impress me.

The snap of a branch several yards to my left makes me freeze in my tracks. I stand as still as a hunted deer, listening. The Romanovs won't be here for several hours yet, but it's essential I'm not seen.

I wait, holding my breath. Listening. Is someone else here, or is it just an animal?

Another beat passes. Another.

Nothing.

I move on. I know exactly where to go: The abandoned warehouse, deeply hidden past a hiking trail in The Cove, is heavily secured with video surveillance. If the Romanovs see me on any security camera, they'll just see a random dude going for a hike off-trail.

They might wonder how their security footage was destroyed, but by then, I'll have everything I need.

The darkness and silence amplify every sound, making me hyper-aware of my surroundings. I only have about another mile to hike before I get to the entrance, but the night is young. I couldn't risk driving anywhere near here for fear of being seen.

"Who's there?" The deep male voice booms in the quiet woods. My heart stops for a split second.

*Fuck.*

I stand still and pull my hoodie over my head, sidestepping so I'm hidden behind a huge tree trunk. My heart beats faster. Did they send people here ahead of time? They have never brought guards to the warehouse before.

Maybe they're getting wary.

My breathing's shallow as footsteps approach. Thankfully, my vision is excellent, even with the hoodie pulled tight. My hand tightens around my knife as I zoom in on my target. I don't need to *kill* any of their guards. Not yet, anyway. I just need to incapacitate and possibly maim.

He comes within ten yards but scans around and shakes his head. Is he alone? I take out the tiny pair of night vision goggles I brought and peek through them. Must be a new recruit. He looks young and scared enough to shit his pants.

Ah, Romanovs, why did you make it this easy for me? I thought we'd be a good match.

He turns away from me and heads back to the warehouse. *Green light.*

The back of the warehouse is camera-free, with no entrances. But for me, I welcome the challenge. It's perfect.

I scale the side of the building using a rusty drainpipe and ledges. My fingers grip tightly, my body tense with the possibility of being seen. I'm in the zone when I'm climbing, mentally placing my feet and hands into positions I can't see.

A thrill races through me when I reach the topmost window, partially opened on the second floor, the hinges rusted. It's far away from the main patrol paths or any surveillance equipment. Since they use this place rarely, they haven't really secured it as heavily as their residences. I never would've dreamed of trying to infiltrate one of their private homes.

I carefully pry the window open and slide inside just as the beam of a flashlight illuminates the leaf-covered ground below. My heart leaps into my throat. I crouch down, peering from the edge of the window as the useless guard walks past, leans against the wall, and pulls out his phone.

When *I* get into a place of leadership in this family—and I fucking *will*—I'm going to fire that lazy son of a bitch. When my breathing slows and he's gone, it's time.

The door to this vacant room is locked. Good. Thought this would be boring. I'd be disappointed if I couldn't pick any locks today. With practiced ease, I do my magic and pick the lock in less than a minute.

Tsk, tsk. Really, boys, a bit of a challenge would be nice.

I move quietly down the dim hallway, testing every footfall for creaky floorboards. I ease myself into shadows in case someone came in here unseen until I find a shadowy loft area right above the main floor. I quickly climb the ladder. It's a perfect vantage point to observe them without being seen.

I mean, I could've done something a bit safer, I guess. Planted a bug, maybe. But Jesus, what's the fun in that? This is late night, the entire surrounding cast in shadows illuminated only by moonlight—it's eerie, tense, and danger-ous. My favorite.

I settle into my hiding spot. I've got a few hours before they arrive, but my heart still hammers in my chest. I've waited *so long* for this. The entire trajectory of my life is at stake.

I lean back against the wall. It smells a bit musty in here, with the lingering scent of motor oil and metal. It reminds me of hard work and manual labor. No one would ever suspect what they really do in a place like this. Only me, maybe. It wouldn't take much imagination for me to figure out exactly what sort of double-crossing, traitorous losers and enemies they bring here to torture and interrogate. I would know. Torture was my father's speciality and is still my brother's favorite sport.

I close my eyes and think ahead, beyond where I am. They say visualization is the key to leaning into a goal, for really making shit happen. If that's true, I have got it *made* since I can already imagine what it feels like to give orders, to snap my fingers and watch grown men cow to me. I can already hear the respect in their voices and feel the surge of power coursing through my veins when they call me their queen.

I'm pulled out of my reverie when I remember my father's cold, disapproving eyes. He would kill me for what I'm about to do.

Literally.

It's half the damn reason I'm here. I frown at my hands and pick at a recalcitrant cuticle. I trimmed my nails and removed the blood-red polish for my disguise.

*"Si pudieras verme ahora, padre."*

*If you could see me now.*

To my father, women were a means to an end. A lower class of citizens, useless in his quest for domination, save their ability to provide offspring. I knew from a very young age I was viewed as less than because of my status as *female*. My brother Javier, on the other hand, was much more highly valued.

I shake it off and focus on the task at hand.

I take mental notes and go over my plan again.

I went to Viktor and tipped him off. My brother would beat the living shit out of me before he murdered me with his own hands, but if he ever finds out, it will be too late for him. If my plan goes well, anyway.

That's one of several reasons he needs to go. I'll see to that.

They're all coming—Mikhail, the eldest and one of the most dangerous. He took over when his father died and now rules the entirety of The Cove, the area between Coney Island and Manhattan. Next in command is Aleksandr, the computer geek, followed by Nikko, the group assassin. He's got the eye of a sniper and a perfect shot, but I won't give him a target.

Viktor will be here, too. The largest one of all, heavily covered in tattoos and scars, Viktor is the group heavy—their loyal pit bull in human form. Ollie, the silent, quiet one who works for international relations, is home from Moscow, thanks to me. He pulled a stint in Colombia, my sources say, and I have it on good authority that son of a bitch is a lot more fucked up than he lets on.

The youngest brother, Lev, will be here, too, but I don't worry about him. According to my intel, he's practically a kid. Javier has it out for Lev, but I'm not entirely sure why, and I'm not sure it matters. Javier hates everyone he sees as a personal threat.

I take out my goggles again and scan below. There's a table with detailed maps and documents. Huh. Interesting. I'd like to take a closer look at those but don't dare risk moving out of my hiding spot.

I stifle a scream when an ear-piercing screech cuts through the night. I hold myself as steady as possible. Human?

No... no. A bobcat, I'd guess, or whatever the hell wild predators they have here. When my breathing steadies again, I go back over what I know of the Romanovs.

The most challenging part of all this is that the Romanovs are so damn loyal. Any one of those brothers would lay down their lives for the others, including their wives, children, sister, and mother. It makes it nearly impossible to plot against a family so dedicated to each other. There's no weak link to exploit.

My family? Ha. Luckily for me, we're power-hungry animals eager to kill for a meaty bone. It's only a matter of knowing whose hunger to stoke and stepping out of the way for the kill... *and* making sure you don't end up the one devoured.

I didn't learn my skills for nothing, though.

I lean back in the loft, hidden in the shadows. The rain beats down harder on the tin roof, the relentless sound drowning out anything I'd hear going on outside. It doesn't matter. They'll show. I close my eyes, just for a little rest. I can't risk falling asleep and someone finding out I'm here, but it feels good to take a bit of a breather.

I wrap the oversized hoodie tighter around myself. It's fucking ice-cold in here. The chill in the air and the drumming rain lull me and I must fight to keep my eyes open. It was a long day, and the night is just beginning.

My focus wavers when a memory surfaces unbidden.

I'm a child, only ten years old, standing in front of my father in his study. I'm swallowing back tears because of what I've seen and heard: another fight between my father and mother. He won. He always won, and even then, I knew it was only because he was stronger and more powerful.

I made a vow then—that would *never* be me. I would never let a man walk all over me, no matter how much money he had, no matter how powerful he was, no matter what he tried to hold against me.

"No crying," my father snapped, his black eyes merciless and unblinking. He scowled at me as he sat back in his chair, his arms folded across his chest. *"Las emociones son para los débiles, Isabella. Serán tu perdición si las dejas."*

*Emotions are for the weak, Isabella. They will be your downfall if you allow them.*

I felt a chill at his words even as I made a solemn vow to rebel against him. One of the first steps toward adulthood is realizing that adults aren't always right. It wasn't true. Emotions are not for the weak.

*Cowardice* is for the weak.

Emotions are human.

My resolve hardens.

*I am not my father, and he has no power over me anymore.*

I set my jaw and reaffirm why I'm here: I will not let my father's legacy of hatred and cold detachment define me or the people of Colombia.

I will use my skills to safeguard the people whom I love, and

I will serve my brother the justice he deserves. I will protect the throne and my family's legacy.

But first... the Romanovs.

I sit up straighter when the sound of heavy footsteps approach. I catch my breath at the sound of deep male voices. I grin to myself in the dark.

Below me, the door creaks open.

# CHAPTER TWO

*Lev*

"WHO ELSE IS HERE TONIGHT?" Ollie walks beside me, our steps muted on the damp forest floor. A light rain punctuates the cold autumn night, the drops spattering on Ollie's leather jacket as we approach the entrance to our abandoned warehouse. Nestled deep in the woods, far from any main highway, this location ensures the privacy and discretion we need. In the distance, the faint scent of smoke mingles with the damp moss, hinting at a campfire.

"Everyone," I reply, my voice low but firm. Ollie's brows shoot up silently, acknowledging the gravity of the situation. It's rare for all of us to gather like this. Viktor received a disturbing message recently, and when he relayed it to Mikhail, our *pakhan*, the alarm was sounded. We were all summoned back to The Cove.

A crackling sound to my left catches my attention. I swivel sharply, my eyes scanning the dimly lit surroundings. "Just an animal," Ollie mutters. To anyone else, that might not be reassuring, but I'd rather face a black bear or a poisonous snake than one of our enemies.

No one knows about this hideout, and we intend to keep it that way. Years ago, this warehouse was used ostensibly for repairing heavy machinery and industrial equipment, a plausible cover for its remote location and the noise it generated. Its real purpose was far more clandestine: a covert arms manufacturing and assembly plant. After my father's death, we acquired it through a friend of a friend. A gift, he said.

As we approach the entrance, I spot Aleksandr's large black truck, nearly hidden in the shadows. Now I know how everyone else arrived. Aleks, our second-in-command and tech genius, and his wife share a home in The Cove. The young guard Aleks hired stands sentry by the main door. I nod to him, and he returns the gesture. If anything were amiss, we'd know by now.

Ollie steps aside, allowing me to access the security panel. I slide my thumb along the identification screen, casting one last glance over my shoulder as Ollie does the same. It's instinctual by now, ensuring we weren't followed. The screen flashes green, and the door unlocks. I push it open, bracing myself for what lies ahead.

"Stay sharp," I whisper to Ollie. "We don't know what's waiting for us inside." Could be just my brothers. Could be someone they brought, or several someones. We can't afford to let our guards down.

Inside, the warehouse is dimly lit, shadows stretching across the concrete floor. The familiar scent of oil and metal hangs in the air, a reminder of its original purpose. We move quietly, every step calculated. This is our domain, but I never let my guard down.

Aleks is already here, hunched over a table covered with maps and documents. He looks up as we enter, his sharp eyes flickering with recognition and concern.

"Mikhail's waiting," he says, his voice a low rumble. "We need to move quickly."

I nod, my mind racing. The message Viktor received was cryptic but alarming. Something big is coming, and we need to be ready.

"Lev. Ollie." My brothers nod their greetings, one at a time. We nod back but don't have time to fuck around.

"Let's get to work," I say, taking my place at the table. My brothers gather closer, each of us falling into our roles seamlessly. Mikhail, the leader, big brother to all. Aleksandr, second in command and fiercely protective, he monitors any cyber threat against our family. Viktor, our family bodyguard, Nikko our personal assassin.

This is our family, our legacy. I'll do whatever it takes to protect it.

Under the dim overhead lighting, my oldest brother Mikhail's golden-brown hair nearly covers his eyes, his tanned skin showcasing ink that marks him as Bratva. I feared him as a kid, and for good reason, but now that we're all grown, it's different. Still, Mikhail will be our leader for life.

"Someone paid Viktor a visit," Mikhail says.

"Right."

Mikhail jerks his head toward Viktor, who tugs one of the folding chairs over and sits down. It sags under his weight. Beside him, our older brother Nikko jerks his chin in greeting and folds his massive arms across his chest. Nikko was the one who taught me and Ollie how to shoot. He's an excellent teacher and an even better marksman. But in matters of strategy, he prefers to take a backseat and observe.

Viktor scowls. "Lydia and I had a visit from none other than Isabella Morales."

I nod. The Los Sangre Dorada Cartel, or LSD, is one of the most-feared cartels in all the Americas. A visit from Isabella is not good news, though it would be fucking disastrous if her brother Javier paid us a visit. Especially for me.

"And?"

"She said our enemies are closer than we think. Said we need to pull everyone in, close to home."

Ollie scowls. "And this is why you had me come home from Moscow?"

Mikhail nods. "We wanted to check the veracity of her statement before we made any assumptions or moves."

Ollie watches everyone thoughtfully but doesn't speak.

"Closer than we think," I repeat. "Does she mean a mole?"

"Possibly, yes, or she could mean her brother is planning an attack," Aleks says thoughtfully.

"Oh, she said that, too." Viktor scowls. "And she said when he does attack, it will be swift and merciless."

"Now *that* I believe," Mikhail says, leaning back in his chair, his eyes dark but thoughtful. "Javier Morales knows exactly what he is doing. There's a reason we don't fuck around with any of them, even though an alliance would serve us well."

My mind whirs, adrenaline sharpening my thoughts as I try to slide details into place like a jigsaw puzzle. "Javier Morales is stationed in Colombia. Has he been sighted anywhere near here?"

Aleks, the tallest and arguably most imposing figure in the room standing over all of us. shakes his head. "No. As soon as Viktor alerted me, I zoned in on the surveillance we have in Colombia and found Morales still there."

I nod. Of course he doesn't have to be the one who attacked us. He could command an attack or call a hit anytime. The momentary relief from his intel doesn't last. The danger Morales represents is ever-present. His reach extends far beyond physical proximity.

"Then someone else is playing this game for him. Someone close. Someone who can act on his behalf."

Mikhail's gaze sharpens and he nods slowly, a dangerous glint in his eyes. "Yeah. We need to find out who and fast."

The room is silent for a beat, the weight of the situation pressing down on all of us. Aleks breaks the silence, his tone determined. "I'll increase surveillance and see if we can trace any unusual activity. If Morales has an agent here, we'll find them."

"Isabella came to my fucking *home*," Viktor snaps.

I frown. "How did she get in?"

Ollie shakes his head. "It's what she's known for, brother. Word on the street is that the woman is made of vapor and smoke. One moment, she's there, and the next, she's gone. She can pick any lock, escape any prison or shackle."

She'll be small, then, most likely. Lithe. Nimble.

Jesus, I'd fucking love to put her to the test. See what she's *really* capable of.

"Do we have any leads?"

Silence. Aleks shakes his head.

"And where's Kolya?"

Mikhail shifts, scowling, before he answers. "He's still in Moscow. His flight was canceled, and I thought it best not to push answers on this right now with him."

Viktor tips his head to the side curiously. "What does that mean? What the hell?" The icy tone of his voice makes the rest of us go still. We're brothers, but no one talks shit in front of Mikhail without repercussions.

Mikhail holds Viktor's gaze as Viktor's hands clench into fists. Though all of us are loyal to Kolya, Kolya took Viktor under his wing like the son he never had, even though he's only about twelve years older than him. Our father couldn't bully Viktor like the rest of us because of the sheer size of the guy, so he passed Viktor off to Kolya to train under the premise of Viktor being "too willful." We all knew the truth, though.

Kolya was a brother figure to Viktor, even more so than to the rest of us. Still is.

"It means that we keep as much as we can to ourselves," Mikhail snaps, his gaze on Viktor, challenging him to defy him.

Viktor gets to his feet. "Bullshit. It means you don't trust your fucking *mentor*."

Both brothers are on their feet now, their toes touching. Viktor's eyes are narrowed, and Mikhail's hands are clenched into fists. There's no telling who would win in an actual fight—Viktor is stronger than the rest of us combined and would absolutely wipe the floor in a fistfight, but Mikhail's the *pakhan,* and if Viktor raises a hand to him, he'll lose that hand.

So yeah, this is *not* gonna happen.

I push myself between the two of them and slap a hand on the chest of each of them. "We start fighting amongst ourselves, and *everyone* bests us."

They both glare at me, but I'm not a kid anymore, and they might be older, but I'm their equal.

I shake my head. "What the fuck are you going to accomplish with a pissing match? Mikhail kept this intel inner circle, so I'm assuming there's information he doesn't want to get out. It's not a slight to Kolya, and we're wasting precious time."

Only the leadership is here, none of our subsidiaries or captains.

"That's right," Mikhail says. "And anything we unearth of importance, we'll tell everyone immediately. So sit *down,* brother."

There's got to be another reason he chose this place and the inner circle, but I'll wait to find out. We all will.

Viktor's jaw clenches, but he finally sits down. The chair bends and creaks this time.

"Refresh my memory," Aleks says, clearing his throat. "The primary method the LSD uses for earning their money?"

"Drugs," Ollie supplies. As our primary director of international relations, he knows the ins and outs of our rivals better than anyone. "They're pushing heroine hard. LSD is spreading like a damn virus."

"They've grown, haven't they?" I ask.

"Yeah," Aleks confirms, his fingers sliding across his tablet. "After those busts last year, they're trying to solidify their power. The Cove's a prime target."

They're known as a ruthless organization originating in Colombia, but with factions now spread throughout the Americas. They're mostly known for their extensive drug trafficking, particularly cocaine and heroin.

"Oh, right," I say. "They were the ones extradited for those high-profile drug busts last year, weren't they?"

"Yep. And word on the street is that they've expanded their influence into New York. Targeting The Cove because of our location and connections."

I nod. "Not to mention our affiliation with various groups." Due to several recent nuptials with my brothers, we've become close contacts with several other underground powerhouses but still have no contacts south of the border.

"Exactly."

I stroke my chin and think this over. Aleks goes back to his tablet, and his fingers fly over the keys.

"The cartel is led by Javier Morales Junior, son of the late Javier Morales. Javier is infamous for his ability to evade law enforcement while keeping a steel grip on his operations," Aleks mutters, shaking his head.

I nod, continuing to snap puzzle pieces into place. "They're not just known for drug trafficking, are they? And they have a mole in law enforcement here in The Cove."

Aleks nods. "Money laundering, arms smuggling, and human trafficking. Their presence here in America taints everything. We need them fucking exiled from The Cove."

Still, none of what we've learned here we couldn't discuss in our headquarters in The Cove. Interesting. There's more.

"But to really evict them, we must know their next move. What's our in with them?"

Aleks nods. "We've had one of our new recruits in their ranks for the past three months. Isabella's warning came on the heels of his intel."

Ah. There we go. This is why we're here.

I'd bet money on Dmitri. Dmitri Petrov joined our ranks after the death of our enemy several years ago and after passing numerous tests to prove his allegiance to us. He'd rather die than betray us.

"Jesus," I mutter, shaking my head. "If they discover he's one of us…"

"Yeah, he's capital-F fucked," Aleks supplies. "He said it was a risk he was willing to take to prove his loyalty. Right now, he's managed to convince the sister of Carlos Cabrera that he loves her."

Ollie speaks up. "Carlos Cabrera is the cartel's chief enforcer, right-hand man to Morales. Our buddy has used Carlos's sister to get intel we otherwise wouldn't have."

"Such as?"

"Such as the locations of their safe houses here in America, the schedules of their shipments, contacts of their supplier, and even the name of one of the corrupt officials on their payroll."

"Shit. He's playing a lethal game, but that's invaluable information." I nod.

"Yeah. We've already managed to intercept two major drug shipments because of information he's gleaned for us. We've let a few slide, even local ones, because we obviously don't want them knowing we're onto them."

"Fuck."

Aleks suddenly goes so still that I want to check to see if he's still breathing. It's like someone's just pressed the pause button on our conversation. He turns toward me and takes out his phone. I watch with interest.

My phone buzzes.

> We have a visitor.

There's a reason he's texted me first and not the group chat. Viktor would already be prowling, ready to smash skulls, and Nikko's weapon would be drawn. He knows I'm slower to react and more methodical in my approach.

A chill skates down my spine, and I immediately sit up straighter. Have they found us so soon? Have they tracked us here? We're not ready.

I keep my shit together.

Oh?

Biometric feedback in the loft. Someone's here.

Aleksandr takes safety so seriously, he always has biometric readings on all of us. Apparently, he has the scanner on his iPad as well.

"Lev." My gaze snaps to Mikhail when he calls my name.

I nod.

"Put your damn phone down and pay attention." I blink at him slowly and look at my phone, then back up at him. Understanding dawns on him as Nikko and Viktor talk quietly to each other.

Aleks to group chat: No one moves. Do not respond. Someone's watching from the loft. Let Lev handle it. He's the fastest and most lethal in tight situations. Lev?

A strategy snaps into place, the strategy laid out in front of me. We have to move.

Viktor, keep talking. Say some bullshit about Lydia and her family or the wedding or something. Mikhail, pretend you have to take a call. Nikko, go to a secure place where you can draw your weapon out of view of the loft and as soon as Ollie and I approach, spot me. Ollie, you and I will go. What do we have for weapons here?

Mikhail: got a gun and blade

Aleks: same

Nikko: carrying two fully loaded guns but fucking arsenal in the car

Aleks: you brought your shit in my CAR?

Mikhail: drop it, stay focused

Ollie: smoke bomb in my jacket pocket, could come in handy since it's a loft. Gun.

Viktor: my fucking fists

At least one of you standby with Nikko, Ollie, get ready with the smoke bomb and for Christ's sake tell me later why you have that shit with you

Ollie: club last night. Let's go

Ollie might look like a nice guy but he's one kinky mother-fucker. I don't even want to know what else he's got with him.

Viktor starts talking some nonsense about gardening and Lydia and fireworks and shit. Mikhail excuses himself to take out his phone and makes a fake call.

"I'm going to use the restroom," I tell them. "I'll be right back."

I walk in the direction of the loft to gauge the location. Is it near a window? How high is it? Is there a way for us to get the ladder away from the loft easily? I walk by it and quickly note everything—tucked away from any windows, it's at least ten feet off the floor, and the ladder looks nailed in place. In this case, that is not good.

I walk into the bathroom and pretend to use it, quickly coming back into the room where my brothers are located. None of them even look at me, but my phone quickly vibrates with another text.

Mikhail: Plan?

I have to admit I fucking love that he's actually deferring to me with this. My father is turning over in his grave. *Imagine that, you asshole, the one you hated most, actually knows his shit.*

We have two options given that it's a loft with only one way up. Either one of us goes up and forcibly drags him down, or we demand he comes down of his own accord. There's no way for us to get there unannounced and there's no other way to get to him.

Viktor: Bring him down. Drag him down here and let me show him how we deal with a traitor.

I shake my head and reply.

My preference would be to demand he come down on his own. Anyone who went up after him would be at a disadvantage. Death wish. Ladder's secure, no easy way to shake him loose. If he won't comply, we smoke him out, force him to crawl down. Once he's here... we make sure he regrets trespassing.

Nikko: Ready.

Mikhail: Let's go

Aleks: On it

Ollie: I'll spot you

I lift my head and stare at the darkness above the loft ladder. I feel kind of dumb because it looks like I'm glaring into blank space, but I trust Aleks. If he says someone's there, then someone's there.

I nod to my brothers and face the loft.

# CHAPTER THREE

_Isabella_

SHIT.

_Shit._

Something's shifted in here. The chatter's died down, and one of them is heading over here. Lev?

I move as quietly away from the ladder as I can. I can't risk peeking down below, not now. Even as I consider my choices, something inside me thrills at the thought of being caught by a passel of pissed-off, heavily tattooed, dominant Bratva. It's the thrill of the chase, the hit of adrenaline when I put my foot on the gas pedal and watch my speed creep up into three digits. The utter certainty of excitement.

I slide my phone off in case that's how they detected me. As soon as I heard we had a mole in our group, I went to alert Carlos's sister. I don't give a shit if the men know, but she's my friend, and I don't want her falling for a liar. God, how could she? I can't risk sending a text, though, not now, when my message could be intercepted.

I quickly assess my situation.

I'm the one in the loft, which gives me an advantage. I can pretend I'm not here and force them to come get me, obviously, and when they do, I take them down one at a time. All it would take is a swift kick to the neck or head if they come anywhere near me.

I'd have to incapacitate them, though, and the worst part of it is, if I hurt them and don't kill them, it's like wounding a rabid animal. They'd come after me with a thirst for blood. And if I *do* kill any of them, as soon as they find out who I am, they'll bring war to my family.

That may be an inevitability, but I'd like to time it just right.

A deep, authoritative, decidedly angry voice snaps below. "We know you're up there. Show yourself."

*Fuck.*

At least my instincts were right.

I flatten myself and peek down below as quietly as I can. Which one is it? I have a better chance with some of them than others. If I get anywhere near Nikko or Viktor, I'll jump out a window.

I concentrate. That isn't Viktor's voice, though, so I look again. I do a double take. Is that... Lev?

Based on my research, Lev Romanov was young, still a teen, but I obviously missed some crucial points. Lev is most decidedly *not* a child, neither in age nor stature. Though he isn't the size of a small elephant like Viktor, he's not *small*. Tall and muscular, he prowls like a lithe tiger, ready to pounce, and there's a coldness to his gaze and countenance that sends a shiver down my spine.

What do these guys *eat?*

He has a commanding presence and sharp, ice-blue eyes that appear cold and calculating. His short, dark hair has a hint of a curl. Wearing a form-fitting black tee, his carved chest and biceps are on display, and his stance suggests he's ready to pounce into a fighting ring.

In other words, I've got my work cut out for me.

*¡Mierda!*

What if I don't show myself? What then?

"You heard something you shouldn't have, and we know it. This doesn't have to end badly for you, but it could." Goddamn liar. I'm not that dumb.

I don't respond. "You have five seconds before I'm coming up. One."

There's no fucking way he's telling the truth. You do not eavesdrop on the Romanov brothers and live to tell about it. I wonder how he'd define "badly."

I look around as if I might've missed an escape route earlier, and looking again might make one magically appear.

"Two."

I close my eyes and grit my teeth. I am not coming, and if they want to come and try me, I'm going to—

Something hits the floor at my feet, and the air in front of me is instantly filled with burning, acrid smoke. I fall to the ground a few seconds too late before ingesting a toxic gulp of the fumes.

I sputter and cough.

*Remember, you're a man. Do not give yourself away.*

Jesus. Who the fuck carries smoke bombs with them?

I'm on all fours, trying to crawl away from here and toward the loft ladder, but I've lost my bearings. My knees ache on the cold, hard floor, and when I crawl forward, I stifle a yelp when a splinter shoots into my palm. I'm wheezing, the air in my lungs painful. I'd do anything for cool, fresh air.

I reach blindly for the ladder and force myself to remember to stay strong, to remember that I can't cave now. I'm a fighter, and just because I'm outnumbered by a bunch of boys means shit. I'll let them take me into custody, and then, at the very first opportunity—I'll escape.

I always do.

*Always.*

Strong hands grip my wrist mercilessly. I stifle a yelp. I can't sound like a woman or act like one in any way.

"Let me go," I growl in the deepest register I can muster. "I'll surrender." I'm seized with a fit of coughing.

When he doesn't let me go, I wrench my wrists away, trying to get free, but I'm dragged toward the ladder. The splinter in my palm aches, and tears from the smoke stream down my face. I turn away so they don't see me. I throw myself bodily down, freeing myself, and *shove.*

"*Jesus.*" I see the silhouette of whoever it is fall a few steps but grab onto the bar and hold on tight. He swings his legs back on and starts climbing toward me again.

I can hardly see from the burning smoke, but I take a quick moment to rear back and kick at him. My kick is off the mark, missing by a mile. *Jesus.* I'm normally so much better than this.

He yanks my arms and pulls me toward the ladder. I throw my body weight at him. He struggles, wobbling, but uses my body weight as leverage. The smoke has compromised me. It's clumsy, fighting with everything I've got, but then I can't see a damn thing and can hardly breathe.

I writhe and scream, and when a hand comes into view, I bend and sink my teeth into flesh. He curses and bellows but doesn't let go.

With a firm arm on me, he pulls me toward him and onto the loft ladder. He shouts below to his brothers. "He's small and fighting like a motherfucker. I'm throwing him down. It'll take forever to wrestle him down this ladder. *Catch.*"

I stifle a scream when the men quickly form a human net with their arms. I claw at Lev and manage to gain an inch or two but don't scream for fear of giving myself away. With a grunt, he tugs me toward the edge of the loft again. We wobble. He's standing on a ladder, for God's sake, the chances of both of us falling—

He yanks me and throws me bodily. I go hurtling into the air. I nearly bite my tongue in two to prevent me from screaming myself hoarse. I close my eyes and fall into a pile of arms that only slightly sways with the heft and impact of my fallen weight.

My heart is beating so fast I can't breathe.

*This is the worst possible scenario.*

I've seen Viktor beat people beyond recognition. I've seen footage of Nikko shooting from an impossible distance, and that man never fucking misses.

I have video evidence of Aleksandr strangling a man who threatened his wife with his bare hands, his face completely devoid of any human emotion as the life drained from his victim. Mikhail once tore through a rival's hideout with nothing but a handgun, decimating everyone in his wake, leaving behind a trail of blood and earning him the nickname *The Siberian Tiger*.

And Viktor—good God, they call the man the Iron Fist for a reason.

But Lev... Lev is different. By no means is he kinder or gentler. I can tell just by the first look into his eyes that he commands respect like the rest of them do and will lay down his life out of loyalty. I mean, I hope it doesn't come to that, but let's not lie. He seems calculating, though. He's observing before he reacts.

I see a brief flare of surprise before Viktor grabs both of my arms, barely protected from the thick hoodie, and stands me upright. He raises a fist, and the others give him a wide berth.

"You dared to invade our privacy," he says in a growl. I can't run away. If he decks me, I'll... Lev launches himself at me from behind, knocking me to the floor as Viktor's fist flies. He came so close to punching me that I felt the whizz of air as his palm flew by.

"Don't!" Lev shouts. "You didn't see what I did."

Viktor roars and decks the wall, unloading the punch that was meant for me. A puff of dust goes up as drywall piles on the floor. My insides clench.

Lev holds me at arm's length and gives me a teeth-chattering shake.

"This is no boy."

*Fuck.*

With a sudden movement, he runs his thumb along my jawline, showing a dark smudge of eye makeup left behind on his skin like a fingerprint in ink. "Unless the trending thing to do is to draw stubble with makeup." He shakes his head. "Kids these days."

Grabbing my arm firmly, he pulls me closer.

"No!" I scream, forgetting to use the lower voice, as he reaches for my ball cap and yanks it off my head. He tears the elastic straight down, pain exploding along my scalp. *Fuck.* Thick, glossy waves tumble down around my shoulders. My stomach plummets, but I keep myself together. I will not cave now.

Lev, still holding me tightly, narrows his eyes. "You're not a boy," he says, more to himself than anyone. I swallow as his grip tightens, and he seems to be processing this new information.

I swallow. "Neither are you."

I'm not sure which of us is more surprised.

"Secure the perimeter," Mikhail snaps, jerking his chin at Ollie and Nikko. They run outside.

I smile at Lev and laugh. "Go on. It'll make it so much easier to fight if a few of you leave. I'm alone. Though honestly, boys, you should fire that useless watchman you hired out front. If he worked for me, I'd put a bullet in his head."

Lev scowls and narrows his eyes. I run my fingers through my hair. Now that they know I'm a woman, I have a reputation to uphold. If only I had a tube of lip gloss.

"Who are you?" he demands, his voice a dangerous whisper.

I lay my hand on his cheek, his hand still cuffed at my wrist. "I'm so disappointed you don't know me, *mi querido jefe.* I'd bow to greet you, but you are holding too tightly for me to do so." I grin at him. "Though honestly, I'm no one of any importance." I toss my hair.

He narrows his eyes. "We'll see about that."

Viktor shakes his head. "If it isn't the Colombian princess herself. *Princesa loca.* Lev, meet Isabella Morales."

I clench my teeth. The audacity of him using my brother's pet name for me in front of them. I *hate* that name.

Mikhail steps forward, his dark eyes sparking at me. "Meet your new prisoner, brother. Thank me later."

Prisoner? Well, I'm still alive, and by all accounts and purposes, that's a positive spin on being captured by the Romanovs.

Lev's jaw tightens as he circles me, drawing my hands behind my back. I wince in pain, but that doesn't stop him. I guess it's better than getting a face full of Viktor's iron fist. I like my nose.

He holds my wrists against my lower back. "Who else came with you?"

"No one," I say honestly, angry that my eyes dance with unshed tears because he's holding me so tightly. My palm throbs with the splinter still stuck beneath the surface of the skin, but my mind is racing.

*I can let him take me. I can pretend he's hurting me, and I won't go easily. I'll have to fight, which might even be fun. And then I'll be right there, in their headquarters, and I can find out everything I possibly can.*

Oh my God. If they don't kill me, which is still a distinct possibility... This could work out quite well.

Nikko and Ollie come back in. "Coast is clear. She told the truth. She's here alone."

Lev nods. "Ollie, sweep the loft and make sure she has no phone or any other comm devices."

My belly dips. Obviously, they'll have to take my phone. But that doesn't matter. I'll find a way to get in touch.

I must.

"I only have a phone," I tell them. "You'll find it up there. I have nothing else."

"Don't believe a word she says," Viktor growls, his huge arms folded over his chest.

I blow out a belabored sigh. "You don't have to. Go ahead,

check me for bugs or whatever." I look at Lev and wink. "You might want to strip me to do that."

Undeterred, he leans in closer to me and holds my gaze. "Oh, believe me, I will absolutely make sure you have nothing on you."

A pang of fear stabs me in the chest.

"I thought you were still a teen," I say to him, my voice a low purr. I let my gaze skate from the strong cut of his jaw down to his neck and the breadth of his powerful shoulders, the line of muscles visible even beneath the fabric of his shirt. His body is tightly coiled and finely tuned, with curved biceps. Strength personified. I lick my lips. "I've never been so happy to be wrong in my life."

His gaze grows menacing as he grips my wrists tighter. "You eavesdropped on my family. You heard intel that has nothing to do with you. You know your life is mine for what you've done, don't you?"

Mikhail chuckles, and the sound makes a shiver skate down my spine. "Fucking love how loyal and hardworking you are, brother. Take her back to your place. Interrogate the shit out of her while Aleks runs intel to see if LSD knows anything about her presence here."

I toss my head. "You call the most powerful cartel in all of Colombia *LSD* like the stupid drug lowlifes use?" I scoff. "Los Sangre Dorada Cartel deserves more respect than *that*. And no, they have no idea I'm here. Don't you know that in my family, I'm expected to put out then spit out little brats?" I make a face of disgust. "You men act like you've discovered the Holy Grail. So sorry to say, I'm really no one of importance."

Lev smirks and shakes his head. "Oh, we'll see about that."

I wink at him. "I look forward to it."

Viktor takes a step toward me. "She has no fucking respect for any of us." He grits his teeth and glares at Lev. "You know how this would go if she were in anyone else's custody."

Lev holds himself to his full height, still holding me in an iron grip. "She's more dangerous than she appears, and I intend to find out exactly who she is and what she knows. And believe me, brother." His voice lowers to a menacing pitch. "I don't take this responsibility lightly."

Uh-oh.

Viktor nods, appeased, and shoots his gaze back to me once more. "You sure you don't need help with this? I'm happy to lend a hand." If my hand were free, I'd blow him a kiss just to see that vein throb in his neck.

"How's Lydia, big boy?" I watch with delight as his face turns beet red.

"Thanks so much for the offer," Lev says with dripping sarcasm. "But I promise you, I have everything under control. Including her." Ollie comes down from the loft with my phone in his hand. He gives it to Aleksandr, the tall one.

*Fuck.*

If my brother knew about this, he would *murder* me. I swallow hard.

"Scan it," Mikhail says. "We'll meet tomorrow morning

after you've had a chance to find everything you can from her phone and Lev's had a chance to interrogate her."

Aleksandr scowls at the phone and in seconds, has managed to bypass the password. *My God,* what we could do with a brain like that in my family. I stare, half horrified and half awed. "Wow, princess," he says, shaking his head. "They don't love you at all, do they? No location tracker enabled at all."

It's the first thing any of them have said that stings.

Asshole.

He slides my phone in his back pocket.

"Open Snapchat, will you, while you're on my phone? I hate to lose my streak," I say with an exaggerated sigh. "A hundred *days*."

None of them bother to reply. I hope Lev lives near Polina, their sister. She's probably the only one in this whole family I'd get along with, though she probably hates my guts because I *am* an enemy.

"Tomorrow," Mikhail says. "Meeting adjourned. Lev, you need a guard here?"

"Yeah," I say. "Why don't you hire that useless douchebag who let me practically walk right past him? That'll be fun. Maybe he'll take pictures when you strip me."

"Alright, that's it," Lev says, clearly at the end of his rope. He holds both of my wrists in his left hand and, with his right, manages to unfasten his belt and tug it through the loops. I stare in fascination bordering on horror. Is he going to hit me in front of all of them, just like that?

At my response, he has the nerve to chuckle.

"Oh good, the hint of a fear response. I was beginning to worry I'd kidnapped a sociopath. I'll keep that in mind. Sorry to disappoint you, but this time I just want you to shut the fuck up."

He tugs me to his chest and loops the belt around my mouth, forming a gag. The warmed leather bites into my lips. I chomp down on it. I feel like a goddamn horse.

"Here," Aleks says, reaching for his waist. In one quick movement, he unfastens his belt. "In case you need another." He tosses it to Lev, who catches it in his fist midair.

What the fuck would he need *another one* for? Argh!

"I've got a knife," Viktor says, tossing it to Lev. It's like they're all pitching in for a gift, and the gift is me, served up on a fucking platter.

"Here are some zip ties," Ollie says.

Lev smiles. "Aw, you shouldn't have."

I sigh and roll my eyes. I'd have a deliciously sarcastic response, but sadly, I really can't talk with this damn bit between my teeth. He shoves me toward the door, then seems to think better of it. "Could interrogate you here," he says thoughtfully. "But if I take you home, I have so many more tools at my disposal." He nods. "Yeah, let's get you home, little spy. We need to have a chat."

# CHAPTER FOUR

*Lev*

IT'S my lucky fucking day.

Mikhail told me after Viktor and Lydia's marriage that I was up next. My brothers have gotten married in rapid succession—our plan to overtake The Cove as the most powerful Bratva group in full swing. The most efficient way of solidifying ourselves as a force to be reckoned with is to expand our ranks. The second, most lasting way, is to put down permanent roots.

Marriage. Vows. Children. None of the marriages in my family thus far have happened the "usual" way—at least the usual way in Western culture. Here, we take what we want.

And right now? I want a leggy Colombian princess with tanned skin, a sharp mouth, and a body that rivals an Olympian gymnast. The image of her thick, glossy hair falling from her baseball cap and around her face like a veil will stay with me forever. Her eyes, bright and inquisitive with just a touch of batshit crazy, are unforgettable. That cute little button nose and bratty mouth beg to be tamed. Her fit, lithe body, small but powerful, is like a tightly wrapped package of dynamite.

I bet she tastes like whiskey and sin.

I'll find out.

She sits beside me in rumpled male clothing. That needs to go.

I reach for the belt behind her head and unfasten it. "What do you have underneath this shit?" I ask her, gesturing to the rumpled sweatshirt and cargo pants.

She winks at me, her grin revealing full, cherry-red lips that draw my attention like a magnet. I'm mesmerized by the seductive curve of her mouth. No longer disguising her voice as a man's, her natural higher pitch resonates, each note a tantalizing aphrodisiac that stirs something deep within me.

"Nothing but my birthday suit and this stupid torture device meant to flatten my breasts." She leans in closer to me, her warm skin brushing mine. I swallow, my dick hard already just by her nearness. She's fucking gorgeous. "Why don't you see for yourself? You have to check me for bugs, anyway, don't you?" She leans back in her seat, a placid look of curiosity on her beautiful face. "I can't fucking wait to take this off. I feel like I'm wearing a jockstrap over my breasts."

"I can't fucking wait to see for myself. Believe me, that's happening." So far, my techniques are absolute shit. Not only does she not look intimidated, but she also looks fucking excited.

Maybe it isn't just the look in her eyes.

Maybe she actually *is* insane.

I'll have to get Aleks to do a background check.

A part of me thrills at this thought, though. I've never been attracted to normal women. Give me a taste of fire and ice, and I'll fucking fall to my knees and worship.

I'm not saying it's a good thing.

We're not far from my home, a newly purchased house I bought after Viktor's marriage. I didn't want to set roots down here right away, not with Ollie overseas and the work Mikhail needed me to do in various cities throughout the world. But after Lydia and Viktor got married, I knew I belonged here. And after Mikhail made it clear I'd be up for marriage sooner than later I knew The Cove was where I'd put down roots. Most of my other brothers live nearby at this point, so when this home hit the market, I snatched it up. I suspect Aleks had something to do with that, but who knows.

We pull up to my house in the dead of night, my estate lit with spotlights. "Wow," Isabella says beside me. "Not bad for the youngest."

I clench my jaw and don't respond. I won't let her bait me. Being the youngest of a family of pythons doesn't make you any less a python.

This house is a bit much for a single guy, but I knew when I bought it, the location was the most important. I'm five miles from headquarters and near Viktor and Lydia, with easy access to the highway. I hardly had to make any modifications except for a handful of security details, including wrought iron gates installed at the entrance, flanked by stone pillars.

When the gates open, a long, paved driveway lies before us lined with trimmed hedges. All along this path are discreetly placed security cameras, hidden along with infrared motion detection. With a click of a button, I can access every camera in my house and often do.

"Just you in a place like this?" she asks in a teasing lilt. A part of me wonders if she takes anything at all seriously. "Surely you've got a mistress, some concubines tucked away, no? You'd get lost here, wouldn't you?"

"I'll fill it with a wife and children someday," I tell her. "I'm not worried."

A shadow crosses her features, and her jaw clenches. I wonder why.

The house itself is three stories, built from stone so dark it seems to absorb moonlight. Tall, with arched windows and a heavy front door reinforced with iron bands, it's simple but sturdy.

Floodlights illuminate our way, casting shadows that dance across intricate stonework. The driveway curves around a blank area where a fountain used to stand. That was a bit much for my tastes.

I've got motion sensors hidden in the landscaping, a state-of-the-art alarm system, and the thick walls are reinforced.

The one balcony off the master suite is secured with iron railings.

If it were daytime, you'd see the garden and benches carved of stone. I love this home. It's mine. As the youngest in the family, that matters to me. Growing up, I got everyone's hand-me-downs. I never went without, not since the Romanovs took me in at an early age, but my parents were pragmatic and made good use of everything they owned.

"It will be hard for someone to escape a place like this, won't it?" she says in a teasing voice, her head tipped to the side. She doesn't seem intimidated or fearful at all... but excited.

I have my work cut out for me.

Bring it.

"Not difficult. Impossible."

She laughs lightly, a pretty, musical sound. "Oh, definitely not impossible, *mi cariño.*"

It's a challenge, then. *She's* a fucking challenge.

I park the car in front of the house. I'll move it in the morning. "Stay there," I order. She smirks at me. I lean in close and rest my hand on her upper thigh, pressing it down to hold her still. "You're mine, Isabella. You'll do what I say. Do not test me. Do not provoke me. You forfeited your life to my family with your choices, so what happens next is all a mercy." I squeeze her upper thigh. My dick aches. "Is that clear?"

"Mmm, *si, señor,*" she says in a thick drawl. "I hear and obey."

*Fuck.*

I lick my lips and swallow, bringing my mouth to her ear. "Good girl. I'll come around and get you."

I open her door and take her by the arm. Her muscles tense in my palm. I imagine what it would feel like to have her tight, lithe body pinned beneath me.

We'll get there.

She's mine now. She broke universal law between the cartel and Bratva. I have the right to kill her for what she's done. That would trigger an attack from her brother, but even he'd do the same thing if the situation were reversed. If Polina ever attempted anything as dangerous as she did, we'd extradite her to keep her safe... if we even got her back.

When we get to the entrance, I bend and grab the little package Aleks left for me.

She walks obediently beside me, taking it all in. "I'm impressed," she says as we head inside. "My family hardly lives in poverty, but this... this is stunning."

I roll my eyes. As if flattery will get her anywhere.

"Just look at this. You can tell it's a luxury home. Those floors. Are they mahogany? Those high ceilings and crown moldings. My God, Lev, you have a crystal chandelier in the dining room."

Forgot about that.

"But it's secure, look at this. Those windows look reinforced, and I'd bet you have cameras trained on every inch of this place. And those mirrors are for more than show, aren't they?"

Yeah, of course they are. Mirrors give an immediate view of every visible angle of the house.

"Listen, if we go out to dinner, you're paying," she says. "Obviously, you can afford it."

My lips twitch.

"Cat got your tongue, handsome?"

"Do you ever talk without flirting?"

"Who, me? Of course not. Why be so mundane?" She smiles, her golden eyes alight. "Glad I finally got you to open up."

I half regret removing her gag and simultaneously regret ever gagging her in the first place. I feel like my thoughts and actions are muddled like scrambled eggs. There's something intoxicating and enigmatic about her.

I love hearing her talk. I love watching her move. I'm entranced with the way her mind works.

And I can't fucking wait to break her.

# CHAPTER FIVE

*Isabella*

AY CARAMBA!

I can hardly believe my luck.

Yes, yes, I've been abducted by one of the Romanov boys. Er, men. And yes, yes, I know that those ironclad rules we've established since the Stone Ages *technically* mean my life is forfeit.

Whatever.

The bottom line is I'm *in his residence.* I've leaped straight from the observation tower into the shark tank.

I can hardly believe I didn't think of this myself. If only I'd seduced him from day one. I mean, this might be most helpful, though, because this way, he thinks this was all his idea.

I must keep him thinking that way.

I take in every detail. While my family hardly lives in poverty, none of the property was *mine*. No woman has ever been allowed to claim ownership of property in the Los Sangre Dorada. Where I'm from... *we're* the property.

So, it isn't just the opulence and beauty of his home that appeals to me. It's that it's his. His property. His castle.

I'm half in love... until he brings me to the basement.

Down a flight of stairs, we leave the brightly lit luxury of the main floor. It's darker and cooler here. I shiver, still wet from my run in the rain to the warehouse.

I've honestly had better days. He yanked my hair pretty good back there. My scalp still tingles. My hair is so thick and heavy, even wearing it in a ponytail can give me a headache, and I had the start of one up in that loft. Can't remember the last time I ate anything. Now, my head's pounding like someone put a box over it and is slamming their fists against it.

My hand is throbbing from the damn splinter, and he's been tossing me around like I'm a doll.

And something tells me he's only warming up.

It's fine, though. You don't get to be me without some serious practice learning to lean into pain and discomfort. Hell, in the right circumstances, I might even like it.

It's dimly lit here, shadows playing on the walls as he marches me down a flight of stairs. The air is cooler, and it's dark down here. Ah. This must be his workout room. When my eyes adjust to the low lighting, I can identify various pieces of high-end workout equipment—a weight bench, some dumbbells, and pulleys. The walls are lined with mirrors, amplifying the space and making me feel eerily on full display here. The cool air smells like any gym would, a blend of metal, rubber, and a tinge of perspiration.

It's spacious, with low ceilings and a cool concrete floor. Ahhh. Maybe that's why he's brought me here.

Whatever he's planning on doing to me, he doesn't want to harm those gorgeous floors upstairs.

Exposed pipes run along the ceiling, and along one wall, a row of weight racks gleams, filled with hand weights and kettlebells of various sizes.

I hope he gives me enough freedom to let me explore this a bit more. He isn't the only one who likes to lift.

The opposite wall is dominated by a large, full-length mirror, slightly fogged, and in the center of the room, there are several workout machines—a treadmill, a bench press, and a cable machine. Not a speck of dust anywhere suggests frequent use.

"Someone takes his workouts seriously," I note. He doesn't respond.

My heart comes to a sudden stop when I see the left of the room. Beside a thick punching bag suspended from the ceiling are a few other things—heavy iron chains and ropes, obviously used for workouts but suitable for... other purposes as well. Yeah, those ropes are great for a core workout but... can be used for other things.

Mmm. My captor has a kink streak. *Of course* he does.

It just keeps getting better and better.

Next to the punching bag are a few more suspension hooks, likely intended for hanging punching bags originally, but they for sure can be used to suspend a *person*. Those weight benches have leather straps attached, the kind someone might use to hold a foot in place for a workout, but I am confident he could use those for another purpose as well.

I look around and note medicine balls and that pulley system near the resistance bands could be put to good use. In the corner is a water filter.

The dual-purpose nature of this room is clear. I'm not sure if he's ever previously used it for what he's going to do to me, but he's absolutely thought about it before.

It's too bad I'm not the interrogator. I could have some fun here.

I swallow, suddenly nervous, when he brings me over to the punching bag. "Alright, now. Let's get to work."

My heart beats faster. My mouth feels dry. I remind myself that it's essential to stay calm and not let fear best me. I blink rapidly, breathing in through my nose and out of my mouth so I stay focused.

"Stand," he barks. "If you try anything, I'll tase you, so don't get any ideas."

Ah, I'm that much of a threat, am I? Excellent.

I stand and nod. "Going to check for bugs?" I ask, wagging my brows at him.

He purses his lips and holds my gaze. "Mmm."

"I told you I have none, but if that's how you want to start this party, let's go." I wink at him.

With a frown, he stands me in front of him and reaches into the waistband of his pants. I watch as he draws out a blade.

*God.* Am I slipping? How did I miss that before? I swallow hard as he approaches me with it, slicing through my disguise until it falls to ribbons at my feet.

"You weren't lying," he says, almost surprised when I stand before him in just that band around my chest, no underwear.

I shrug. "Why wear underwear? They only get in the way if you catch my drift."

He doesn't take the bait but flicks the blade and presses it to the bottom of the band. I draw in a sharp breath as he slices clean through it. Damn, that's one sharp blade. I can't help but shiver when it grazes my skin, but he leaves me fully intact.

The band falls to the floor, and my full breasts swing free. My nipples pebble when he draws closer, and his breath tickles my skin.

"Thank God," I say in a thick voice, affected by his nearness and the threat of a blade. "Lucky for you, you'll never know the torture of wearing a bra, and that little torture device was about a hundred times worse."

"Stand still," he snaps. "And be quiet, or I'll gag you again."

I sigh and nod. I'd give him a *yes, sir,* just to mock him, but he told me to be quiet.

Now for the fun part.

He removes something small and compact from the bag on

his front step. Ah. It looks like some kind of a scanner or some such device that you might find at an airport.

"You're strong," he says thoughtfully. "I'd bet most of the equipment here's familiar to you."

I nod. It is, and I'm not allowed to talk. Not that I follow rules all the time, but there's a time and a place, and I need to keep up my energy, so I don't miss anything. My stomach growls with hunger.

"Hungry? Good. That might come in useful."

Dammit.

Well, lucky for me, I'm well versed in fasting, so he can starve me, and I'll be fine. If he keeps me from water, though...

Taking the device in hand, he scans from the top of my head down the side of my face until he reaches my neck. He carefully scans my neck. It emits a soft hum as he runs it over my body, the screen lighting up as he goes. This is some high-tech shit.

The scanner beeps occasionally, but he doesn't pause. Apparently, the little beeps are normal, probably telling him I'm alive but not much else. As he passes my lower abdomen, though, he looks closely.

"No IUD," he says as if surprised.

"Nope. I don't want one of those damn things inside me."

He nods. "Good. I don't want one of those damn things inside you either."

Is he some kind of healthy maniac or... does he have an issue with birth control?

"You aren't a virgin?"

I snort. "Hell no. You really thought I was a virgin?"

He gives me a withering look before rolling his eyes. "No."

"Well, you didn't have to answer *that* fast."

The grip on his scanner tightens, but he takes a deep breath. He seems thrown off, somehow. I wonder why.

He smacks the inside of my thigh for me to spread my legs. My pussy clenches, and my clit throbs at the nearness of his strong hand and the bite of pain from the little slap. Mmm. Goddamn, we could have some fun together. I've never been interested in regular men, but the criminal type? Now you're talking. None of the men at home tickled my fancy, though. Too macho and too familiar. This one, however...

He scans the inside length of both of my legs. I swallow as my nipples become painfully hard, and wetness gathers between my thighs. It's been way too long since I've been touched by a man, and the last time was hardly memorable.

When he reaches the top of my left thigh, he stares at the tattoo I have, a tight wreath of vines in an elegant, flowing script that reads *Fuerza y Libertad*.

I got it on my eighteenth birthday, and no one in my family was the wiser. Carlos's sister Renata was the only one who knew about it.

"Interesting choice for a tattoo," he says. "What does it mean?"

I swallow. "Strength and freedom."

It feels oddly intimate to tell him that.

He scans all the way down to my toes, back up my legs, and across my ass until he's finally satisfied.

"Maybe you were telling the truth," he says thoughtfully. "Maybe you weren't. Let's see."

I know he hasn't found anything, but that doesn't stop him from bringing the scanner to my breasts again. He brushes it along the top of my hardened nipples. I keep myself in place with effort, trying hard not to show how much he's affecting me.

He could try lots of different tactics, but this might be his most effective method. I can't let him know.

Wordlessly, he cups my ass in one of his strong, rough hands, the calloused palms scraping across my delicate skin. "And this scar," he says when he notes the white pucker on my shoulder blade. "What is that from?"

"You'd have to ask Javier," I say with a sad smile. Yes, that one's my brother's souvenir.

"Your brother gave that to you?" he asks in a low growl. Is he... angry? Upset that his "prize" is marred? Affronted that he didn't give it to me himself?

"Mmm. What a man, isn't he?" I can't keep the venom from my voice.

He's the devil incarnate, and I hate him.

"I'll fucking kill him," he snaps.

"Not if I get to him first," I retort, and I fucking mean it. I won't let anyone else exact the revenge that belongs to me.

*I* was the one he hurt. I was the one pressed under his thumb. I was the one thwarted by his chauvinistic tactics, and *I* will be the one who claims his throne.

Lev gives me a curious look but doesn't respond.

"No bugs," he says, with a satisfied nod. "Now let's get to the good part."

My heart thumps madly. I'm instantly wet. I must be insane.

This might not work out so well for me. Or him, really.

I swallow hard and toss my head as if scoffing at his threat. If he sees right through me, he doesn't let on.

"Come here."

I'm restrained and stuck in place as if someone's flicked a switch and frozen me. With a scowl, he spins me around and claps his hand across my ass. Under normal circumstances, that'd turn me on, but it only serves to unfreeze me. I yelp and hop to, walking over to where he instructs me to go.

The cable system looms in front of me. It might as well be the stocks or a medieval torture device under these circumstances. The cold, metallic glint of the pulleys and weights reflects the harsh light of the basement, casting eerie shadows on the walls.

What time is it? It's got to be the middle of the night, maybe even into the wee hours of the morning. I'm tired and hungry and in pain, but I will not break.

*I will not.*

When I cast a glance at him, his dark eyes are unreadable. The weight of our situation presses down on me. At any moment, he could end my life, but then where does that leave him? The irony is that the only thing keeping me safe is my identity... which is also my greatest condemnation.

The tension in the air is palpable. I shiver, not from the cold, but from not knowing what's coming next. He doesn't seem tired like I am at all but energized and almost excited. I mean, he's got a naked woman at his mercy. I don't really blame him.

"Enjoy the view?" I ask, somehow managing to keep my tone light and not betraying the fear that thrums through my veins with a life of its own.

"You seem to be enjoying the attention," he says smoothly.

I roll my eyes, trying to mask my growing terror. "Well, it's not every day I get such an audience for my workout routine."

His low, dark chuckle makes my frayed nerves quiver. "This is no workout routine, Isabella."

I give a mock gasp. "No," I say, my voice dripping with sarcasm. "Are you going to make me confess my addiction to sweets and my appalling lack of cardio?"

A hint of a smirk tugs at his lips. "It's more your extracurricular activities that interest me."

I toss my hair, but he's got me in a tight grip. With deft moves, he lifts both of my wrists over my head. I crane my neck to see what he's doing but can't really get a good view.

I don't need to, though, as the next moment, my wrists are pulled into restraints.

Uh-oh.

Here we *goooooo*.

"I'm just trying to learn everything I can about you, of course. You intrigue me."

He snorts. "Right."

"Go ahead, Lev. Give me your best," I challenge, dropping the teasing lilt of my voice. "Whips and intimidation tactics won't break me. And honestly, I'm not scared of you."

"Good," he responds. "Fear makes people weak. I prefer my women strong."

*His women.* Why does a sudden need to know exactly who *his women* have been grip me? He's nothing to me. I don't care.

I'm not *jealous. God.*

He pulls a lever, and I stifle a gasp when my wrists are lifted above my head so high I'm on my tiptoes. He has complete access to my naked body.

And something tells me he's going to use that to his *full* advantage. I squeeze my eyes shut and brace myself for something. Anything. But when long minutes pass, I finally venture to open an eye.

He's standing in front of me, his face unreadable as he looks at his handiwork. When he meets my gaze, he doesn't speak, but something warm and delicious unfurls in my belly.

*It could work,* my instincts purr. *We could conquer every-thing together.* If only I could get him to come to me, to bow just the tiniest bit, I could have this man eating out of the palm of my hand. I want him. I want *us.*

I blink, trying to shake the spell he has over me. It doesn't work.

Slowly, methodically, as if he's polishing specks of dust off a prized possession, he runs his hand down the length of my body. He starts at my shoulders, his hands hot to the touch. Down my back he goes, to the small of my back, until he gets to my ass. I watch the outline of his arousal with appreciation, his thick cock taut in his pants. I lick my lips.

Next, he runs his hands down the length of my thighs, all the way down my calves, down to my feet.

"What's your training regimen?" he asks me, taking me by surprise. "Your body's an absolute pillar of perfection."

His praise warms me. I didn't expect it.

"I eat clean. Run for cardio. Swim at every opportunity. Strength train five days a week. But really, *mi querido jefe,* it isn't fair. Here I am, all naked and on display, and I can only guess at what's beneath your clothes."

A corner of his lips quirks up, but he doesn't bite.

He comes in front of me and steps so close, the warmth of his breath brushes my skin. He weighs my breasts in his palms and brushes his thumbs across my nipples. I do my best but can't completely stifle a hum of approval. My God, it feels good to be touched like this.

Thankfully, I'm good with the knowledge that I'm crazy. Most women would likely berate themselves for craving the touch of their captor. Me? I've never been more turned on in my life.

# CHAPTER SIX

*Lev*

IF KOLYA, our mentor, were here, he'd warn me to watch out for this one. She reminds me of a Venus flytrap. It'll lure you in with its sweet, seductive nectar, but when an unsuspecting insect lands on the trap, it snaps shut, ensnaring its prey before it sucks the life out of it. She's stunning, the most beautiful woman I've ever laid eyes on, and yet every instinct in me tells me to turn and run in the other direction.

Kolya didn't just train us physically, showing us how to hone our bodies to become finely tuned instruments as powerful as a weapon; he taught us mental resilience, too. In all honesty, that training's been way more useful than the physical stuff. Any lout can teach you how to shred with macros and protein. This guy taught us how to persevere.

I've put his training to good use, and I'm gonna have to do it now. Because it doesn't matter that her eyes are like molten chocolate, warm and sensual in all the best ways, framed in long, thick black lashes. It doesn't matter that she's so beautiful, she makes my heart ache—the kind of woman men lose their religion over and the type of body that makes them sell their souls to the devil.

It doesn't matter that Isabella Morales is lust and sin wrapped up in a bow. I'm gonna break this woman if it kills me.

I must.

So far, she's responded favorably to being manhandled, so that's likely not going to work. Still, it can't hurt to try.

She's suspended with her arms up above her head, giving me a stunning view of her slender but sculpted back and tight, round ass that I want to lick and bite and *fuck* until she screams. Toned, tanned legs curved with feminine lure. And that's just the back view.

*Fuck.*

I've found no evidence of anything on her, not so much as a tracking device. It really does bemuse me. I can't believe the LSD would allow a woman of her stature and beauty out of their sight. Surely, someone will come looking for her at any moment.

Won't they?

But no. No tracking on her phone. Nothing on her person. And even though Isabella schools her features well, she didn't hide the flicker of pain that crossed her face when Aleks said something about her family not knowing or caring where she was.

She's an independent woman, but there are holes in her armor... I mean to take full advantage.

Just for good measure, I do one more sweep with the tool Aleks left for me, but she's hiding nothing.

Now that that's over with, I get to move on to bigger and better things. First, I'll try physical intimidation. It's the easiest method, and something tells me she might like it.

I circle her, taking everything in. The hardened nipples and the way she bites her lip when I breathe on her. I cup her ass, my large palm holding her in place. I watch as she swallows, and her pupils dilate.

It's so easy getting her excited. If only it were this easy to get information from her.

Maybe she truly doesn't have anything to tell me, but I doubt that.

What's her weakness? How will I break her?

I step behind her and slowly reach for the buckle of my belt. I remember the look of it tucked between her teeth as I unfasten it and pull it slowly through the loops.

I wonder if she's ever been whipped. If I were going to give her a spanking, I'd use my hand. But I'm not here to turn her on, or me, for that matter.

I wonder if it will make her talk or arouse her? Maybe it'll piss her off. Maybe both.

I'm already hard as fuck by the time the leather's through the loops. I make sure to take my time, so she hears the sound of the belt unbuckling and the whir of it being pulled completely off.

I loop it and fist the buckle.

"Let's go, Isabella. Let's hear what you have to tell me."

She tries to look over her shoulder as if to make sure her senses haven't betrayed her.

"I told you. No one knows I'm here. I have no more information to tell you."

I don't know if she'll ever actually tell me the truth. She lies as easily as she breathes. I suppose it's part of her charm.

It's go time.

The first strike snaps against her ass, a measured, deliberate stroke. Though she comes up on her toes, she barely makes a sound. The sight of the red stripe across her ass makes me hard as fuck.

"Are you sure about that?" I ask, bringing my hand back before I lash her again. I lay down two, three, four hard slaps across her ass until the skin is striped a red-hot pink, but she only shakes her head and wiggles her butt.

"I told you," she says in a singsong voice. "And whipping me is only going to turn me on, not get more information." She sticks her butt back out. "So go ahead. Give me all you've got. Please tell me you're just warming me up, and you've got more than *that*."

Saucy little bitch.

I won't let her bait me, but I won't let her shame me, either. I snap the belt again and again, still careful not to hit too hard, even as a little voice inside my head asks me *why?*

Why am I afraid to break skin? To really, truly hurt her? I need answers, and I fucking need them *now*.

The next lash makes her cry out. I open my hand, let the belt's tail loose, and snap it again. She flinches but still only wriggles in her restraints and taunts me. "Now that's what I'm looking for. There you go. If you're trying to turn me on, you're doing an *excellent* job." The low purr of her laugh makes me smash my teeth together before I slap the belt across her ass, the hardest strike I've given her yet. It satisfies me to see the raised welt of the leather. To hear her cry of pain.

"Tell me," I snap. "What do you know? If you know nothing, why did you come to Viktor? You're contradicting yourself, Isabella."

I whip the belt across her butt again, crisscrossing where I left off. The good thing about a belt is that it builds in intensity, each strike magnifying the last. I'm no stranger to a little bedroom kink. I know how to make it sting and how to make that sting last. A man can be questioned with muscle. A woman needs a much finer touch.

When she still doesn't answer me, I kick her legs apart, loop the belt again, and slap it against her bare, perfectly pink pussy. She hisses in a breath and squeezes her eyes shut, but I don't miss the glint of wetness on her pussy lips. I swallow hard, ignoring the heady haze of arousal that threatens to blind me.

I slap her again and again, but she doesn't move. I fucking swear, with her low moan and the way her eyes have fluttered closed, she's on the edge of subspace, for Christ's sake.

I toss the belt down and reach for her hair. I fist it and yank her head back. "Tell me."

Her mouth flies open, but she doesn't say a word.

"If you don't tell me, I'm going to find out who matters to you. I'll try different methods to get the truth out of you. Pain, fear, maybe even well-earned pleasure."

I'm determined to break her down mentally, the most effective way of extracting information from most prisoners. At that, her eyes fly open, her pupils dilated with heated arousal. She licks her perfect lips.

"Please do," she says in a breathy whisper.

Alright, this isn't working.

I go back to my knife and slowly, deliberately sharpen it in front of her. The sound of metal scraping metal heightens the tension in the room, and I swear she looks *excited*.

"Knife play?" she asks in the same voice one might croon about a delicious delicacy. "Mmm."

I press the blade between her breasts, the cool metal making the skin it touches turn white.

Her breath quickens, her chest rising and falling. Her eyes, wide and luminous, lock onto mine with a mixture of fear and arousal.

"Are you going to tell me anything now?"

She swallows hard, her tongue flicking out to wet her lips. My dick aches, imagining how fucking good it would be to have that gorgeous, pouty, full mouth wrapped around my cock.

Another option, if I need it. I'll keep that shit in mind.

I drag the knife downward, just enough to leave a trace of a line on her skin. She gasps, her back arching toward the blade.

"What do you want to know?" she whispers in a hoarse voice.

"What is your brother planning?" I twist the blade and trace the curve of her breast. She whimpers softly, her hands fisting. It's the first sign of any weakness. She isn't impermeable, then.

"Stay still, Isabella," I snap, my voice a low command.

I love the way her name rolls off my tongue. I love having her at my command. To win the attention of a woman like this would be a man's crowning joy. To win her devotion, his absolute triumph. Beauty is fleeting, but her fire and brilliance, her indomitable spirit and fierce intelligence behind those captivating eyes—now that's what drives a man to his knees.

Her breath becomes erratic as I continue my slow, tortuous path with the blade. The knife passes over her stomach, and I watch her emotions play out on her face—excitement, definite arousal, and something that hints at fear.

"Good girl," I praise softly. Still testing. Every word and move a litmus test. I pause with my knife just above her pubic area. I let it rest there, a silent threat. When she bites her lip and stifles a moan, I turn the knife so the hard nub of the handle is at the vee between her thighs. I press it down. It slides easily through her slick folds. She bucks and whimpers.

"Do you want to come, Isabella? Do you want a *reward?*" I circle the handle of the knife and press it further down between her legs.

Her mouth parts open in a silent gasp, her eyes filled with horror and anticipation. Holding her gaze, I press the handle deeper in. Her breathing hitches as I slide it in and out.

"You like this," I say in a low whisper. "You dirty, dirty little slut." A wicked grin lights her face, and she spreads her legs wider.

"Takes one to know one," she says in a breathy whisper. A trickle of arousal wets my fingers. I slow my pace and watch her reaction, then draw the handle of the blade slowly, so slowly, until it's nearly out. She whimpers and writhes, her pelvis arching when I shove it back into her hot, slick folds. I twist it and press my thumb to her clit this time.

"Oh God," she moans as I build a rhythm.

"Let's hear it," I whisper in her ear. "What was your brother planning?"

I hold the blade still. She tries to force friction, but her position makes it impossible. I move it just a slight bit. She parts her legs and whimpers.

"I don't know," she says, but this time she won't look in my eyes.

I shove the handle fully in, and her head falls back. I toss it to the floor, kneel in front of her, and spread her legs wide.

I've found my method of interrogation that just might work with her. I part her legs and slide my tongue between her pussy folds. I let the tip taste the tiniest drop of her arousal. I swallow, keeping myself in check with effort.

"Oh *God,*" she says, her wrists straining with the effort of keeping herself in place. She whispers a stream of something in Spanish I can't quite identify, but I hear a few curse words mingled in.

I'll break this woman, no matter what it takes—spanking, pain, sexual intimidation.

"What do you know? Who sent you?" Anger creeps into my voice. I realize it isn't just her presence that's a threat but the mental challenge she presents.

"I can't tell you," she says on a whimper. "Stop fucking asking me."

I grip her thighs and nip her clit. She screams and shakes, but I don't miss the way her pussy clenches around my fingers when I shove into her. I lick her, a slow, deliberate stroke of my tongue through her folds before I pull back and hold her gaze with mine.

"You know," I say lazily. I shove my fingers in her core but hold them still. "Tell me what you know."

She shakes her head. "I can't."

"Oh, sweetheart," I say, shaking my head before I lick her clit again. "You can and you will. None of them know where you are, remember? There's no one here to save you. No one to rescue you."

Her eyes flash at me, and she clenches her teeth. "I don't need a fucking man to save me."

I chuckle. My breath on her thighs makes her skin pebble. "You're naked and tied to chains in my basement. No tracker on you. No one who gives a fuck about where you are or what you're doing." I shake my head. "I don't know why you're holding out."

"Maybe because I have nothing to tell you," she snaps.

I spread her wide, swallow hard, and lick her again and again until her clit throbs and she's moaning on the verge of climax. She bites her lip as if holding on for dear life.

"Why are you so afraid of the truth, *mi querido jefe?* Tell me, Lev. What happened to you?" She grins, her eyes glinting at me dangerously even as they water. *"Who hurt you?"*

She's way too in control here. Goddamn, she's naked and restrained in *my* basement. I'm the one who's whipped her, threatened her, and brought her to the edge of climax with no release, yet the seductive purr of her voice and I'm hard as fuck.

*Jesus.*

I'm done here.

For now.

I'm both frustrated and intrigued by her resilience. I'm wary but curious. How can she stay so in control?

"You're a fucking liar," I say. I breathe against the sensitive, damp skin of her inner thighs. I lay the flat of my tongue along the edge, and she tries to roll to me as if silently begging for my tongue where she wants to relieve pressure. I spank her ass and hold her in place. "*I* am in control of this situation, baby. *Me. Not you.* You'll do what I say. And since you haven't given me any information..." I give her one more stroke of my tongue that makes her quiver before I lean back and stand. "You'll have to be punished." I shake my head. "This isn't over. I *will* find out everything you know."

I turn and walk away. I chuckle to myself at the sound of her scream of frustration right before the door to the workout room slams shut.

The woman is a threat, a ticking time bomb that could destroy everything we've worked so hard for. I won't allow that.

She's maddening... and intriguing. But above all, my duty is to my family.

She will remain a prisoner.

I *will* break her.

# CHAPTER SEVEN

*Isabella*

THE DOOR SLAMS SHUT, and my scream echoes through the dark, damp basement, still tainted with the lingering scent of sweat and iron. My wrists ache from the cold metal of the restraints, but the discomfort fuels my resolve. I refuse to be broken, not by Lev or anyone else.

Minutes pass. Hours. I wait for him and allow myself to imagine what he's doing. Eating a steak? Watching a football game?

Jerking off to the image of my naked body suspended from his ceiling and the taste of my arousal still on his tongue?

*Asshole.*

My mouth feels as dry as a desert. I have to pee. He left me throbbing for release and nearly begging. I'm cold, my ass is killing me, and I'm so hungry, I'd eat damn near anything he'd give me, even those gross *kholodets* they like to eat, some jelly-like, gelatinous delicacy served in Russia.

Okay, maybe I wouldn't eat *that,* but I'd stoop damn low right about now.

Ha, who am I kidding? I've already stooped lower than I ever thought possible. Chained up in the basement of my enemy, fighting against the man who holds my fate in his hands.

Even if he were to be smacked by some fairy godmother's stick and he decided to grant me freedom... what he doesn't know is they wouldn't take me back. I'm damaged goods now, and my brother's probably already dancing with glee at his good fortune. Imagine his luck, no need to split our inheritance.

I cannot allow the Romanovs to think they've bested me.

This *must* be on my terms.

I draw in a deep, calming breath. Blink.

*Focus.*

Hell, I've been in worse situations than this. My late father once tried to marry me to a Colombian crime lord. I was fifteen years old, planning my *quinceañera,* one of the most pivotal events in a young girl's life as it marks the transition from childhood to adulthood.

Apparently, my father thought that meant it was time to sell and breed me. He and my mother fought. She threw the vase her mother had given her across the room. It shattered into pieces. In response, my father shattered *her.*

After she was discharged from the hospital, she left. I don't know how she managed it. I don't blame her for leaving, not really. I blame her for leaving me behind.

I blink my eyes and focus again. It isn't going to help me to think about that now. I've risen above that. I'm better than the past I left behind. I *will* leave a legacy behind me, and it won't be a woman who ever cowed to a man.

I take a deep breath and come up with a plan. So, I'm chained. He'll be back eventually, either to torture me again or let me go and try something else. It was kind of cute how he called me a little liar. Of course I'm lying. I could tell him so much information it would fill reams of notebooks and systematically decimate everything my brother has built and hopes to build yet.

I can't do that, though, and it has nothing to do with any half-assed loyalty to my family. *I'm* the one who will take over that cartel after I do away with my brother. I won't give away the keys of the kingdom for all the money in the world, much less a threat of pain.

*Ha.* It amuses me he even entertained the thought of intimidating me into giving up anything. I live for pain. It turns me on.

I calm myself and focus on my breathing. Of course, I know exactly how I'm going to get out of here, but he might have a camera on me, so I must play it safe.

I look around the room, searching for a source of video feed. It takes me a minute. It's hard to focus when I'm so starving. My vision keeps blurring in front of me. And the *thirst.* My God, I can hardly swallow.

Lev Romanov underestimated me. He thought he could chain me up and leave me here, and I don't see any evidence of recording going on. I suppose he was pretty confident in these chains he has.

But he has no fucking idea who he's dealing with. They call me *La Sombra* back at home—the shadow. I can be elusive and silent, capable of escaping anything.

And even naked, I'm prepared. With deft, quiet fingers, I maneuver the pin in my hair. It will take a little time, but I can undo this lock.

As I work, my fingers moving with muscle memory, his parting words echo in my mind.

*This isn't over. I will find out everything you know.*

Not everything, *mi querido jefe.*

He thinks he can break me? I trained my entire life for situations exactly like this—to resist and to survive.

I grit my teeth and concentrate. I stifle a chuckle when I feel the lock give way under my fingers.

Yeah, baby, I'm *that good.*

*Click.*

The barely audible sound is the sweetest music to my ears.

I slide the chains off quietly. Now that I'm free, I have to move fast, every movement calculated so he doesn't notice. My heart races with a thrill of defiance. I am not some helpless damsel. I am Isabella Morales, and no one will ever keep me in a cage.

I quickly assess my clothes. Wrecked. *Shit.*

I slide into my shoes. They're clumsy, and I'd give anything for a pair of slim-fitting leggings and a tank top, but it'll do for now.

I silently move toward the door, every sense on high alert. The basement is tricky to navigate, but I've observed enough of the basic layout. I push the door open, a sliver of light guiding my way. I hold my breath as I step into the hallway, turn, and shut and lock the door behind me. That'll slow him down, anyway.

I move through the darkened basement, my feet silent on the cold floor. Every sound seems amplified: the creak of a floorboard, the distant hum of machinery. My heart pounds in my chest, adrenaline surging through my veins. I must get out, to find a way to freedom. The adrenaline makes me feel like I could scale a wall if I had to.

I might have to.

He has video surveillance and guards, that much I know, but what I don't know is where *he* is. That could kill me. Do his guards have patrol routes? Where are the cameras trained?

Freedom is so close I can taste it. My hands tremble as I work another lock, but I force myself to stay calm.

Heavy footsteps approach. I quickly and silently duck into a closet filled with brooms and cleaning supplies. I hold my breath, the familiar lilac scent of *Fabuloso* overpowering.

The steps pass by me. Is that Lev returning, or someone else? If he finds I'm gone...

When the coast is clear, I exit the closet and head as fast as I can toward another door near the windows, telling me that this one will lead to freedom. I try the lock. My pulse races when the handle turns.

*Yessss.* I push it open. The cool night air hits my face as I step outside. It's early morning, dawn on the horizon. I'm so tired and so hungry, yet my heart races with exhilaration. *I've made it.*

I still have to get to the exit and then find my way out of here. I don't even know where he lives.

But as I near the exit, a shadow looms ahead. I freeze. I can't breathe. Is that... one of his guards or...

*No.*

A grim smile plays on Lev's lips. He stands, his hands anchored on his hips. "Going somewhere, are you?"

His voice is hard and cold, and his features show no sign of surprise.

*Dammit.*

Panic and frustration surge through me, but I force myself to stand tall. "You can't keep me here."

His eyes narrow. "Can't I?"

Frustration mixed with admiration flicker in his gaze. "You are *very* resourceful, I'll give you that. I was sloppy with the restraints. But no, Isabella, you're not going anywhere."

I move quickly. When he reaches for my wrists, I deflect, and when surprise registers in his eyes, I take my chance. I shove at his chest, pushing him off kilter, turn, and run.

I'm faster than he is. He curses behind me as he chases me, huffing and puffing, but lock picking isn't the only skill I've learned for a quick escape.

He's gaining on me. I can feel the heat of his breath behind me, and he's at an advantage because he knows something I don't. I have no damn idea where I'm going. And in the end, that's my demise. I nearly run straight into a chain-link fence in front of me. I come to a crashing halt.

Before I can react, he's on me, his grip ironclad around my arm. "Let me go!" I scream, but it's no use. He's too strong, and he's *pissed.*

"No," he snaps. "You're lucky I've let you live. If you think

for a moment I'm going to let you escape, you're mistaken." He curses in Russian. "If any of my men saw you...." He grits his teeth and whips off his tee.

It hits the top of my thighs. It's warm and it smells like him, but I'm fucking pissed.

I meet his gaze, defiance burning a hole in my stomach. I consider kneeing him between the legs, but he's got such a hold on me I'm afraid he'd easily deflect and then hurt me even more than he's planning to already. I'm in major trouble and I know it.

"You're staying here."

"You can chain me up, but that doesn't make me yours." It feels childish and petty to spar like this, but I can't help myself.

A glimmer of a smile plays at his lips. "You're so full of your-self. You think it's all about you, don't you?"

I don't respond. The rebuke stings.

"What makes you think I can't keep you here?"

I snort. "You plan on keeping me chained up here forever?" I retort, my voice steady despite my shaky nerves. "Even then, I'd find a way. A lock is only a game for me. You'll see."

"I have other methods of keeping you under my thumb."

My *God*. I want to smack his smug, handsome-as-sin face.

"You don't intimidate me."

He pulls me closer to him, his eyes flashing. "I haven't even tried yet."

I smirk. "Bring it."

He smiles, baring his teeth. "Oh, I intend to. But first, let's get you back where you belong."

Where I... belong?

He leans closer to me, his presence overwhelming. I didn't realize how big he was until now. Compared to his other brothers, he looks a bit smaller, but... compared to me, the idea of using the word "small" to describe him is damn near laughable.

And I'm definitely aware of how strong he is now.

*Damn it, focus, Isabella.*

I blink, caught off guard by his sudden proximity. Despite everything, I can't ignore how good he smells: warm and spicy and masculine. His face, now inches from mine, highlights his sharp jawline and heavier stubble. His eyes pierce straight through me.

"You're wasting your time. I'm not going to break." It's

getting harder to fight him, though. I'm in pain, I'm famished, and I'm so damn tired and thirsty.

His eyes flash with chilling amusement, a challenge dancing in their depths. "We'll see about that," he murmurs, his voice a low, dangerous whisper that makes me shiver. I turn away from him and wobble. I fall to my knees. The air in front of me seems to shimmer. I'm dimly aware of him cursing behind me before he bends to me. I grit my teeth, ready to fight him if he's going to hurt me again, but instead... he doesn't.

He lifts me. The world grows a bit hazy and unfocused. I blink my eyes, half expecting I've fallen into a dream, but it's definitely not that.

Maybe he wants me to get stronger again so he can question me more. Fair enough. If his plan involves food and some water and sleep, this will be perfect.

I didn't get far from the house. I tell myself that if I were *well,* I could've nailed this. I would've slipped through his fingers like fine sand. I'm compromised. That's the only reason he caught me.

But even as we walk, my mind is churning with possibilities and a glimmer of hope surfaces. This doesn't have to be a simple, predictable game of cat and mouse... does it?

In the dim light of early morning, a light breeze kisses my cheek. I chance a glance at Lev to find his face stoically set, determined. He's a man on a mission, but he doesn't seem angry or resentful as I'd expect him to.

I've done my research with these guys, though. I know what they're like. I know what their strengths are. Their weaknesses. Lev Romanov is a strategist at heart. He's cunning and ruthless, and I can't ever let myself forget that. Lev is like a master chess player... always several moves ahead of his opponent.

I'd do well to remember that.

It smells faintly of burnt wood and damp moss as we make it up to his front porch. This house is stunning, so different from what I've grown up with. At home, I grew up in a large, colonial-style home with stucco walls and terracotta roof tiles, traditional where I'm from. His home, though, is secluded from the city. A large, imposing structure with a fortress-like appearance shows his need for security and control. It's modern and minimalist and somehow seems perfectly fitting for a man like him... at least what I know about him.

His arms are warm around me.

*That doesn't matter.*

He's so strong, he walks with me in his arms as if I'm a little waif. I'm small, yes, but still, there's something undeniably attractive about being overpowered like this.

When we get to the door, it opens of its own accord. I'm a little confused as I try to see how he did that—before I note a guard at the door. Glaring at me.

I wonder if he's friends with the loser I ratted out. Whatever.

"Look away," Lev snarls, and the guard practically gives himself whiplash when he obeys.

He walks with me toward a room with a wide-open door, then lays me on a large, upholstered couch. Like everything here, like *him,* the room is minimally furnished and practical, but everywhere I look I see hints at high-end security with a modern flair. The walls are a stark, utilitarian gray, only a shade lighter than the couch and coordinating armchair nearby.

Discreet cameras blink at me from the corners of the ceiling, their lenses following every movement. A reminder there's no privacy here, and he trusts no one. The floors are varnished hardwood, and in the far corner of the room sits a sleek, modern desk made of straight black lines with monitors and computers and all sorts of gadgets. I'll have to look more closely when I'm rested and fed.

He taps a watch on his wrist and barks out orders in Russian. I don't know a lick of Russian, but a moment later when the door opens and the security guy comes in with a bottle of water and a plate of food, I can hazard a guess at what he was ordering.

"Drink," he orders, thrusting bottle of water at me. I take it gratefully and must wince when I hold it without realizing it because he frowns. "What's wrong with your hand?"

I look down at my palm. The splinter from earlier is tightly wedged beneath the flesh, the skin around it raw, red, and swollen.

"*Maldita sea,*" I curse under my breath. "I got a splinter in the damn loft." I give him a smile. "I was so distracted by your enjoyably effective methods of torture that I forgot all about it."

Frowning, he stands and lifts his phone again, barking out another order.

"Do you always talk to your staff like that?"

"Like what?"

"Like they personally offended you, and if they don't do what you say, you'll kill them?" I smile sweetly and take another gulp of water before eyeing the food on the tray—bread, butter, and a wedge of cheese. Typical prisoner food, but with flair.

"I don't get offended. That's childish and a waste of time. As far as doing what I say, they know better. Now eat." His tone is gruff. "We'll eat a proper breakfast after you rest, but you need to eat something now."

"Fattening me up for the kill?" I ask sweetly before I slather butter on the bread and take a large bite. My mouth waters, and my belly churns. The past month before I came here, I put myself on a strict diet regimen so I could shred. I haven't eaten bread in ages.

His expression remains stern, but there's a hint of something softer in his eyes. "Just eat. You need your strength. We have a long day ahead of us."

The effort of holding my head up is becoming too much, and though I'd never let him know it, even talking is exhausting to me now. I enjoy the simple food, even under his impassive, penetrating gaze.

He doesn't talk or ask questions, and for that, I'm thankful. After I have food and water in my belly, I lie back on the couch. It's warm in here, and I'm so damn tired. My back and ass ache from where he struck me, and this damn splinter—

"Give me your hand." My eyes fly open. I didn't even realize I'd closed them, and I have no recollection of him retrieving first aid supplies, but here we are.

I let my eyes close again and give him my hand. My eyes are so heavy. Did he drug me? I don't even care at this point. I need rest, and tomorrow, I'll make my next move.

His warm, rough hand holds mine. It hurts like fuck when he opens my palm, so I crack an eye open, but I don't flinch. I'm not afraid of pain or discomfort. I've learned to cope with both. Instead, I eye him curiously as he pokes at my palm with metal tweezers.

The painfully reddened skin screams as he digs in deep, but I don't move. I watch his concerted effort, the way his brows snap together.

"Don't take this as me hitting on you, but you really are the most handsome of all your brothers. Do you know that, or are you one of those guys who has no idea he's gorgeous?"

The Romanov men are delicious specimens of masculine perfection, and their one sister is absolutely stunning. But this guy... there's something about his brooding countenance, the warmth in his eyes, the fullness of his stern mouth and the coiled strength in his muscled body that checks off *all* my boxes.

I hiss in a breath when he finally grasps the splinter in the tweezers and yanks it out, but a second later, there's almost instant relief. I let out my breath slowly.

"Looks are fleeting," he says with a shrug. "We'll all be worm food one day." He dabs disinfectant on my palm before he slides a bandage on it.

I close my eyes and snicker. "Worm food. I like that." It's like a pragmatic way of living the whole YOLO thing. If you only live once, you might as well make the most of it.

I close my eyes, and my head falls back. I'm so damn tired. I'm just going to rest my eyes for a minute. He's saying something to me, but his voice is distant. It sounds like I'm underwater, and he's talking above me.

Something warm and soft falls over me. My subconscious starts putting pieces and parts together.

The Romanovs. I'm alive. My brother. The cartel. Power.

Visions of weddings and rings and crowns fill my head, and I fall into a deep sleep.

# CHAPTER EIGHT

*Lev*

I GLANCE at the clock and stifle a groan. Nine a.m.

I can't keep doing this, sleeping in shitty positions and places just to keep an eye on her. I have things to do, and keeping tabs on her, even if I have the help of my team, simply will not work.

Something has to give.

I get to my feet and note she doesn't stir. Mikhail will expect me on a call to update, and I have almost nothing to tell them except Isabella Morales is unbreakable.

Is that true, though?

If I really wanted to get through to her, I could push harder. She buckled under the sexual tension I put on her, and if I leaned into that—yeah. Yeah, that would very likely work. But it doesn't seem like she's actually hiding anything.

I check on her before I go. In sleep, her hands are underneath her chin. She looks almost childlike, with none of that reservation and ballsy energy that defines her. She wore herself out. I take no small measure of satisfaction knowing I had something to do with that.

Here, she'll be safely confined and under close surveillance.

Not that that stopped her yesterday. She'll try to escape again, no doubt, but probably not right away. She likely wants a shower, some food, and maybe some money before she does.

I keep a wad of cash in the desk drawer.

I want her to get this out of her system. Let her push on the walls of that cage now because the sooner she does, the sooner she'll realize she won't ever escape.

If she were a man, she'd already be six feet under, and we'd be planning our strategy to take on the LSD. But she isn't a man.

Oh, hell, she is *not a man*.

I take the call at the kitchen table—my iPad set up with a dual screen with Isabella's sleeping form on the left side, my brothers on the other.

"Morning," I tell them while I fire up the espresso machine.

"Well, good morning, sunshine," Aleks says with a smirk. "How was *your* night?"

I snort and pull out a mug. I wonder if she drinks coffee and, if she does, how she takes it. I set my mug in place and hit the button, the rich, decadent smell of hot espresso filling the room. I turn to face the camera. "Exhausting," I tell him honestly. "But I can't say this is the worst job I've ever had."

Mikhail smiles grimly. "Did she reveal anything to you when you interrogated her?"

I warm milk and frown, thinking it over. I hit the froth button and watch the milk churn. "More than she knows," I say with a shrug. I pour the foam into my mug, turn, and sit back down at the table. I glance at the screen before I elaborate. She turns over in her sleep, maybe thinking of waking up. The blanket's fallen to the side, revealing her perfect form. She starts to stretch.

"Gonna fill us in?" Viktor says darkly, leaning over in front of the screen with a scowl. He will never forgive her for sneaking onto his property unnoticed. He takes it as a personal threat against his wife.

He's not wrong.

"Yeah. I'm monitoring her on another screen. So, there's no tracking device on her at all. She really is on her own, which is telling in its own way. I know nothing else about why she's here."

Mikhail stares at the video camera in front of him. "Did you really interrogate her, brother? I know it's harder with her being a woman."

I take a sip out of my mug before I answer. I nod. "I did. I could've continued, but she was exhausted and worn out. So was I. It was a long fucking day. She almost escaped, too."

Mikhail chuckles. "And how'd that work out for her?"

I shrug. "She didn't get far."

"I found out some shit," Aleks says, looking down at his tablet. "And it corroborates what you're saying, Lev."

"Go on," I say, leaning back in my chair, my gaze locked on Aleks.

He looks up from his tablet. "Isabella's brother has been making some moves. His alliances are shifting, and he's burned some big fucking bridges. It looks like he's preparing for something huge."

I tense, my grip tightening on my mug. "Like what?"

Aleks taps a few times on his tablet, pulling up a series of documents and photos. "He's been in contact with some of our old enemies. There's talk of some kind of seismic power shift, obviously it's something to do with dismantling what we've built here in The Cove."

Mikhail curses. When he took over as *pakhan* in the wake of my father's death, his first plan was to destroy our biggest adversaries. However, it was like eliminating fucking weeds from a garden. As soon as we removed the threat of the largest one, smaller, resilient ones popped up. No one wants to see us get stronger, but with each year that passes, that's exactly what we've done.

We've come to expect challenges. But the LSD may be the most significant challenge we've faced.

Mikhail's expression grows serious. "And Isabella? How does she fit into all of this?"

Aleks shrugs. "I don't know. Maybe her brother's using her

to be eyes and ears for the cartel. Maybe she's more involved in his operations than we initially thought."

I shake my head. For some reason, I don't believe that to be true. Isabella is not the type of person to be used by any man, and she can't disguise the raw hatred she has for her brother. Aleks continues. "Maybe her presence here isn't a coincidence. Perhaps she was sent to gather intel, to find our weaknesses."

"No... I don't think that's it. Regardless, she's still absolutely a threat to us, but I haven't gotten to *why* yet. I'd bet my life she's not working for her brother. Did you find out anything else?"

"Yeah," Aleks continues. "Well, Aria did anyways." Mikhail's wife Aria is even more skilled than Aleks, often finding hidden layers of information that give us a broader, more holistic picture of the world around us and the threats lurking therein. "She dug deep into her background. You may be right, Lev, because it seems she hasn't been entirely loyal to her family. There are rumors of her sabotaging their operations. Things like freeing captives, especially women who were meant to be sold. Going against direct orders, etcetera."

"Jesus," I mutter. "I bet her brother loved that."

"Yeah," Aleks says. "There's a record here of an emergency visit last year. Looks like she had a broken arm and black eye." My vision turns hazy red, and my cup clatters to the table. Only a fucking pussy raises a hand like that to a woman. A fucking pussy.

"Easy," Mikhail says. "Think about it. What would we do if Polina sabotaged our efforts?"

"She fucking *has*," I say, shaking my head. My sister's penchant for being compassionate and fair has gotten her in loads of trouble. "You wouldn't beat her, Mikhail."

"Of course not," he says.

"Then what are you saying?" I snap.

Viktor growls, and Aleks's brows shoot up to his hairline. Mikhail clears his throat. "Watch it, Lev."

I draw in a breath and let it out slowly.

"What I'm saying is this. You are not going to lose your shit on her brother because of some kind of misplaced chivalry." He leans forward. "Am I clear?"

I'm shaking with the effort of controlling myself. They don't know what she's like. I've never seen a woman as tenacious and fucking brilliant as Isabella Morales. If some small-minded, tiny-dick asshole thinks hitting her is the way to get her compliance, I absolutely *am* fucking going to remember that.

I blow out a breath.

"Lev," he says warningly. But he can't intimidate me like he used to. When I was young and wild, before I'd sown my oats and been fully inducted into the Romanov Bratva, my older brothers acted the part of guardians. They kept me in line, made me obey the rules, and taught me discipline and respect, and as an adult, I'm grateful for that.

But sometimes, they don't remember that I'm not that fucking unruly, unpredictable kid anymore.

Still, Mikhail is my *pakhan,* and I do owe him my allegiance and respect. I know I do.

I nod. "Yes. I understand. Isabella is a wild card."

"Exactly," Aleks says. "Which makes her both dangerous and highly valuable." He sets the tablet down. "We need to decide how to handle her. If her brother finds out she's here, things could escalate quickly."

"It isn't a matter of if," Ollie says softly. "But when." I almost forgot he was there.

I nod. He's right. I take another sip of espresso, my mind racing. Her fierce resistance, her skills, and now this new intel paints an interesting albeit complex picture. She isn't just a pawn. My suspicions about her are correct—she has her own agenda.

"I'm gonna watch her closely," I say, determined. "Make no mistake. If she tries to betray us, she'll learn what happens when you cross the Bratva."

Mikhail nods. "Good."

I won't let anything jeopardize my family, not even the most beautiful woman I've ever seen.

I glance back at the screen where Isabella lies and lift my mug. I blink. Look harder. *Shit.*

She's fucking gone.

"Motherfucker," I mutter. "I'll be back." The alarm indicating she's crossed the edge of my property blares. One of my brothers chuckles, and another one curses in Russian.

I tap the surveillance footage and can see clearly where she's escaped. She's a sleek little mouse, easily moving from one place to the next undetected. *Christ.* How am I going to keep this woman under my thumb?

I force myself to stay calm while I watch the footage to see how she escaped and how I'll get to her. She moves silently through my house, using her lock-picking skills to bypass several locked doors. Her movements are precise and calculated, and there's a small smile on her lips and a gleam in her eyes that tells me she's enjoying herself immensely.

Fucking brat. We'll deal with that later. She's a few paces from the courtyard with no possible escape. She'll trigger the security lights and alert the guards.

I'll have to find another way to keep her shackled.

I take off at a run and reach her just as the blare of a second alarm sounds. She swivels to me, her eyes momentarily widened.

"Jesus," she mutters.

I walk toward her, my steps deliberate and measured, flanked by my men.

"You have no idea how badly I want to drag you across my lap and whip that ass until you're screaming for mercy," I mutter as I reach her. I deftly nab her wrists, secure them to her side, and toss her over my shoulder. "If only you didn't fucking like it."

"Oh, do I?" she says in a teasing tone. This is a game for her, a fucking *game* as if lives and entire kingdoms don't hang in the balance. My resolve snaps, and I crack my hand against her perfect, taut ass. "Mmm," she croons. "Do it again please."

I clench my hand into a fist, itching to spank her again, but not if she's begging for it.

"You don't know when to quit, do you?"

She sighs. "I will never stop trying to escape. You won't be able to keep me here forever. You know that."

"As if your brother will come and rescue you? I don't think so." We're steps from the house now. She may have tried to escape twice, but she hasn't gotten very far. "We investigated your background. We know where you stand with him."

I take the steps to my back door.

I battle growing respect and reluctant admiration for her spirit. I can't afford to show weakness, though.

"Oh? You think you know everything now, do you?"

I squeeze her ass in my palm, remembering how she almost caved when I turned her on. Maybe *that's* my key.

I spank her again, this time lighter before I run my palm along her ass. "Not yet, but I will. I do know this."

"Mmm?" she says in a low, seductive voice. I didn't know a woman could flirt while lying over my shoulder, but she does it with perfection. "What's that, handsome?"

I take her off my shoulder and slide her down the length of my body. My cock stiffens. I pull her to me and firmly grasp her chin in my hand. "There are other ways for me to keep you bound to me."

She blinks, confused. I don't bother to explain but take her by the hand and march back into the kitchen, where my brothers are still waiting, chatting among themselves. I sit down and hold her in front of me, my grip on her wrist firm and unmovable.

"Ah, you found her," Mikhail says. "Well done." He clicks his tongue. "You're playing with fire, Isabella."

"Your point?" she says haughtily. "It's the best type of play there is, *Pakhan*."

I stifle a smile. This girl is ballsy as fuck.

Viktor releases a long-suffering sigh. "My wife would agree."

*Wife.*

*Yes.*

*Wife.*

Mikhail looks at me, as if the realization hit him the same time it did me. "Having a hard time keeping her restrained, are you, Lev?"

I nod, a wicked smile spreading across my face. "Yes and no. I could chain her to the bed. I could keep her suspended in my basement. I mean, it's an excellent view while I work out."

Isabella rolls her eyes, but she's tense.

"I need a way to bind her to me permanently."

"Yes," Mikhail says, nodding, as the rest of them sit up straighter, our next move clear. "There *are* other, more effective ways to shackle her to you, aren't there? It's time, Lev."

I nod. The others in my family have done their duty.

Mikhail married Aria when he'd been newly inducted as our leader. She'd infiltrated our ranks and needed protection, their union mutually beneficial. Aleks married Harper in an arranged marriage between two families. Nikko married Vera, another strategic power move to align both families, and Viktor's marriage to Lydia had a similar impact on us.

None of the unions we'd forced, arranged, or otherwise compelled were out of love but necessity. Every marriage strengthened our family and deepened our roots here in The Cove. Every child our family welcomed became a thread in the intricate tapestry of our legacy, binding us together and solidifying our reign.

It's my turn.

Conventional methods aren't going to keep Isabella bound to me. I need something permanent. And if I know her and her dedication to the mafioso life, the best way to ensure that is to make her mine, whether she likes it or not.

"You're thinking what I am," Mikhail says, his gaze locked on mine.

I nod and grip her wrist tighter. "Of course. Vows. Marriage." I put my mouth to her ear. "She takes my name and I knock her the fuck up."

Isabella stills. A low murmur ripples through my brothers.

"Yes," Mikhail says. "Most of us have taken this step. It will absolutely infuriate Morales, and there won't be anything he can do about it."

I pretend to think about it. "I agree."

Isabella's gaze grows wicked and calculating. She smirks at me, fury in her glare. She's trying to pretend like she's above wanting to murder me. "I really, really need to talk to your sister."

"You really, really don't."

Something in me thrills at having her bound to me in a way she can't control. While "love, honor, and obey" are laughable with a woman like her, she will be tied to me in a way even she, with all her skills, can't thwart.

My tone is cold and calculated when I look back at the screen. "She's left me no choice. Since I can't control her through fear, I'll have to bind her to me with something stronger."

Isabella seems stunned by my words. It may very well be the first time I've actually surprised her. She narrows her eyes and clenches her small but tight little fists.

"If you think forcing me to marry you will make me obedient to you, you are fucking delusional."

Viktor clicks his tongue. Aleks snorts. Mikhail, however, smiles. "I have zero doubt about your exceptional ability to make this work, Lev. I have full faith in you."

I stand, release the hold on her wrist, and bring her to my chest. She tries to pull away, to break free from the tight grip I have on her, but I won't allow it. She fights fiercely, her desperation evident.

"Prepare for the ceremony," I tell Mikhail. "I want this to happen as soon as possible."

Isabella screams, kicking and struggling, but she can't get away. "You can't do this! I will never be yours willingly!"

Interesting that she says nothing about her brother. I lean into the screen. "Can you make that happen, Mikhail?"

He nods. "Of course. Consider it done. Get her to family headquarters."

"Good. I'm going to sign off so I can help my fiancée... *prepare.*"

I click off and shove the iPad away.

I turn her around to face me. My voice is low and threatening when I grip her jaw like a vise and make her look into my eyes. "You know I have the right to kill you. But that would be a terrible way to ruin the potential benefits our marriage could bring to my family."

Her beautiful eyes widen even as she presses her lips together and refuses to respond. "I don't need your willingness, beautiful. I need your compliance."

"Forcing me to marry you changes nothing!" She tries to push away but can't. "Neither does calling me beautiful."

That protest is weaker, though. So much weaker.

I loosen my grip and move my hand down the length of her neck. Her pulse quickens beneath my fingers, a tangible sign of her fear and defiance.

"That's where you're wrong. A marriage between a Romanov and a Morales changes *everything.*"

In one swift move, I yank her in front of me. She screams, thrashing and fighting with all her might, but her struggles barely register. My grip tightens. I hope she knows how futile fighting me is.

"You say it as if we aren't even individuals. As if *I'm* not Isabella and *you're* not Lev." Her voice catches. "As if our identities are meaningless and the end justifies the means."

I scoff and shake my head. "You don't get it, Isabella. But you will. Who you are, who I am, that doesn't matter in the grand scheme of things. None of it does." I grit my teeth. "And the sooner you stop fighting the inevitable, the better off you'll be."

Her eyes meet mine, a mixture of fury and something else swirling in their depths. Understanding? Resignation? I lean in, my lips brushing against her ear as I murmur, "We both know what we have to do now." This forced union will ignite a chain of events almost out of our control.

She lets out a ragged breath as if she understands the gravity of our situation. "We're in this together now, whether you like it or not," I say, my voice softer now but no less resolute. I feel a slow smile curve my lips. Being married to me *will* force her to be shackled to me... and so much more. "We can either fight it..." I brush my lips against her cheek. "Or welcome it. Make it ours."

I don't know why I feel the need to offer a hint of an olive branch. Fuck knows she doesn't deserve it.

She stops struggling, her body tense against mine, and for the first time, I feel a shred of something like compliance.

"I take *very* good care of what belongs to me," I say softly before I pull away. "Let's get you ready. I won't hold you captive anymore, either. You have free run of the place." I let her go and head to the door, pausing just before I leave. A fleeting look of desperate hope crosses her perfect face. "Go ahead and try all you like, Isabella. There is no escape.

I'll catch you. I'll hunt you down. And I'll drag you back where you belong now."

I give her a final, lingering look, leaving the door open behind me on purpose. I want her to know freedom is an illusion; the real binds that keep us together are inevitable.

I can't fucking wait to see her in a wedding dress.

Wearing my ring.

Taking vows.

Bearing my child.

The more I think about it, the harder I fucking get.

I don't know why I didn't think of this earlier.

# CHAPTER NINE

*Isabella*

I STARE at the open door.

I stare at his retreating back.

My stomach clenches. The events of the last few days have spiraled out of control. I hardly know what I want anymore.

But I know who I am. He can say what he wants. He can force me to take his name, and he will. But I'm Isabella Morales, and I will *always* be Isabella Morales.

And I have never, ever, no matter how powerless and beaten down I was, let my circumstances dictate my future. I may have been born into a family that valued me as a second-class citizen, *but that doesn't make it so.*

Fine. Lev Romanov is going to marry me. I turn over the possibilities in my mind and think it through.

Yes. Yes, I can absolutely use this to my advantage, *and I will.*

The tension still lingers in the kitchen when my belly aches for an entirely different reason. I'm *starving.*

Well, then. Make myself at home, he said.

Happily.

Lev maintains his body like a finely tuned sports car. Well, guess what? So do I.

I open the fridge and am not at all surprised to find it well stocked and immaculately clean. Excellent. Someone's watching his macros—we have at least one thing in common. Not that he cooks... It looks like most things in his fridge are prepackaged meals he gets from some kind of delivery service.

I grab a banana and yogurt before I hit the basement workout room.

I'll need my energy for the day ahead.

I look around the kitchen. Will this be *my* kitchen? Will we live here?

In that case, I could like it. Could use some color, maybe some greenery or plants and definitely more coffee cups, but it's a large, open-concept kitchen with high-end appliances.

I make myself a cup of strong, black coffee and drink it slowly while I consider the possibilities.

I fought him. I'll fight him still. But he isn't wrong. The two of us marrying might be exceptionally advantageous. He says he wants to do it to keep me chained to him or whatever, but it takes two to tango, and I am *not* going to lie down and give up. Nope.

This could be the perfect way to neutralize my brother. Once I get seated on the throne of the Los Sangre Dorada as the wife of Lev *Romanov?* Holy *hell* will heads roll. He can be king all he fucking wants as long as I reign as *queen*.

I find a single set of clothes in a guest room that will do for a workout. The tension from earlier still lingers in the air as I make my way to the gym.

I *do* need to work out. I need to clear my head, and working out has always been my way of finding focus. I need to stay strong, too.

His guards step inside as if they know better than to underestimate me.

The gym is spacious and well equipped, a testament to Lev's dedication to his own training. I get a quick vision of the two of us working out together and quickly squash it.

He isn't my friend.

*But he could be.* We could rule together.

Every time I entertain the idea, I wonder if I'm crazier than I thought. Still, though...

I take a quick look around and head straight for the punching bag, wrapping my hands with the practiced ease of someone who's spent countless hours in training. Each punch lands with a satisfying thud, the rhythm soothing my restless mind. Fuck, but it feels good to break a sweat.

My knuckles are numb, my hands aching, but I don't care.

"Carlos, for being a male chauvinistic prick and hurting my best friend," I mutter.

*BAM.*

"My father, for thinking he could teach me to be a mindless robot and for hitting my mother."

*BAM.*

"Javier, for not having a shred of human decency." I could make a litany of accusations against him, but instead I let my fists do the job.

*BAM. BAM. BAM.*

I narrow my eyes at the bag. "For Lev, for having the nerve to be so fucking hot and total fucking asshole."

I hit the bag again, and again, losing myself to the repetition until sweat blurs my vision and I'm gasping for breath.

"Wow," a deep, amused voice, says behind me. "I don't know if I should kiss you or take you over my knee."

I swivel around to see Lev standing by the entrance, watching me. His gaze is intense, a mix of curiosity and something else I can't quite decipher. A corner of his lips tips up and his eyes lazily take me in. I'm surprised when he swallows hard, his Adam's apple bobbing, as if I'm affecting him. I'm covered in sweat, the little tee riding up my belly. My hair sticks to my forehead and neck, and these boxing gloves are twice my size. I've had better days.

Well, two can play at this game.

*Kiss you or take you over my knee.*

I lick my lips. It doesn't help that blood is pulsing through my veins and I already know what he can do with that mouth. I can only imagine what it feels like lying over his lap. I would kick and scream and fight him and he'd overpower me.

And I would fucking love that.

Now that I've decided I'm going to lean into this and make the best of it, I'm giving myself permission to really appreciate the upside here. The guy is hot as hell.

Women always talk about men's arms, or their backs, or how hot they are when they take their tees off. But me? Goddamn, give me a man with *shoulders*. Shoulders I can anchor myself on when he pounds into me or bite when I wrestle my way on top.

Now it's my turn to swallow and take *him* in. Jesus, people underestimate the effect of a plain white tee stretched over well-defined shoulders, carved biceps, and a six pack.

*Rawr.*

Still, I probably shouldn't let him sneak up on me like that.

"Don't you have better things to do than watch me?" I snap, acting mildly annoyed by his intrusion.

He steps closer, his movements calm and deliberate. "I didn't realize you were so skilled."

I roll my eyes, turning back to the punching bag. He calls whacking the shit out of a punching bag *skilled?* "Yeah, honey, there's a lot you don't know about me."

He doesn't leave, instead moving to a nearby weight bench.

Out of the corner of my eye, he pops a few weights on a bar that likely equal my entire body weight. Shocker.

For a moment, we work out in silence, each lost in our thoughts. Despite myself, I can't help but glance at him. His movements are fluid and precise, his form textbook perfect —a testament to his own training and discipline. He's disciplined as fuck, and that's kind of a turn-on to a woman like me.

After a while, I stop, wiping the sweat from my brow. "Why are you here, Lev? Are you trying to keep an eye on me?"

He sets the weights down, wiping his hands with a towel. "It's not all about you, beautiful." He winks at me.

Is he... flirting?

"I'm here for the same reason you are. Or maybe I just needed a distraction."

I narrow my eyes, skeptical. "From what?"

He hesitates, then looks at me, his expression unexpectedly open. He looks away and doesn't answer at first. I wait. Finally, he shrugs a shoulder. "From everything." He lifts the bar again.

I don't know why, but his honesty catches me off guard. For a moment, I see the man behind the ruthless exterior and the weight of his burdens. It's a fleeting glimpse, but it's enough to stir something within me.

"You're not the only one with burdens," I say quietly. "We all have our own battles."

He nods as if acknowledging my words. "I know. And sometimes, it's easier to forget them for a while."

We fall into a comfortable silence. Tension ebbs away like the passing of a rainstorm. I start to understand that beneath our mutual animosity, we have a few things in common—pain, responsibility, and a drive to survive.

Today is core day, but who's keeping track. I'm sore, but that doesn't stop me from hitting planks and sit-ups with gusto. We don't talk.

Finally, I want a shower and a proper breakfast, so I head to the door.

As I go to leave, Lev calls out, "Isabella."

I turn, waiting.

"You're not alone in this," he says, his voice softer than I've ever heard it. "Remember that."

I don't respond, but his words linger as I walk away. For the first time, I wonder if there's a way through this mess where we might find a sliver of understanding. A sort of truce.

I mean, we're fucking getting married.

"I need some clothes. And... things," I tell him.

"Make a list," he says, in between bicep curls. I watch the sheen of sweat on his forehead and the carved muscles in his arms. I swallow.

"Then what?"

"I'll take care of it."

I frown. "How long will you treat me like your prisoner? Even if I do marry you?"

He drops the weight to the floor and draws himself to his full height, his hands anchored on his hips. "As long as it fucking takes. Forever if I have to."

I stifle a growl.

He lifts a ridiculous amount of weight and starts bench pressing.

Show-off.

He starts lifting. I need to find something that will distract him.

Oooh. Glutes.

I stand in front of him, feeling the weight of his gazes as I grasp a bar. With deliberate slowness, I position it across my shoulders. I glance in his direction to make sure I have his full attention then focus on the mirror in front of me. I make sure to capture his gaze in the mirror as I descend into a deep squat, my form perfect and my movements controlled. I rise, the muscles in my legs and glutes tightening with the effort, knowing he can't look away.

I repeat the motion, each squat a blend of controlled seduction. His focus shifts entirely from his lifting to watch me, a smirk playing at the corner of his lips. I add a little extra sway to my hips as I come up from each squat, my eyes never leaving his. The tension in the room thickens, charged.

His reaction is immediate and intense. He pauses mid-lift, the weights hovering as he struggles to maintain focus.

"I didn't know you were so skilled," I taunt.

His eyes narrow on me, a mix of amusement and admiration flashing in his gaze. He shakes his head from side to side. "You're not making this easy," he mutters, the low growl of his voice carrying in the quiet of the room. I watch him set his weights down with a controlled click, never breaking eye contact.

"What?" I ask with mock innocence. "I'm working out. It's not my fault you can't keep your mind out of the gutter."

He leans back against the bench, crossing his arms over his chest, and openly watches me, his eyes darkening with every squat I do.

Is it hotter in here?

"Impressive form," he finally says, his voice laced with challenge. "But can you keep it up?"

His words feel like a dare. I know as well as he does that he isn't talking about squats.

I can't look away and neither can he.

My lips curve into a playful smile as I do another squat, holding the position a beat longer just to tease him. I rise slowly, my movements fluid and deliberate. When he approaches me, there's a flicker of challenge in his eyes. He steps behind me, grabs a few more weights, and adds them to the bar, his movements deliberate and calculated. I raise an eyebrow at him.

This isn't about the weights, and we both know it.

"Think I can't handle that?" I tease. I chose lighter weights than normal just so I could taunt. I also didn't really want him knowing just how fucking heavy I can lift.

"Let's find out," he says, leaning back against the wall and folding his arms again.

I shake my head and begin another squat. It's *heavy*. I manage the first few reps easily, but I'm getting tired.

Wordlessly, he grabs two more plates.

"Keep going," he orders, his eyes on me. "Let's see what you've got."

*Bastard.*

I squat again, straining with the effort. Again, I make it down and with effort push to the top, only to find him waiting for me with two more plates.

"What the fuck are you doing?"

"You said you could take it. Show me."

I do another squat, then another. I can't breathe. My legs are shaking.

*I will not let him win.*

I explode to the top with a shot of adrenaline, fury racing through me. I lift the bar off my shoulders and before I can throw the damn thing his way, he braces it with one hand and lifts it effortlessly. He turns from me and hurls it away where it slams to the ground and rolls away, the plates spiraling away like tightly wound springs unraveling.

Before I can react, he spins back to me, eyes blazing. He moves toward me with predatory grace. I back away, but I waited too long. He's too fast. I struggle, but I'm exhausted from working out and my reaction time is impaired. In seconds, he's got me pinned to the floor.

"You don't fuck around with weights."

"You started it!"

Jesus, what am I, twelve?

"You think you can do whatever you want?" he growls, his voice a low rumble in my ear. "You think you can taunt me, workout half naked, and expect me to keep my hands off of you?"

I open my mouth, unsure of how to respond. Of course I thought I could taunt him. I thought I could workout half naked. Not sure if there was ever an assumption he'd keep his hands off of me...

He flips me over with ease, his hand crashing across my ass. The sting is immediate, and I jolt. Heat sears through me.

"You need to learn some discipline," he murmurs, his tone dark. I'm vividly aware of how turned on he is. How turned on *I* am. My God, I'm aching. He spanks me again, each strike sharp enough to make my clit throb but just enough that the pain doesn't eclipse the delicious arousal coursing through me. I'm breathless and trembling.

He flips me back over and cups my chin, tiling my face up to meet his gaze. The intensity in his eyes sends a shiver down my spine. I'm on *fire*. I touch the side of his face, my palm meets stubble, and he leans in, claiming my mouth with a punishing kiss that leaves no room for doubt. Lev Romanov wants me, and I have his fucking number.

Our tongues tangle and our breath mingles. He tastes like mint and vodka. I want more. My hands find my way to his hair, and I pull him closer as he deepens the kiss. My body arches beneath his and one large, warm palm cups the small of my back and holds me to him. The length of his erection presses against me belly.

When he breaks the kiss, his breath is ragged. I stifle a moan. I want him back.

"You drive me crazy," he mutters.

"Good." My own voice shakes. "I like keeping you on edge."

With a growl, he claims my lips again. Our bodies mold together. I'm vaguely aware of him pushing the thin layer of fabric between us aside and reaching for my pussy. I bite his lip as he strokes my clit which earns me a tight pinch.

"Fuck!" my hips jerk.

"Behave yourself," he grates.

"Never."

That earns me a nipple tweak, the asshole. My clit aches. His hands roam my body, his touch possessive and purposeful. I shiver when his fingers trace the counters of my waist and the curve of my hip before slipping under my shirt. I gasp when his palm slides upward. I've never wanted my breasts touched so badly in my life. His thumb skates over my nipple, drawing a moan from me.

"You're mine now," he whispers against my mouth.

"Is that a promise or a threat?" I don't recognize my own voice. "Prove it."

He captures my lips again. His hand leaves my breast and trails down my stomach before hooking into the waistband of my leggings. "Mmm," I moan, eager for more. My God it feels so damn good. I gasp, my nails digging into his shoulders as he strokes me with practiced ease. I'm on the edge of madness with every touch.

He moves lower, his mouth leaving a trail of fire in his wake. When he reaches the vee of my pussy, he gives me a wicked grin. And that does it. I can resist many things, but the wicked grin of a sex god ready to eat me out is my kryptonite.

I nod, wordlessly begging.

"Tell me everything," he drawls.

"Mmm." I'm aching with need. There's no need to hold back from him. We're going to fucking crush Javier and take over the cartel. He can have anything he wants from me. Only I'll spoon feed it to him to maintain some semblance of control.

"What do you want to know?" I whisper. He doesn't wait any longer. His mouth descends on me, flicking and circling and driving me wild. I cry out and my hips rise to meet his mouth.

"Javier's next plan."

"I don't know but I can find out. I have sources. People on the inside. I know he's got men in The Cove watching you. They know where your headquarters are."

He rewards me with another delicious swipe of his tongue.

"His number one lieutenant. Who is it?"

"Carlos Cabrera." I frown. "You should know that."

He bites my clit and I scream. "Hey!"

"I do know that. It was a test. Next in command."

I smack at his shoulders, but he only reacts with another lick that makes my toes curl.

"Tell me about Carlos," he orders.

"He's ruthless, loyal to Javier, but has a weakness for money. Bribing him is an option."

Another swirl of his tongue makes me gasp. I tangle my fingers in his hair.

"Javier's hideout?"

"It's a compound in the hills outside of town, but you won't find him there," I manage between breaths. "It's his safe-house and meeting point. Heavily guarded. I can get you the schematics, though."

"Security rotations?"

"Mmm."

He licks me again. Goddamn, Lev has my number. He can intimidate me all he wants but the real key is holding sex above my head.

Whatever.

He hums approvingly, sending a jolt of pleasure riding through me. "Shipments? When and where?"

"Every other Thursday. Midnight. Docks on the south side. New shipment next week – drugs, weapons, you name it."

"Good girl," he drawls. Oh, damn, I like *that*. When he licks me again, I practically see stars. I'm so on the edge.

"Javier's biggest weakness?"

I bite my lip, trying hard to concentrate through the growing haze. "Paranoia. He hates betrayal. Threatens his men's families. If you can turn someone close to him against him, it'll dismantle everything."

He grins. "I think I already did."

"You can hold onto that belief. I'll give it to you," I say magnanimously. "If you let me come on your mouth now."

His mouth returns to its task.

My body trembles and my hips rise as he licks me to completion. I explode into pleasure. Bliss floods my veins and I scream his name as I tangle my fingers in his hair. I moan, drowning in pleasure that courses through me over and over in waves of perfection until I collapse to the ground beneath him.

"You're incredible," he whispers in my ear. "Together, we'll take him down."

He pushes himself up on his elbow. Gives me a long, lingering look. Bends and brushes a kiss to my cheek before he stands and walks away.

I stare at him.

I'd say he used me, if I didn't know full well I completely let him.

I push open the door to my temporary quarters, a luxurious room that feels more like a gilded cage with each passing hour, the lingering memory of what we did making it hard to walk.

What. Just. Happened?

# CHAPTER TEN

*Lev*

I WANDER the dimly hit halls.

I took a shower. Got something to eat. Tried to sleep but all I could think about was Isabella sleeping in the room down the hall from me.

But my mind's racing with what happened today.

What happens next.

Marrying Isabella is a strategic move, but she's way more than I anticipated.

I want her. All of her. The image of her coming beneath me is burned into my memory forever. I want her so fucking bad.

Everything about her haunts me. Her defiance, her spirit, her beauty.

As I pass the office with an attached library, I notice a faint light seeping under the closed door. Curious, I push it open gently and find Isabella sitting on one of the plush chairs, a book in her hands. She looks up, startled.

"Can't sleep?" I ask, stepping into the room and closing it behind me.

She shrugs, as if trying to appear indifferent. "It's lovely here, but it's still a prison."

I can't help but smile at her. "So dramatic. I see you've made yourself at home."

She's wearing nothing but an oversized white tee and a pair of panties.

She shrugs a shoulder. "It's a particular talent of mine." Her gaze darkens and drops to my groin. "Did you make *yourself* comfortable?"

I grunt and don't respond, which makes her laugh out loud. There aren't enough showers in the world to eviscerate the need for her.

Her telling smile says everything. Little brat. "Your book collection is impressive."

I walk over to the bar cart and pour myself a drink. "Drink?"

She doesn't hesitate. "Whiskey, neat, please."

"The books were here when I bought the house. I don't touch them."

Except when I do, but I can't help wanting to hold back, to not tell her everything about me.

I hand her the glass and sit down opposite her. Our needs almost touch. We sit in silence for several minutes, the weight of what's happening next hanging between us. Finally, I break the silence.

"You're not what I expected," I admit with a shrug, swirling the liquid in my glass.

She raises a brow. "Oh? What did you expect?"

"A scared girl. Someone who would either cower and beg for mercy, or someone who would come in with a chip on her shoulder and a thirst for blood."

She tips her head to the side. "Aw. I've been too nice."

I shake my head. "No, nice isn't a word I'd use to describe you. But you're a lot easier to get along with than I expected."

She takes a sip of her drink thoughtfully before responding. "We have a common enemy, Lev."

I take a sip myself. We do.

"And what about you? You know loads about me, and I know hardly anything about you. What did you have to become to survive in your world? You aren't what I expected, either."

That surprises me. For some reason, I hadn't considered the fact that she'd have any expectations about me at all. "What did you expect?"

"I thought you were an awkward teen."

I laugh out loud. "I was. Once upon a time."

She gives me an appreciative grin. "Well, sir, I can say with confidence those days have passed."

Mmm.

I lean back, studying her. "People in my world – *our* world – they don't stay innocent."

"No," she says sadly. "You have to either die or become a monster yourself."

Exactly.

"Yeah."

We fall silent again, both of us lost in our thoughts.

"Marriage isn't just a strategy." I polish off my drink. "It's a way to protect you."

Her eyes flash. "I don't need a man to protect me. I can take care of myself."

Jesus. Here we go again. "But maybe you don't have to. God, woman, we're in this together now."

She clenches her fists and turns away.

I push myself to my feet. Over the proverbial pillow talk. We're getting married whether she likes it or not. I finish my drink and look over my shoulder.

"Get some sleep. Tomorrow, we're heading to my family home."

I swear as I leave. I hear her glass shatter into shards behind me.

# CHAPTER ELEVEN



I SIT IN THIS... *prison.* A well-decorated, very comfortable prison, yes, but it's still a fucking prison.

The room in his family's home is extravagant... from what I've seen, anyway. It's impeccably clean, too. My mama would approve, though she never understood the American love of neutrals and whites. But even though this room is gorgeous, I still feel as if I'm caged.

I practically am.

He made sure to remind me of that before he left to go help with preparations or whatever, our earlier conversation forgotten.

All day, I've heard people coming and going outside my door. Lev's men scurry about, making arrangements. He's leaving nothing to chance, ensuring there's no possible way for me to escape. I've tried the windows, the locks, even the ventilation ducts. He's covered every possible escape. I met with his family, we discussed the wedding, then he brought me to this room.

I guess the whole freedom thing doesn't apply *here*. The truth is, though, I could escape even this room if I put my mind to it, but breaking out of here doesn't hold the appeal it once did.

I stare out the window when the door swings open, and Lev steps in. He's calm, composed, every bit the cold and ruthless strategist I've come to despise. When his eyes meet mine, the fire in them stokes flames of my own.

He's cunning, wicked and fearless... *and I want him.*

I so fucking want this man all to myself.

Yes. Yes, we're going to do just fine. I mean, we'll have our growing pains.

"It's all set," he says. "We're almost ready."

I'm glad he doesn't ask, *Are you?* Because that would be a 'hell no'. I try to remember the glimmer of whatever I saw in him earlier. I try to remember my promise to myself to make this work.

I clench my fists, fighting the urge to lash out. "You're making a mistake," I spit. "I'll never be yours willingly."

He steps closer, and for a moment, I see a flicker of something in his eyes, but it's gone as quickly as it came. "You don't have a choice," he replies. "The sooner you accept that, the easier this will be for both of us."

I manufacture a glare at him... playing along, my mind racing.

I'll let him think he's won.

As he turns to leave, I let my posture relax slightly, a hint of defeat in my stance. There's some kind of surveillance in here. I know it. It's all part of the plan. The more compliant I appear, the more likely he is to let his guard down. And when he does, I'll be ready.

"I'll be back soon."

I open my mouth to stop him, but the door clicks shut behind him. What is taking so long?

I take a deep breath, forcing myself to stay calm. I can't afford to lose control now. This marriage may be a trap, but it's also an opportunity. I'll use it to learn everything I can about the Bratva's operations and his weaknesses. I'll gather every piece of information, every scrap of intel, and I'll use it to bring not only Lev down but fucking *everyone else*. My brother won't even know what hit him.

Tonight, I'll be his bride, but that doesn't make me his. Not truly. I'll bide my time, play my part, and when the moment is right, I'll strike.

Lev thinks he's the only one playing a game, but he's wrong. So fucking wrong.

Sun breaks through clouds on the other side of the heavy drapes. Hope. There's hope.

I stand in front of the mirror and make my decision. I'll play along with him. I'll let him think he won. He'll expect me to fight, so I'll give him that, and I might even fucking enjoy it.

Yes. This might work really, really well.

I *could* get out of here if I really wanted to; I know I could.

Then what? No matter how hard I try, no matter what resources I secure, I'll never be able to take over my family on my own and claim my rightful position of power. If I could, I'd have done it already.

The odds are stacked against me. But with the help of the Romanovs...

I thought he said he was ready? Now that it's go time, I'm growing impatient.

Finally, the door creaks open, and I tense, expecting another guard. Instead, it's Lev. He steps inside, closing the door softly behind him. For a moment, we just look at each other, the silence heavy and charged. This time, he doesn't glare at me as he did before but looks a bit more... contemplative.

"What?" I ask, my voice sharper than I intended. I swallow hard when his brows draw together and his lips purse.

I remember what it was like being chained in his basement. I remember the erotic charge between us.

He doesn't respond immediately, just walks over to the window and stares out. His presence is a bit unnerving. I don't know what to expect.

"They tell me you're not eating," he says finally, his tone surprisingly gentle. "You need to keep your strength up."

It's the last thing I expect him to say. "Somewhere between 'you'll be my prisoner, oh, just kidding, how about my wife,' I lost my appetite." I roll my eyes.

"Watch it, woman," he says in a low purr that makes my skin heat.

I can't let him see that he's affected me. I scoff, crossing my arms. "Why do you care? I'm only a pawn in this game. You know that. All you need is a warm body."

He turns to face me. "Maybe you don't have to fight this so hard." He rests his hand on mine. "We've received word that your family knows you're marrying me today. Let the adventure begin."

My *God*. So soon, they know? I flinch, unprepared for the sudden wave of anxiety that grips me. The room feels too small, the air too thick. I gasp, trying to steady my breathing, but the panic takes hold. I can almost feel my brother's hands around my neck, squeezing the air out of my lungs. He tried once before, but one of his beefy captains shoved him off and told him my father would kill him for losing his temper with me.

There are no barriers now. Though I celebrated the day we buried my father, I knew it meant I was fair game to Javier. I can still feel his hands around my neck. My eyes bulging as I clawed at his fingers and gasped for breath. The heat in my face and the bruises on my neck I had for weeks.

I'm struggling for breath. Reminding myself that won't happen again.

There are many ways to kill a man, and I've rehearsed damn near all of them. He *won't* hurt me again.

Lev's expression changes. Frowning, he holds my hand. "Isabella, breathe. Look at me."

I try to focus, but it's hard. The walls feel like they're closing in, and my chest is tight. "I can't... I can't breathe."

"Listen to my voice," he says, his tone steady and calming. "Inhale slowly, hold it, then exhale."

I follow his instructions, my breaths shaky but gradually slowing. His eyes never leave mine. After what feels like an eternity, the panic begins to ebb.

"What happened there?" he asks.

I let out a breath, still lightly caught in the panic attack. I shake him off and try to brush it away. "Nothing. I'm fine."

"No, you're not fine. I mentioned your family. Is there something you need to tell me?"

There are lots of things I need to tell him and even more that I don't.

I shake my head. "It'll go away." I turn to face him. It's time to give him a bit of the truth. If the two of us are going to conquer together, he'll need to know. I swallow hard. "Suffice to say, my family is nothing like yours."

His gaze darkens, and he leans in closer. "I know this. But once you're mine, they can't touch you. They can try, but I won't allow it." He drops his voice. "None of us will."

For a moment, we stand there in silence. I'm not sure how much of what he's telling me is bullshit and how much is truth. He's still the man who's forcing me into this marriage, but right now, he's also the man who helped me through a panic attack.

"Why are you being kind to me?" I ask, my voice barely above a whisper.

He looks away, staring out the window. "You're going to be my *wife*."

In my world, that explains nothing. In his, there's no more to say.

Maybe Lev isn't just a monster. Maybe he's as trapped as I am.

His words hang in the air, and for the first time, I see a crack in his armor.

I don't need a man to protect me. I never have and never will. It matters to me to take care of myself.

"Even as your wife, I don't want your sympathy," I say, though the words lack their usual venom.

"I know." He opens his mouth as if to say something else, then shakes his head. "We're ready now. Get dressed."

With that, he turns and leaves the room, the door closing softly behind him. I'm left standing by the window, my mind a whirl of conflicting emotions.

I stare around the room. I feel like I've just run a marathon.

Somebody left a white dress wrapped in plastic for me. After carefully putting it on, I stand in front of the mirror, the silk of my wedding dress smooth under my fingers. It's beautiful, an intricate design of lace and satin that clings to my curves in all the right places. But to me, it's nothing more than a symbol of my captivity.

Lev has outdone himself in making sure this wedding is perfect. The room is filled with flowers we'll use for the wedding, their cloying scent heavy in the air. I glance at the door, knowing there are guards posted just outside, ready to pounce at the slightest hint of rebellion.

A knock at the door startles me. His sister Polina, steps in. I knew I'd find sympathy with her, which is probably why he didn't want me meeting her right away.

"Oooh. It's gorgeous, Isabella." Tall and willowy with white-blonde hair, she looks nothing like her brothers, but this family is unlike others. Maybe the only thing that makes the men look like each other are the scowls and muscles.

She's carrying a small bouquet of roses, her expression a mixture of sympathy and resignation.

"You look beautiful," she says softly, handing me the bouquet.

"Thanks," I reply, trying to keep my voice steady. "Not bad for a fake wedding." I laugh, but it sounds a bit choked.

Polina gives me a sad smile. "Oh, there's nothing fake about this."

I nod. That's not what I meant.

She clears her throat. "This might not make sense to you now, but I promise—my brothers aren't as mean as they might seem. I won't make excuses for what they do, but... well, anyway. Maybe he'll surprise you."

Her words give me a flicker of hope. She doesn't seem like a liar. It doesn't matter, anyway. We can still rule together if we call a truce.

We'll be much *stronger* if we forge an alliance...

"It's my own fault," I tell her. "I was the one who broke the rules." I shrug. "They could've killed me."

She winces. "I've heard a lot about you. I know you're *strong*. It takes incredible strength to do this. Don't forget that."

I nod, taking a deep breath. "I will."

"Alright," she says, brushing an invisible speck of dust from the length of her dress that falls to the floor in rippling silver. "What can I do to help?"

I stare at my mop of hair and face. "I can tell you how to pick any lock or find an exit in the tightest of situations. I can show you how to become invisible and stay resilient under pressure." I tug at my mass of hair. "But something tells me a messy bun isn't gonna work for this ceremony, and I don't know highlighter from foundation from concealer, so... help a girl out?"

She claps her hands together with glee. "My God, yes. *Yes*. This is like giving a master painter a blank canvas in front of a breathtaking sunrise. I am honored." I can't help but smile. Her enthusiasm lifts my spirit. She sighs and tucks a wisp of hair behind my ear. "You and my brother will have *the* most *gorgeous* children on *the planet*."

Children. Yikes. I've barely gotten past the part where we'll have to consummate this shit, something I have to admit, I am very much looking forward to. But... children?

She does up my face with some magical potions or whatever, and when she's done, I nod appreciatively. "Impressive," I murmur. My eyes are brighter and my complexion flawless. My lips are fuller and a bit pouty. She even put this shimmery thing on my cheeks so when I turn to the side, I feel like I'm glowing.

"You are *so pretty*," she says wistfully. "Now, they're waiting for us. We've kept them waiting quite a long while, so there's a nod to your Colombian heritage." She's not wrong. Colombians have what may be called a leisurely concept of time. "*Hora Tipicia*," Colombian time, means that a bride might show twenty or thirty minutes late for her own wedding.

The preparations outside this door have died down, so now is as good a time as any. Plus, who knows how long this makeup will last.

Polina winks. "Let's get this over with."

It feels like she's on my side.

Maybe I have more choices than he thinks.

The ceremony will be held in a grand hall, every inch of it screaming wealth and power. Lev stands at the altar, looking every bit the formidable Bratva leader. His suit is perfectly tailored, his posture rigid, his eyes fixed on me as I walk down the aisle.

My heart leaps in my chest when his gaze locks onto mine. God, why does he have to be so irresistibly handsome? That blend of ruthless bad boy, dominant male, and suave charisma makes it impossible to look away. My self-protective instincts scream at me to run, while my primal instincts bow down in submission to this alpha male who promises to take good care of what belongs to him.

I force myself to meet his gaze, to show no fear. Each step feels like a march to my doom, but I hold my head high. I won't give him the satisfaction of seeing me break.

Yeah, I can be a little dramatic, but it's in my blood.

A priest stands nervously in front of us as if sensing the tension in the room. We didn't do any of that dramatic walking down the aisle pomp and circumstance.

"This won't change anything," I say in a low voice, playing my part.

Lev's response is icy, his jaw tight. "It changes everything. As my wife, you'll be bound to me in every way."

Is that so, Mr. High and Mighty? Heh.

The priest drones on and on, flipping through a well-worn book with tattered pages. The officiant begins the ceremony, his voice a dull drone in the background. I barely hear the words, my mind focused on my plans. I need to gather information, find allies, and wait for the right moment to make my move. This marriage is just a means to an end.

When it's time to exchange vows, Lev takes my hand. His grip is firm. Possessive. "I, Lev, take you, Isabella, to be my lawfully wedded wife," he says, his voice steady and unwavering. "To have and to hold, from this day forward, for better, for worse, for richer, for poorer, in sickness and in health, until death do us part."

I'll remember that, Mr. Romanov.

I swallow hard, fighting back the scream rising in my throat. I never thought I'd be here. Here goes nothing.

"I, Isabella, take you, Lev, to be my lawfully wedded husband," I say, the words tasting bitter on my tongue. "To have and to hold, from this day forward, for better, for worse, for richer, for poorer, in sickness and in health, until death do us part."

The rings are exchanged, cold metal slipping onto my finger. I stare at the physical reminder I'm shackled to him.

*D'aw. How sweet. A mini handcuff.*

When the officiant pronounces us husband and wife, Lev leans in, his lips brushing mine in a chaste kiss. I brace myself. I remind myself to stay aloof, not to allow him to have any power over me at all, but the touch sends a shiver down my spine. He's hot, and I'm not dead. And now that we're married… there's no telling what he'll do to me next.

When the ceremony ends and we turn to face the crowd, the applause is deafening. When I glance at Lev, his expression is inscrutable.

*This is just the beginning,* I remind myself. The game has only just begun.

His hand grazes my elbow. I stifle a shiver at his touch, even as my body tingles and my heart beats faster. I swallow, quickly scanning the room to anchor myself. I catch Polina's gaze, and she winks at me. I wink back, take in a deep breath, and march forward beside my *husband.*

Means to an end. *Means to an end,* I chant in my head. I can do this.

As we walk down the aisle together, side by side, I vow silently to myself that I will find a way out. Lev may think he's won, but he doesn't know what I'm capable of. I will bide my time, gather intel and strength… and when the moment is right, I will make my move.

"Phew," I mutter under my breath. "Something about being held captive and being forced to marry a Russian gives a girl an appetite, I guess."

Lev's large, rough, warm hand squeezes mine just a bit. His eyes spark at me. "I get it. There's something about keeping a Colombian firecracker princess hostage that's made me a bit peckish, too."

I can't help it. A corner of my lip twitches. He's told me we're in this together, but I am not so sure about that. I need cold, hard evidence before I will believe it.

I'm more than a little pleased, though. It's nice to know I haven't been the easiest to keep prisoner. I haven't lost my touch. Maybe he isn't quite as hard to read as he thinks he is.

"You shine up nice," I say appreciatively when he shrugs out of his suit coat and leads me into the dining room. I can throw him a bone.

The room is set up with large vases of flowers in deep reds and oranges. The air is filled with the warm scents of cinnamon and clove, making my heart ache just a little. I don't miss my family, but I do love my homeland. The colors and scents remind me of the markets in Colombia.

I'll get back there.

There's a small table set for two a bit apart from the rest, and he leads me over to it.

"I shine up nice?" he says with a smirk. "I'd say the same for you, but you never lost your luster. Even when you're angry, you're beautiful." He sighs. "*Especially* when you're angry. You're glowing, but it doesn't take much to spark your eyes, does it?"

I stare at him before responding. There's no hint of foul play or sarcasm in his tone.

He pulls out a chair for me while I stand frozen. "Did you just pay me a *compliment?*"

"Definitely not," he says, shaking his head. I unfreeze and fold myself into the chair, giving him a curious look. "Just an observation," he finishes.

"Right," I say, remembering how my father would rant about my looks and scream about keeping me away from predators and men who would use me. I wasn't allowed to wear anything tight or remotely appealing. I couldn't wear makeup or two-piece bathing suits, and the day he caught me trying on lip gloss, he gave me a fat lip. His "protection" had nothing to do with me and everything to do with his own pride.

On the surface, it might seem Lev's appreciation of me is something I would want. But I know better.

"Any word from my brother yet?" I ask, hoping he doesn't notice the way my hand trembles when I reach for the wine glass. Before answering my question, he asks one of his own.

"Wine?" I blink at the label, taken aback. *Marqués de Villa de Leyva.* A nod to my homeland.

"Mmm. Please," I say. He pours me a generous glass, and I close my eyes and inhale. My father died when I was eighteen. While others drank this exact wine to honor his death, I drank for another reason altogether—in celebration of the end of tyranny. The first layer of it, anyway. "So? Anything?"

"Yes. Javier has a few associates lurking nearby, but none of them have made a move yet."

I smile at snapping cameras. We hold our wine glasses up next to each other as if they're kissing and clink the rims. "He will," I say, smiling at the camera. "Get me the names of who's here and I can tell you exactly how. We're not impermeable. He will either think you've captured me against my will and our marriage was a power move or that I've betrayed him and given myself over to the enemy, plotting an attack against him." I shrug. "In both cases, he'd be right. Still. We have to be careful."

He nods but doesn't otherwise respond as his family enters the large room. I notice Viktor first, because he's so huge it's hard to miss him. I wonder idly if he books two plane tickets when he flies. His wife Lydia stands next to him, a full-figured, stunning woman with thick, wavy brown hair, wearing a red dress that shows off every curve and dips dangerously low, all the way to her navel. She catches my eye and blushes, wiggling her fingers at me. I smile and hold my glass to her.

Cheers to the women who married into this family because they had no other choice.

Aleksandr, the tall one with dark black hair, is sitting, talking to his mother, his wife Harper on his other side. I know them mostly from research. Harper was a Bianchi before she married into this family, and I know for a fact she can outshoot every damn person here.

I find all the brothers from the warehouse, but someone's missing... hmm. Who's missing? Oh, right, Nikko, the assassin. His wife Vera is often off somewhere doing fieldwork, and even though he was here earlier, he's likely off on the trip with her.

And Mikhail. Where's Mikhail? The eldest brother and leader of all, I need to keep my eye on him.

Wait... there he is. Walking in here now.

Others are present—people I don't know and people who don't matter for my purposes. Cousins and aunts and uncles, or associates and paid help, smaller, less powerful men from the Romanov Bratva, businessmen and women. Who knows, and who cares?

The one who matters the most is sitting right next to me.

Mikhail nods and gives Lev and me a little, informal bow before he reaches for his wine glass and clears his throat. His wife Aria, with a slim pair of glasses perched on her nose and her wild mane of curly hair momentarily tamed in a bun, eyes me with curiosity.

"Tell me again about Aria," I whisper to Lev. "I couldn't find much about her online except that she's good with computers and married to Mikhail."

Lev leans in. It feels somehow intimate whispering like this as if we're friends. Allies. And even though we're married, we're neither friends nor allies... yet.

But we could be.

"Aria's the world's best hacker," he says with no hint of exaggeration. He simply states this as fact, which gives veracity to his statement, in my opinion. "There's no one she can't find, nothing she can't do. She sees the world's most impermeable firewalls and encryption as a personal insult and challenge."

"Oh, wow." Oooh. Now, that is awesome. The more I think about it, the more it would make sense for me to lean into the Romanov family and all they bring to the table. Here, each one of their skills builds a solidified front, whereas in my family, one only sees another's strengths as a personal threat to their safety.

World's best hacker... world's best hacker. Hmm. I could do something with that.

I take a sip of the wine and look at Mikhail.

"A toast," he says, clearing his throat as he waits for the ensemble of guests to quiet. "Ever since Lev joined our family, he's had to make a show of himself. Prove his worth as younger and smaller than the rest." Mikhail's lips twitch. "It was nothing we demanded of him but something he did on his own because Lev is fierce and proving himself mattered to him."

The room quiets down. Viktor looks at Lev with pride, and Aleks sits up straighter in his seat. "And some of us thought we were better by sheer age and brute force until Lev taught us otherwise."

Lev smiles, but there's a sadness in his eyes. I, too, have borne the pain of not being enough for my family based on where I came in the lineup and having nothing at all to do with my actual talents, gifts, what I could do, or who I am.

"I know what that's like," I mutter to him in a low voice.

"Having to get stronger than five brothers?" Lev asks, his brow lifted teasingly. "Glomming endless YouTube videos on how to best someone bigger and stronger than you in a match like David defeating Goliath? How many of your older brothers did you have to beat up?"

I shrug and stretch, mimicking buffing my nails.

"All of them," I say with a yawn.

He snorts. "I thought you only had one brother."

"Well, yes, but that's all of them."

Mikhail continues and Lev's eyes twinkle a bit. He whispers in my ear, "I'd like to hear that story sometime."

I whisper back, "It seems we both have some stories to share."

"And now," Mikhail says, holding his glass up. "We've seen the youngest among us rise to the top. He's fought every adversary that's come his way and proven himself tirelessly the most loyal, the most dedicated, the most dependable brother we could ask for."

"Hey," Aleks says with mock effrontery.

Mikhail ignores him, and his mother, a regal woman with gorgeous silver hair and twinkling blue eyes, laughs. "It's not a competition, son."

"Oh, but it is," Lev whispers to me. "I might have to knock you up with triplets. You game?"

I bury my face in the wine glass and pretend I didn't hear him. I absolutely love sex. *Love. It.* I swear to God, people who don't aren't doing it right. But the thought of other little humans occupying my body—well, I'm not quite there yet, especially if said humans contain Romanov blood.

What have I gotten myself into?

"Do you have like... breeding competitions?"

Lev seems to be mulling this over. "Well, that's a crass way to put it."

I feel my brows shoot into my hairline. "Is there another way to put it?"

"Mmm," he says but nods toward Mikhail, who's finishing up. We're putting a pin in this conversation, pronto.

"On behalf of the entire Romanov family, we want to thank you, Lev, and welcome you, Isabella. Though our future is uncertain, know this: By marrying into the Romanov family, you are now one of us, and we welcome you."

My nose feels all tingly, and my throat surprisingly tight.

I guess he maybe, probably, *has* to say something like that, but it doesn't mean I'm not eating it up.

They all cheer, and we clink glasses. I lift my glass for Lev to refill.

But Mikhail is still standing up. "On a practical note," he begins. "Our enemies will be on the prowl."

We all know without him saying that said enemies are *my family*.

"They will be looking for you after word gets out that you've been married. I've decided it's in everyone's best interest for you two to take a honeymoon in an undisclosed location. When we're done here, Aria will give you all the details. Even I don't know where you're going."

"Heavily encrypted!" Aria says with a grin. "But I promise, I found a perfect spot. You're gonna love it."

Lev can't disguise the look of surprise on his face. "A honeymoon?"

I shift in my seat, not making eye contact with him. I know what happens on a honeymoon. He knows what happens on a honeymoon. Whatever happened when he interrogated me in the basement only stoked my appetite. We're going away?

"Yes, a honeymoon. You two will go away for a week, and in that time, we'll keep a close eye on any developments."

I don't need him to tell me exactly what those developments could be. I know as well as he does.

"For now, a toast to the newlyweds." He lifts his glass and pronounces something in Russian.

"What does that mean?" I ask Lev.

"It means may the happy couple have lots of babies and lots of practice trying."

I stare, my mouth agape when I notice him smirking.

"You lied!"

He shrugs. We toast and drink, and the doors open, and staff pour in.

"In *my* family, weddings are practically acts of war."

"Why does that not surprise me?"

"Mmm. During my cousin Eduardo's wedding, someone secretly poisoned the champagne used for the toast. Several guests were in agony after toasting. Another time, when I was a small girl, a bride's brother was kidnapped and beaten before the ceremony was about to begin. We had to reschedule the wedding and negotiate his release. Another time, during a celebration, an older uncle who was kind of an asshole disguised himself as wait staff and launched a surprise attack." I sip my wine. "My family's *fucked up*."

"Got it," he mutters into his wine glass. "Don't expect a wedding gift."

I stare at the platters of food.

"You look shocked," Lev says as I watch the staff mill about, serving salads and appetizers. They lay silver trays of decadent food in front of us. I blink in surprise.

"Lev, is that... *bandeja paisa?*" My throat is a little tight. Someone actually arranged for the traditional wedding feast of my homeland. The platter includes grilled steak, chorizo, fried pork belly, and a variety of other foods that make my mouth water—rice and beans, avocado, and fried plantains. Another platter of *arepas*, delicious little fried cornmeal cakes, accompanies the rest. They even have tamales and empanadas. "Wow."

"I thought you could celebrate a day like today with some food you were familiar with." He shrugs.

I stare at him. There are more layers to him than I expected.

"Thank you." I don't need to be asked twice and make a large plate of food then tuck in. Mikhail said we leave in an hour, so we probably have forty minutes left or so. He eats as well, and even though they've brought some more traditional Russian foods, he tries everything from Colombia.

"What do you think?" I ask.

Do I care what he thinks?

"It's not Russian," he says, his eyes twinkling. "But I could see how food like that puts hair on your chest."

"Excuse *me*," I mutter under my breath. "You've seen my chest, and it's absolutely hairless."

He leans over and plucks a remnant of my fried plantain and pops it in his mouth. "I've seen all of you, and I can indeed confirm you're hairless *everywhere*." My belly spasms, and heat builds between my legs. "But I look forward to doing a more thorough inspection later tonight."

If I were more innocent, I'd likely blush. I only pour myself another glass of wine.

Polina makes us take picture after picture and keeps commenting on our future babies. Lev snorts, but I can tell he's pleased. His brothers each congratulate him, one at a time. I have a growing suspicion that he's been oppressed by his family, just like I have. They may be closer and less hostile, but he's had to prove himself to them.

Maybe we have more in common than we thought.

Time flies by until the chop of helicopter blades catches the attention of everyone.

"Time to go," Mikhail says. He leans and whispers something to Lev, who nods soberly.

"Yeah. I do." What the hell is that about? Probably something about keeping me in line or whatever. Good luck with that.

"Here," his mother says, bringing a covered plate over to us. "You can't leave without your dessert."

"Thank you," I say graciously, taking it. Something in me stirs at the sound of helicopter blades.

I'm escaping. Leaving. And even though logically I know it isn't true—I just took vows to a man who's a sworn enemy—my brother won't be able to find me. Even Lev's brothers won't know where we are.

They all stand and cheer as we make our way toward the exit. I'm barefoot, having kicked off my painfully tight wedges, and when I lift the edge of my gown, Polina squeals.

"Here!" she says, handing me a pair of black flats. "Take these. Mom buys more shoes than she knows what to do with. I grabbed these from her closet. The tags are still on them."

I take them, touched by the gesture. "Thank you!"

She leans in. "And I packed everything else you asked me about, too."

Thank God for sisters. My throat gets a little tight. "Seriously, thank you. I owe you."

I slide them onto my feet. They're warm and soft and fit like a glove. My throat tightens. Lev holds the door open in front of him.

"I could carry you if your feet hurt," he says softly, his brow furrowed. "Are you alright?"

"I'm fine," I tell him, taking his hand and joining him as we head outside to the helicopter. I'm not, though. I'm not at all. I'm disarmed and wary, a decidedly unnerving combination.

"C'mere," he says, shaking his head, and before I know what's happening, he's swinging me up in his arms. "I can't carry you over a threshold so this will have to do."

Everyone cheers behind us, and I actually feel my cheeks blush.

Am I seeing the man behind the mask? The man behind the monster?

## CHAPTER TWELVE

*Lev*

IT'S ABOUT damn time all that formality is over.

We took the first step, and I'm so goddamn ready for the next.

We have shit to do.

Polina presses a bag into Isabella's hand and kisses her cheek, then mine. "You boys do this in the most unconventional ways, but I do love that I have another sister. Be good to her. She has *excellent* energy."

Oh, does she? Whatever the fuck that means. I roll my eyes. I've already hunted her down trying to escape twice, and even now, I'm on the lookout for any escape method she might use because she knows as well as I do that once she gets on the helicopter, there will be no escape.

I took Mikhail's reminder to heart. I know exactly how to keep Isabella shackled to me.

She's behaving for now, though.

I give Polina a quick hug. "Thank you."

"Here," I tell Isabella, pointing at the bag. "She's put clothes in there that you can change into." I snap my gaze to where the pilot sits. "She's getting changed. Close your fucking eyes." I'd kill him barehanded and fly this thing myself before I let him see an inch of her bare skin.

Isabella winks at me and slithers out of her wedding dress with a sigh of relief. "Mmm. Thought you'd never ask." In seconds, her dress is in a heap on the floor, and she's wearing slim black bike shorts and a tank top. "That's so much more comfortable. Going somewhere warm?"

"So I'm told."

I quickly dress, too, and put our dress clothes in my bag. Next, we slide on headsets to drown out the deafening sound of the helicopter blades, and we buckle in. I lean back in the seat and draw in a deep breath. I am so damn ready for a vacation.

A crackling noise sounds in my ears. "We'll communicate via the headset." It's the pilot. I've flown with him before, but he introduces himself to Isabella. "Mr. Romanov and I served in the Russian Army together. I owe Mikhail my life. In other words, you can depend on me." He grins. Mikhail doesn't do anything half-assed.

"We have a two-hour flight ahead of us. Please enjoy the ride and let me know if you need any assistance."

Yeah, I won't be needing any more assistance than making sure the guy gets us safely to wherever we're going. "Thank you," I tell him.

The chop of the blades is muffled but steady as we rise into the air, clouds quickly skating beneath us. I look at Isabella to see how she's doing, but she's frowning.

I tap the headset comms button, but she talks first.

"Lev," she says with a frown. "Mikhail didn't order *two* helicopters, did he? Something's not right."

I glance out the window and spot the rapidly approaching aircraft. It's definitely not ours.

We aren't the only ones who have noticed. Below, I can see Mikhail with his arm up, yelling at everyone to go for cover. *Shit.* We're under attack.

Instinctively, I tap the headset, connecting with our pilot.

"Incoming hostile chopper. Evasive maneuvers now," I command, my voice sharp.

The pilot snaps to and immediately complies, banking hard to the left. We lurch forward in our seats, but his move buys us time. I quickly scan the interior of our helicopter. My brother wouldn't send us alone and airborne unarmed.

*Ahhh.*

I find the emergency weapons stashed under the seat. I pull out a MP-9 submachine gun equipped with a suppressor and pass a Glock 19 pistol to Isabella. Her eyes gleam. She's fucking *thrilled* by this turn of events, grinning ear to ear like a kid in a chocolate shop. I swear to God, I think I just married a psychopath.

"Stay low, and be ready," I tell her, my tone brooking no argument as I reach for the door.

"No, I've got this." She nods, her eyes focused and determined. "This is Javier or one of his friends, I know it. He wants to go out in style? *Bring* it."

As the enemy helicopter closes in, they soar above us, angling slightly downwards so they can get parallel to us, about 30 meters to our portside. We see three men in the door, lining up their shots with wicked looking long rifles.

The pilot continues flying evasively, trying to make it difficult for them to accurately hit our chopper, or draw close but their pilot is persistent and matches our maneuvers with deft skill.

"We need to prevent them from getting a clean shot at our pilot or the tail rotor," I tell Isabella. "Cover me."

"No! Let me! They won't shoot at me."

She's already got her hand on door lock mechanism.

*Fuck.*

I can't believe how fast she moves; how quick and lithe she is.

I nod.

"Cover me!" she shouts again as she unlatches the side door. She doesn't have to ask me twice. She's *my wife.*

The wind roars, and the helicopter rocks with the turbulence, the wind dragging her small frame half out of the helicopter, but she steadies herself and pulls herself back in. I position myself next to her.

The first asshole I see, I pull the trigger. Fire bursts from my gun, the bullets hitting him in the chest. He releases his grip and plummets. The second one's eyes go wide and he hesitates, giving me all the time I need to take him out. The third one, leans out, resting his feet on a landing skid and grasping a handle inside the doorframe, but Isabella leans around me and shoots him in the hand, causing him to lose his grip and fall.

Their helicopter hovers dangerously close. A fourth gunman aims straight at her. I fire and hit him straight between the eyes. His face explodes into a pink mist of chopped meat. He falls. Another chopper pulls up on our starboard side.

"There's another helicopter," I scream to her so I can be heard over the roaring wind. "We need to take them out!"

"Fucking *bring it*!" she screams. "We're gonna do something risky. Trust me." She signals to the pilot to bring our helicopter close to the ground.

"Do what she tells you!" I yell into my headset. Even with the headsets, the noise is deafening.

As we approach the ground, Isabella screams, "Get ready to jump!"

"Are you fucking insane?"

"Trust me!" She looks straight into my eyes. "Husband."

*Fuck.*

"We're getting out," she says. "Keep us steady and don't fucking kill us."

As the helicopter grazes the ground, she grabs my hand. We leap together, landing hard on the grass of what appears to be a park of some kind. I pull her up and yank her behind me.

This caught them off guard. We use the element of surprise to our advantage. They stare, shocked, for a second as their chopper whizzes by, but that was probably her whole point.

We dart for the trees nearest us. The enemy chopper swings back around, lands and deposits four more sicarios on the ground directly in front of us before we can reach safety.

A thin, lithe woman lunges straight for Isabella, but she doesn't even bat an eye at the threat. Elbow to the neck crushing her larynx, knee to the belly, she knocks her attacker down and puts two bullets in her skull, her life ended in an instant. Another shoots at me and misses. I pull the trigger, thankful my brother doesn't cheap out with weapons. His chest explodes.

*Two down.*

I look up and see Isabella riding on the back of a third attacker, plunging a blade into his neck, his blood spraying everywhere. Definitely potential psychopath.

*Three down.*

The fourth takes aim at my wife; I take immense pleasure in pulling that trigger. Within seconds, we've eliminated every damn man and woman who has dared to attack us. They never stood a chance. We secure the enemy helicopter.

I quickly make my way to the cockpit. "Stand down!" I scream at the pilot, my gun jammed into his temple. He scowls and doesn't respond. Isabella comes up behind me, her blood-soaked face a mask of beautiful fury, like an avenging angel.

"*¡Retírate, imbécil!*" she screams. "*Sabes quién soy y sabes de lo que soy capaz!*"

I have no idea what she just said, but he absolutely does. With a whimper, he turns to face us. For a moment, I think he's given himself over, but at the last second, he lunges toward her. I pull the trigger.

She looks at me with wild eyes. "My *hero*.", she says with a wicked smile, her eyes flash with a fire and hunger I could drown myself in.

"Where did you get the knife from?" I ask.

"I took it from that bitch." She laughs, her triumphant smile even wider now.

"Hand it over, now." I command.

Isabella reluctantly places the blade in my outstretched hand.

Breathing heavily, I grab the headset. "We're secure, get back here and pick us up."

A moment passes. Another. My phone is out of control with calls and texts from my brothers. I can't deal with them right now. I need a minute to collect myself.

When we finally climb back into our chopper, the pilot stares, wide-eyed at the sight before him, Isabella's blood-soaked face a mask of pure unadulterated joy is not something he ever thought he'd see in this life. His gaze immediately turns and focuses ahead of us as we lift off into a blue sky dotted with clouds. "I'll make sure you get a bonus for this," I tell him. I turn back to Isabella, who's trying to catch her breath, but her eyes still burning bright. She fucking loves adrenaline.

"Nice work," I tell her.

"You, too, *mi querido jefe*," she replies, a small, grudging smile playing on her lips. "If we were on a plane, I'd fuck you senseless right now. That was so goddamn *hot*."

The pilot chokes.

"Ignore that," I snap. I tap him out of our conversation. He can talk to us if he needs to, but he won't hear us.

Good. We need a minute.

I turn back to her, wrap my hand around the back of her neck, and yank her to me. Without a word, I kiss her, our mouths clashing together. The combination of cortisol and epinephrine surging through our bodies heightens our senses to a fever pitch. She moans, her tongue licking mine, and just like that, I'm hard as a fucking rock. I kiss her until our breathing syncs. She tastes like whiskey, adrenaline and blood, and I want more.

"How much longer?" I ask the pilot.

"One hour, fifty minutes."

We lean back in our seats. "What did you tell the pilot?" I ask her as I hand her a roll of gauze and some saline solution from a first aid kit to clean herself up with. I want to know. Fuck she's fearless.

Isabella grins. She's so gorgeous it breaks my heart a little. "I said you know who I am, and you know what I'm capable of."

I smile at her. Somehow in the melee, the two of us shed a little of our animosity. I suppose it can't be helped as we were allies for a little while.

"Who are you? And what else are you capable of?"

Leaning over, she cups my chin in her small, warm hand. "I am Isabella Romanova. And I am capable of world domination."

I can't help it. I lean over and kiss her again.

We lean back, and finally, our breathing slows.

Our ascent is breathtaking as we soar above the clouds, and the houses below us quickly become so small they look like tiny little houses you might find on an aerial map, the clouds like thin wisps of vapor.

"Southeast," Isabella says with a nod. I can hardly hear her but can read her lips. She's right. We're heading out to sea. After some time, there's nothing but the blue depth of the ocean beneath us. Her brow furrows, and I watch the details as well. Even Mikhail doesn't know where we're going.

I tap the mic so the pilot can hear me. "Can you tell us where you're going?"

"I'm sorry, sir," he responds stoically. "I can't tell you until we land. It's too risky."

"Fair enough."

I watch the pilot closely. I know him, he's been vetted... Still, I've never been *married* before. I didn't have a wife to look out for. I look over to see Isabella's head tipped to the side. She's asleep.

I can't risk falling asleep, not until we've landed, and we're settled.

I stare at the sleeping form of my wife beside me, my chest swelling with the knowledge that she's taken vows with me. It feels surreal. I've never known anyone more beautiful or dangerous than Isabella Morales.

And she's *mine*.

Unlike our private planes, I have no Wi-Fi up here. I lean back in my seat and cross my ankles. It's the most peaceful I've felt in recent memory.

I'm tense and alert when Isabella stirs and opens her eyes. She blinks in surprise but doesn't talk as she quickly orients herself. I watch her stare down at her hand where I placed a thick gold band a few hours ago as if reminding herself it wasn't a dream.

I stare at the ring as if imprinting it in my memory. She gives me a curious look but doesn't make a move to take her hand away. I give her a squeeze and lay her hand on my knee, resting my hand over hers.

I don't care if she's a Morales. I don't care that she's a sworn enemy. I don't care that I forced her to marry me, and our marriage is loveless. She's my wife, and I promised her I would take care of what's mine.

"Minutes now," the pilot says.

As we begin our descent, an island comes into view—a lush, green paradise surrounded by crystal-clear water. It's breathtaking and remote, the perfect hideaway.

"Where are we?" she whispers. "I thought maybe Iceland or Nova Scotia, but it's impossible to tell from this height. And it looks warm, not cold. Thank God," she mutters.

"Mmm. It's impossible to tell even now. There are thousands of uninhabited, remote islands."

We land on what looks like a private helipad near a grand villa. It's perched on a cliff that overlooks the craggy rocks of the ocean below, but to the east lies a white sand beach. God, it looks like fucking heaven, and I'm going to enjoy the hell out of this, our brief reprieve before we're thrown back into the fire.

"Bermuda," she murmurs. "I bet we're on one of the islands of Bermuda. Only a few hours from New York, it's the only place I can think of that would be warm and sunny this time of year." I watch as her lips curve upward in a grin. *Find me now, Javier.*" When she flexes her pretty, delicate hands with well-manicured nails, I imagine for a brief moment she has them sharpened into claws, ready to tear him apart with her bare hands. I blink and she looks delicate and gorgeous again.

No... delicate is the wrong word. Isabella never looks delicate. Fit. Lean. Stunningly beautiful and decidedly feminine. But delicate? Never.

We take our bags and exit the helicopter.

"Thanks," I tell our pilot.

He nods and, without a word, gets back inside to head back. I take our bags and walk toward the large villa in front of us as the helicopter rises, the blades chopping in the air, and leaves.

"You think we're the only ones here?"

I shake my head. "I fucking hope so."

"No one to cook for you? To make your bed? I can shoot a gun, Lev, but domestic duties..."

"My mother raised me to be a man, not a boy," I tell her with a smile. "Yeah, I can handle this shit."

Isabella shrugs a slender shoulder and smiles. "We don't need staff, do we? There's a certain appeal in being alone on an island."

But when we enter the villa, it does appear we're alone. This place is a masterpiece of modern architecture, somehow perfectly fitting with the natural beauty of the island. Floor-to-ceiling windows offer panoramic views of the ocean, and the interior is furnished with elegant but simple decor.

"My mother would cluck her tongue at all the white and beige, you know," she says with a smile. "Though I like the ocean inspiration with the accents." Outside furniture of white wicker features shell decor and pale blues and greens. The clean, simple lines give the place an elegant, pristine look.

All I care about is that it's well-furnished and isolated, perfect for keeping her close and safe.

As we step inside, I watch her take in our surroundings. Her eyes widen slightly, and I can tell she's impressed, even if she doesn't want to show it. A place like this must contrast with what she's familiar with at home.

I take out my phone, not surprised to find I have four bars and Wi-Fi. My brother would never send me to a place where he couldn't reach me the second he wanted to. I shoot him a text.

Mikhail: What the fuck happened???

We took down an enemy helicopter. I'll get her to tell me who they were later but obviously, we know it was the cartel behind it.

Shit. Glad you made it safely.

All good at home?

We're fine. Couple of dumbasses tried to stir shit here but Viktor handled it. Mom never even knew

Perfect. Any staff here?

No. I thought you two would be better off and enjoy it more if you were totally alone. I had specific instructions left when the staff vacated to make sure you have a relaxing stay. Nothing to worry about. You'll find everything you need at the front desk. You two fucking earned it.

Thank you.

Stay in touch

I turn to Isabella. "We're the only ones here. Mikhail says there are instructions for us up front."

She grins. "Alone, on a gorgeous island, hidden from our enemies and stranded with my hot, dominant husband who has a vow to consummate our marriage and knock me up?" She taps her chin. "Hmm. Let me think about this." She pretends to think for a minute before she pumps her fists and hoots. "Woot!"

I watch as she runs to the front desk, where normally, staff might check us in. She picks up a white sheet of paper. "Oooh, look here, Lev. This is what Mikhail was talking about." She reads in her beautiful voice.

*Welcome to Kuznetsov Island Villa. We have made the following accommodations for you.*

*You will find the kitchen well stocked with high-quality ingredients as well as a handful of gourmet meals that can easily be prepared or reheated, a variety of snacks and beverages, fine wines, champagnes, and spirits.*

*There is also an espresso machine and a fully stocked coffee bar.*

*Linens, towels, and anything else you might need are in the hall closet, and your bedroom has been prepared.*

*We have left a few personal touches throughout the villa to enhance your stay. You'll find a selection of books and movies, as well as luxury spa accoutrements on site. Please use the hot tub and pool with caution but as often as you wish.*

*Should you find you wish to explore the island, we have detailed guides and equipment in the shed outside for snorkeling, kayaking, paddle-boarding, and hiking. Outdoors, you will also find a secluded beach picnic area, a hammock for two, and a gazebo beside the outdoor bar.*

*We have a state-of-the-art workout area as well as a recovery room. You'll see everything listed on the map.*

*Everything has been automated—lighting, climate control, and security systems, but should any need arise, please dial the number provided for immediate assistance or security we've established on a nearby island.*

*Congratulations, and enjoy your stay.*

Isabella grins. "Did we die in that helicopter and land in heaven?" For a moment, I stare at her, hardly believing this woman is my wife and I've got her all to myself for the week.

*"Find out what you can," Mikhail instructed. "Anything and everything she'll tell you."*

I smile at her, hoping it doesn't look like I'm baring my teeth. I guess I don't smile very often.

"I'm not the kind of guy who goes to heaven when I die," I say, shaking my head. I can't help but smirk at her.

She takes a step toward me, her eyes smoldering. "Good," she says in a low drawl. "Sinners have more fun, and I'll enjoy the company."

# CHAPTER THIRTEEN

*Isabella*

MY NEW HUSBAND KISSES ME.

I let him.

It feels good to just let everything go for a little while, to relax and enjoy this. My eyes flutter closed, and his hand comes to the back of my neck. I'm not the type of girl who surrenders easily, but knowing what we have to do and who we are—I lean into this.

When we pull away, I'm all kinds of aroused, and I'm not the only one. "You're beautiful. There's something crazy that lights a fire in your eyes."

I grin at him and wink. "Takes one to know one. Now do I get the grand tour or what?"

"Let's settle for the mini tour. I just want to find our room and put our bags away for now."

"Yeah, I need a shower after all that."

"Bed would be nice."

I look around. It is fucking beautiful here. I feel like someone handed me a glossy pamphlet at a travel agency, and I stepped right into the picture. I've never seen anything like this in my life.

Granted, I've never really been on vacation before, but God, we fucking earned this.

I reach for my bag, and Lev grunts and takes it out of my hand.

I frown at him. "Dude, you don't think I can carry my own bag?"

"Isabella," he says in a growl that makes my nipples hard.

Excellent. My new husband has the ability to turn me on with his voice. I guess that's his superpower.

"It's not a question of if you *can*. Jesus, let me carry my wife's bag."

"Alright, alright."

I give him a sidelong look as we head down toward the hall to where our room is marked on the map.

We have to have sex, that I know for sure. He mentioned something about a rivalry between him and his brothers having babies and whatnot as if they need to repopulate all of New York with virile Romanov genes. And logic tells me that sex is the way to get there.

While I'm not too thrilled with the idea of giving birth to children anytime soon, I wouldn't mind a few practice sessions.

Also, this is the God's honest truth... He is hot. Like next level, light up my uterus, can I sit on your face, sir, hot.

I may have thought about being chained up in his basement more than a few times. And the way we harmonized on that helicopter—it was seamless. Beautiful. Thrilling.

We walk down the hallway. I would think it would feel odd to be in a vacant resort, like there are ghosts around here or something, but it doesn't feel odd at all. It feels kind of nice.

I like being alone with him.

"Are you hungry?" he asks. Our footsteps are noiseless on the thick carpet. They've obviously prepared for our arrival, as I can still see faint lines from the vacuum in front of us.

"Not really. You?"

"No. *Shit*. I just remembered we left the cake on the helicopter."

I shrug my shoulders. "Meh, I don't eat cake. It's fine. It was a nice gesture and all, but I'm sweet enough without the extra carbs."

"Sure you are," he snorts.

"And anyway," I say, watching his reaction. "I just married my enemy, so it's really no cause for celebration."

"Mmm. Good point. Honestly, this villa is pretty much like a prison. Looks just like one. You may as well be shackled in my basement still."

Why does that only make me want him more? I'm *thirsty*. Yes. I'm so fucking thirsty, and here I am, striding down a hallway toward the bedroom with New York's ultimate thirst trap.

I swallow hard and try to look away, but I can't help admiring him. Dressed all in black, the defined muscles in his shoulders and arms bulge with the effort of carrying our bags, but he doesn't hunch over. His body is a masterpiece of masculine perfection, and I am so fucking here for it.

I don't have to fight him anymore. I don't have to hide from him. I need to convince him to partner with me. I need to convince him to jam together the well-oiled machine of his family and mine... and then make it all work.

I can do this. I must do this. I have no other choice.

"According to the map... this is ours."

I turn the handle, and the door opens. I stifle a gasp. *"Dios mío. This is beautiful."* The honeymoon suite at the island villa is a dream. Floor-to-ceiling windows offer a breath-taking view of the ocean, so brilliantly blue it reminds me of an aquamarine necklace my mother used to wear. Waves kiss the shore. Sheer white curtains billow with the ocean breeze. A plush, king-sized bed made in crisp white linens stands in the center, a tray on the bedside table welcoming us with rose petals in the shape of a heart surrounding a bottle of champagne nestled in a silver bucket, two crystal flutes beside it.

I swivel my gaze around, trying to take it all in—a spa-like expansive bathroom boasts a clawfoot tub with a view over-looking the ocean and a walk-in shower encased in glass. Thick white towels on a shelf beside glass bottles of lotions and soaps. A basket of washcloths and more rose petals. Every damn detail hints at luxury and peace.

"My God," I say, staring out at the expanse of the blue ocean from the balcony. "I can't imagine anything more beautiful."

A beat passes when his dark eyes meet mine. "Really?" His voice is a low purr. "I can."

I swallow hard. Is this where the Big Bad Wolf takes off his mask and devours me whole?

I remind myself—I am strong. I am fast. I can get in and out of tight spaces with ease. But logic reminds me, there's no escaping him now.

He was right. The best way to keep me shackled to him was to bind me with vows, and I'm sure Mikhail sending us to this island had more to do with keeping me hostage than it did giving us a honeymoon. I can't run. Even if I could escape him in the middle of the night, what would I do? Swim? To where? Both of our families know that I'm married to him now.

*But I don't want to leave him,* I remind myself. My instincts have always been to run. And now... the greatest challenge lies in *staying*.

I meet his eyes. Lick my lips.

"Mmm? What's more beautiful than this?" I ask, aiming for a seductive tone, but instead, my voice sounds small and a bit subdued.

"You. Naked." He punctuates each word by removing an article of clothing. "On all fours in the middle of that fucking bed."

He tugs the end of his shirt straight over his head and whips it toward our luggage. Next, he unbuckles his belt. My mouth goes dry. I watch him tug it through the loops. When he snaps it in his large, capable hands, pressure and need build between my legs.

*I need him. I want him.*

"All fours? Like an animal?" I tease.

"Like my wife."

"You like calling me that."

He shakes his head. "You have no idea."

His eyes are on fire, and when he pushes down his jeans, I can see the long length of his erection in his boxers. Holy hell, he's just as turned on as I am.

Lev's eyes blaze as he stares at me, and the intensity of his gaze makes the pressure between my legs throb. I stifle a moan. He steps closer, the muscles in his torso tight as he pulls me into him. His body is hot to the touch, chiseled; the man's a fucking paragon of masculine perfection. His lips find my ear, the warmth of his breath fanning my neck.

"Strip," he orders, his voice low and commanding. I freeze. When I don't obey immediately, he claps his hand on my ass. I squeal.

My hands shake as I reach for my top and pull it over my head. I let it drop to the floor as his eyes roam over my body. The heat of his gaze warms me like a physical touch.

I tug off my shorts and stare at him. "Do I get to touch, too?"

He narrows his eyes at me. His voice cracks like a whip. "What did I say?"

Oooh, *Jesu.* My pussy clenches, and I stifle a whimper. I'm so exposed in front of him like this.

I project myself as a confident woman, but the years of forced modesty were so beaten into me I can't help but feel incredibly exposed.

I'm not used to being vulnerable in front of anyone, much less a man.

*He's my husband.*

*Shit.*

"All of it, Isabella," he rumbles.

I swallow and hold his gaze as I unclip my bra. "Good riddance," I mutter as I toss that to the floor. Fucking hate those things. I hook my thumbs into the waistband of my thong, sliding it down over my ass and my thighs. His eyes darken with lust as he takes in every inch of my naked, vulnerable body.

"Good girl," he says, his voice a rough purr.

Oooh. Oh, I like that.

"Say that again," I beg. "Please."

He leans in closer and gathers my hair in his fist before he gives it a tug. His mouth to my ear, he whispers, "You like it when I call you a good girl? Do you like it when I tell you that you please me?" He trails hot fingers down my spine.

"I do."

*I do.* What is that about?

"I love how feisty you are. I love how you fight. I've been hard since the helicopter." He bends and kisses my jaw, his voice a low rumble. "Now get on that bed like I told you."

I walk to the bed, holding his gaze, and climb on. Positioning myself on all fours as he commanded, a surge of arousal floods through me. The way he looks at me—like he's starving and I'm his next meal—ignites me.

Yet he doesn't rush. He takes his time, moving behind me. Circling me. Taking everything in.

I bow my head. I hear the rustle of fabric as he removes his boxers. The bed dips under his weight as he climbs on, his hands gripping my hips with a possessive strength that makes me gasp.

"Spread your legs wider," he demands, his voice brooking no argument.

I obey, spreading my knees apart until I'm completely open to him. I'm wet, so damn wet. His fingers trail down my spine, making me shiver, before one hand wraps around to cup my breast, squeezing hard enough to make me moan.

"You belong to me now, Isabella," he murmurs, his voice thick with desire. "And I'm going to remind you exactly what that means."

"Let's see what you've got." I smile to myself, but my sass earns me a sharp slap.

I moan.

He positions himself at my entrance, and I feel the hard length of him press against my wetness. Without warning, he thrusts into me, filling me completely in one powerful stroke. I cry out as he sets a relentless pace, his hips slamming into mine with a force that leaves me breathless.

"That's it," he groans. "Take all of me."

I spread wider and lean my chest on the bed.

His hands move to grip my wrists, pinning them down as he pounds into me. The sensation is overwhelming. I fucking love the way he takes control. I can't move, can't think, only feel the intensity of his possession.

When he leans over me, his chest presses against my back, and I feel his hot breath on my ear again. "You're mine, Isabella. *Say it.*"

"I'm yours," I gasp, my voice barely more than a breathless moan.

"Louder," he demands, his thrusts becoming even more forceful.

"I'm yours, Lev!" I cry out, my body trembling with the force of my orgasm as it crashes over me.

"That's right," he growls, his own release imminent. "You're mine, and I'm never letting you go."

He thrusts into me one final time, groaning as he comes deep inside me. His grip on my wrists tightens momentarily before he releases me, his hands moving to cradle my body against his as we collapse onto the bed.

For a moment, we lie there, our breathing heavy and our bodies damp with sweat. Then he turns me to face him, his eyes softening slightly as he brushes a strand of hair from my face.

"You're incredible," he murmurs, his lips brushing against mine in a surprisingly tender kiss.

I smile up at him, feeling a strange mix of emotions. I feel like he's tugged a zipper down, and I'm completely undone.

"Lev," I say softly. I want to tell him my plan. I want to tell him everything.

But I don't. Maybe I'm not courageous enough yet. Maybe I need to get to know him more before I do.

Maybe...

"Mmmm?" he says, his eyes closed as if he's ready for sleep. It's been a long day.

We're tired.

"Let's get some sleep," I whisper, my eyelids feeling suddenly very heavy.

I wonder what it would be like to really trust him. I wonder what it would be like... to experience real love.

His breathing slows. Mine matches his. I'm warm and comfortable, and the bed is so soft, I fall asleep.

I wake the next morning to Lev's head between my legs.

Oh my *God*. Am I dreaming?

I find myself in a beautiful resort with the sunrise out my window and a white sand beach. The hottest man I've ever met is between my legs, worshiping my clit as if his life depends on it and I'm the queen who can grant him salvation.

"Hands above your head," he commands in a low growl from between my legs, lest I forget he's the one in charge. I immediately comply, my mind wandering to what he would do if I didn't.

I'd probably like it.

Just for fun, I reach down and tug his hair. As if on cue, he sinks his teeth into the tender skin of my inner thigh. I yelp.

"What'd I say?" he growls. "Do I need to tie you to the bed and whip your ass before I make you come? Or are you going to be my good girl and come on my face?"

*Oh shit.* Oh hell. "I'll be a good girl—*this* time anyway," I say as sweetly as I can. He licks my clit lazily, stifling his own groan. "Jesus fucking Christ," he whispers reverently. "You taste delicious. I love this. My God."

He licks me again and again. My hips jerk and spasm, pleasure washing through my lower belly. I'm warm and tingly, and I haven't even come yet.

"You taste like sunshine and sex, like whiskey and sin had a baby."

I giggle and bite my lip. "You're so romantic, you weirdo."

He bites my thigh again, and I scream.

"Now you've done it, bad girl," he says, giving me a stern look. Shaking his head, his eyes are on fire. "Disrespecting your husband?"

He's on his knees, bending down to reach for something on the floor. Oh my God, he came prepared. He has the belt from one of the plush bathrobes in his hand. In one deft movement, he ties my wrists to the headboard and wraps the belt around them, securing it in place.

On his way back down, he slaps my pussy.

I gasp. "You can't spank me there!"

"I can't?" he says, bending over and spanking me again. "Do you really want to test that theory? My belt isn't far off. I can go and get it if you really want me to prove how easily I can whip your pussy."

It's rare that I'm completely dumbfounded, but he's done it. I stare, shivering at the sound of his dark chuckle, before he positions himself between my legs again. My hips jerk, eager for the warm, wet pressure of his tongue. He groans, his muscles tensing, his stiff cock in his hand as he jerks himself off while licking my pussy.

This is the dirtiest fucking thing I've ever seen, and I am so here for it.

"You have my permission to come. This time," he says. He licks me again, and my hips rise. He sucks my clit between his lips.

I shatter. The first spasm of ecstasy crashes through my veins, riding through me. He licks my clit, and I jerk and scream, my wrists tight in my restraints, my hips rising as I come on his face. He grips my ass and squeezes hard.

"Jesus," he says to himself in a reverent whisper. "She's still coming." He licks me again and again. My orgasm is interminable. I think I stop coming and then go into a second one as he drives his fingers into my channel, pumping. I soak his hand, and still I come. Over and over, I climax against his mouth until I'm spent and can't move.

I'm still tied to the bed when he grabs my legs, spreads them wide, and positions himself above me, driving his thick, hot, throbbing cock between them.

I come again as he thrusts into me, over and over, until I can't take it anymore. I'm as weak as a rag doll, lying in the bed as he groans, tightens, and spills inside me. "Jesus," he says. "Never seen one like that before. You're so uninhibited. It's the most beautiful fucking thing I've ever seen. *God*, woman."

"You weren't exactly Mr. Shy when you came either, caveman."

That earns me a bonafide smile from the guy.

"Ooh. A smile. What will you do if I feed you *breakfast*?"

He snorts. "Eat it? But you're not feeding me breakfast. I waited a long time for this. You stay here. I want to eat breakfast in bed with you."

He unties my wrists, and I lean back on the pillows, still warm and pliable after coming like that. "Alright," I say. "If you insist." Good thing he's planning on feeding me since I don't really trust myself to walk right now.

"You'll find out soon that I don't usually make suggestions."

"Mmm," I say thoughtfully as he tugs on boxers and heads to the door. "You'll find out soon I don't usually obey."

The heat of his gaze turns whatever bones I have left to jelly. "We'll work on that."

"I hope we do."

He shakes his head and heads for the door.

"Why are you wearing boxers?" I ask after his retreating back. "There's no one here."

"I can guarantee there's video surveillance in the hallway, and I have no interest in my brothers seeing my junk."

*God.* "Fair enough. So, I guess I can't waltz around naked either, then?"

I wait for what's sure to be a rewarding answer. "I'd have to fucking kill them if they saw you naked, so yeah." He turns around halfway out the door. "And *you* wouldn't sit for a fucking week."

Jesus. I came twice, and now I'm turned on again.

I half fall asleep before he comes back with more food than I could eat in a week, but I'm famished, and the ripe fruit and scrambled eggs are delicious.

"What do you want to do on our first day?"

"Check out the workout room and make our way to the beach." I shrug. "Fuck my husband again."

"You're right," he says with a nod.

"About what?"

"You definitely don't need cake to party."

I smile. "Yeah and it's probably time to talk about birth control."

He blinks. "Birth control? Fuck birth control. We're married."

I stare at him. Jesus. "What? I'm not ready for babies yet, Lev." I checked my bags already and confirmed I have my pills with me. It was one of the first things I asked Polina about and she hooked me up.

"I get it. It doesn't have to happen today." He pauses. "I'll take very good care of you as my wife, Isabella."

My heart thumps. "Even so... I'm not sure how I feel about having children."

"Why?" he asks, his eyes searching mine.

I look away, struggling to articulate my feelings. "I don't know."

I tell myself I don't want to have swollen ankles and heartburn and stretch marks. But the truth is, I really don't know why I don't want children. There's a part of me that really, really *does*. I love holding babies, kissing their sweet little heads. The way they hold your finger when they sleep and how adorably they smile and coo. It's not that I don't want *babies*...just maybe not right *now*.

And I always envisioned having babies with a man I actually love. My voice is a bit tighter than I intend when I snap back at him. "I just don't want babies right now, okay?"

His face grows serious. "My family will expect it."

"Really?" I ask, curiosity piqued. God, of *course* they do.

"We are strengthening our roots by having children. Growing in numbers." He shakes his head. "I want you to *want* the children, though."

I purse my lips. "Why is that?"

A muscle tenses in his jaw. Before he responds, he takes our plates, stacks them, and lines up the napkins before placing them on a tray.

"Because children aren't commodities." Ooh. That touched a nerve. "My father treated us like that, like trophies to win and put on a shelf, and it's not right."

I swallow, looking at him. "You want me to *want* a baby," I repeat.

"Absolutely."

Well now he's really pushing it. I frown at him. "You *want* to be a father?"

His dark eyes grow earnest. "I do. So much."

It is not fair the way he makes me melt like that. What is it about a man that says he wants to be a daddy? I swallow the tingly feeling in my throat and look away.

"Even though you had a bad one..." I guess I'm telling him more than I planned.

I turn my head away, uncertain how to continue. How would that work, me being the queen of Colombia and him in the Bratva and *pregnant*?

Maybe it's time I tell him about my plan. Maybe it's time he knows marrying me comes with decided benefits... *if* we play this right.

I stare at him, unsure if I can trust him yet.

Will there ever really be a time?

# CHAPTER FOURTEEN

*Lev*

I HAVE to hand it to Mikhail.

First of all, this place is fucking awesome.

Second, my wife is fucking awesome.

We had to get to know each other, and we needed to get to a place of trust, but we didn't have the luxury of time that most people do. Being dropped down in the middle of nowhere in an absolute paradise and having to trust each other? It's getting the job done.

Three days into our stay on the island, we enjoyed the private beach area, taking refreshments onto the sand. Kissing under the shaded canopy. Skinny-dipping in the ocean, with nothing but the blue sky ahead and the occasional call of a seagull.

She lives for sex, and if she has a hard limit, I haven't fucking found one yet.

We've taken full advantage of the Jacuzzi and hot tub on site. She even made me do a fucking yoga routine—said something about it opening my chakras, whatever the fuck those are. She tried to guide me through meditation after, but I tackled her and fucked her in the middle of the yoga studio.

She didn't seem too bothered by that.

It's nice, not having technology at our fingertips constantly, notifications vying for our attention. Even though I love my family with my whole heart, it's nice to have a little break from them.

And sex with Isabella is mind-blowing. There is nothing she won't do, she's a savage. I am here for it. Every time she screams beneath me or on top of me because she's all about riding me, I feel like *Superman*.

"We've used up most of those premade meals," Isabella says. She's lying on the beach in a bikini, her eyes closed. I let my gaze roam over her beautiful, finely tuned body stunning.

We've fallen into a routine: working out together in the gym, swimming or hiking during the day, followed by lazy afternoons on the beach. Some days, we eat light; other days, we cook a feast. She has a hearty appetite and isn't picky. Everything seems to excite her. She has a thirst for life that brightens my day. She loves to explore and talk about the future... but there's an elephant in the room we need to address.

Two, if I'm honest.

We'll get there.

"*Mi querido jefe,*" she says, her eyes closed. The sun beats overhead, but the woman doesn't burn. She just becomes more golden.

"Yes?"

"What are we having for dinner?"

"I think we need to cook together. Are we going to survive?"

She opens one eye and gives me a sly grin. "That depends. Can you keep your hands off me?"

Well, that decided it. No.

Doesn't matter, though. We're the only ones here. We have a job to do, which involves me getting to know her body intimately and her getting to know mine. Bonding and all that shit.

I roll her over and kiss her until her lips are swollen and my dick is hard pressed up against her.

"What does *mi querido jefe* mean?"

She grins at me. "All this time, and you don't know what it means? Really?"

"All this time? It hasn't been that long." It has, though, maybe not in days or minutes or hours, but life before Isabella was a lifetime ago.

"It's been long enough," she says with a wink. "*Mi querido jefe* means 'my dear boss.'"

*Jesus.* I should've studied Spanish. "You've been calling me 'your boss' this whole time? Is this some kind of joke?" I flop back down on the sand beside her, scattering some across her skin.

"Hey! It's not my fault you don't know the most basic Spanish."

"Excuse me? Are you sassing your husband again?" I quirk an eyebrow at her. She turns on her elbow and gives me a curious look, lifting her own brow in return.

"Depends. What are you going to do about it?"

"Obviously, I'm going to lift you up off that towel, carry you over to that dock, and toss you in the water. What the fuck else would I do? Brat."

She gets up on all fours, and I stifle a moan when she does one of those yoga moves she did in the studio, lifting her neck and arching her back like a kitten. Fuck, she's gorgeous. I forgot what the hell she calls that move, but I know this is just a distraction. She wants me to see her tits in that tiny little top and her gorgeous ass just begging to be smacked.

I groan. "What the fuck are you doing?" I push myself up to my knees.

And then she's on her feet and off at a run, and I'm cursing behind her because she's smaller than I am but faster, by a lot. Doesn't mean I won't fucking catch her. We're both good at this game.

Sand flies beneath her bare feet as she screams and runs the length of the beach. I follow behind her. Even as I chase her, I know deep down in my soul, I will never actually catch her. It will always be her and me together, fighting for survival, and there will always be a chase.

There's not a submissive bone in Isabella's body, and I'm

fucking loving it. I love the way she poses such a challenge to me. I love the way she runs. I love chasing her.

Finally, I get a break. She trips, and it slows her down for a moment, giving me the chance to catch her. I bend my knees, toss my shoulder into her torso, and slap my hand across her little ass. She squeals and giggles. I love the sound of her giggling. For someone who's been through so much, she's incredibly resilient. She lives life with such gusto, and I absolutely love that.

I march to the dock with her over my shoulder. "Now you've done it."

"Put me down!" She slaps my back.

"You want me to put you down?"

"Lev! What are you doing?" she screams.

"You know exactly what I'm doing." I walk down the dock toward the water. She fights me, kicking and screaming and pushing at me, but I don't let her go. Not until we get to the end of the dock. I smack her thigh, which makes her squeal, then slide her down off my shoulder and cradle her in my arms so I can kiss her. "You're so beautiful," I say with a smile before I rear back and fling her. She flails and screams, then splashes into the water before she comes up sputtering for air.

"You jerk!" she screams, her soaking wet hair straggling in her face. "That isn't fair!" She paddles, splashing at me, but I have the advantage up on the dock. "Come on in, Lev," she croons. She's so pretty with her hair hanging about her beautiful face, water dripping off her. She could be on a postcard for a beach vacation.

"Let's go," she says. "The water is fine, you *asshole*."

I lean back, enjoying the view, when suddenly her face contorts, and she screams. "Something bit me!"

I dive into the water after her without a second thought. Suddenly, I see a jellyfish swimming away, and panic surges through me. I yank her out of the water and swim to the dock. Her leg has a red, swollen mark where the tentacles touched. I quickly swim to her, cradling her in my arms as I bring her back to shore.

"Hold on, Isabella," I murmur, my voice shaking with worry. "I've got you."

She winces in pain, her breath coming in sharp gasps. "It hurts, Lev. Fuck, it really hurts." Isabella has a high pain tolerance, but a full-on jellyfish sting is brutal.

I lay her gently on the dock, quickly inspecting the sting. "I know. We need to neutralize the venom." I remember reading about jellyfish stings and the best way to treat them. I toss sand on her leg and rub to get rid of any residual tentacles, but I must get her back to the resort for first aid supplies.

I make quick work of carrying her back, and she's brave about it. I can feel the tension from the pain, but she doesn't whisper a word of complaint.

"What do you do for this?"

"We need something to neutralize the sting and toxins. There will be a first aid kit."

I sit her on a stool in the kitchen and rummage through

supplies, finding a small bottle of vinegar in the cabinet. "This will work. Put your leg out."

She gasps as the vinegar makes contact. "Is it supposed to burn?"

"A little, but it should help," I assure her.

Tears well up in her eyes, but she stays strong. "Thank you, Lev."

I look at her, and I hate that she's in pain. "I'm so sorry this happened. Let's get you situated. Some hydrocortisone will help."

I scoop her up in my arms and carry her to the living room and gently place her on the couch, propping her leg up. "I'll get some ice to reduce the swelling."

She gives me a weak smile. "You're really good at this, you know."

I sigh. "I've had practice taking care of stubborn people."

As I apply the ice pack to her leg, she winces but then relaxes. "Thank you."

I kiss her forehead. This is my job. I'm supposed to watch out for her.

Back in the room, she lies back with her foot elevated. "This *is* your fault," she says, but I can tell she doesn't really blame me. "If you didn't throw me in the water..."

"If you weren't a brat, I wouldn't have had to throw you in." I do feel guilty, though. "I didn't think there would be jellyfish."

"I guess you'll have to make it up to me," she says cheerfully.

"Seriously, how does that feel?" I ask, looking at her swollen ankle.

"I won't be running away from you anytime soon. I know you're devastated. But the good news is, I don't think I'm badly hurt. I'm fine. I don't know about you, but I'm starving. Let's go cook dinner."

I anchor my hands on my hips and glare at her. "*I'll* go make dinner. You're going to stay right here with that leg elevated."

"I can stand just fine," she snaps.

"You are so fucking stubborn!"

"It takes one to know one," she snaps back. "I don't like people serving me. I like to cook my own food."

"Well, you're just going to have to get used to it."

"Or what?" She challenges me. Here we go again.

"I'm going to tie you to that fucking couch." I glare at her, absolutely ready to do it.

Instead of defying me, she pouts a little, which is more effective than I expect. "Lev, I am not helpless."

"Finally, just a tiny bit. Isabella, you're my wife. Can you just let me fucking take care of you for once?"

She stares at me and doesn't speak for long moments. "You want to take care of me?"

"It's a little different than always trying to tell you what to do, isn't it?" I say.

"I guess it is. But promise me this."

"Yeah?"

"If *you* get hurt, you're going to let me take care of you. This works both ways."

"Sure. But I don't get hurt."

"We'll see about that," she says teasingly.

"What is that supposed to mean?"

"It means, Lev, let's cook dinner."

"Isabella," I say, exasperated.

"Please," she says sweetly. How am I supposed to say no when she asks me like that?

I bend down and lift her. To her credit, she doesn't protest that she can walk or anything; she just lets me.

"I like when you carry me," she says in a little voice, a hint of vulnerability that's unusual for her.

I like it.

"Do you?"

"There's just something about a strong guy carrying me that makes me feel... I don't know, protected. And even I can't help but like that, at least a little bit," she admits.

"Well, I'm happy to protect you," I whisper, kissing her.

"I can help you cook," she says, her voice surprisingly steady. "I'm perfectly fine, Lev. It hurts, yes, but that doesn't matter. I don't care."

Is she really this stubborn? This is going to be my life with her. I have to admit, I like it. I'm not the kind of guy who wants things easy. I like the challenge, and I like to fight.

"I'm making dinner tonight, but I promise you'll get plenty of opportunities to cook for me. Maybe you can chop veggies on a stool or something."

 Her eyes twinkle, and her lips twitch. "Maybe you're not that bad."

I slide her into a chair. "Sit. Elevate that leg."

"I've never had a man cook for me before," she says with a hint of wonder in her voice.

"Seriously? Most of us cook. Who the hell feeds you?"

She tilts her head, a wistful look crossing her face. "Staff." She shrugs. "I cooked for myself mostly."

I rifle through the contents of the fridge and cabinets. "Do you miss Colombia?"

"Yes and no. I miss what used to be in Colombia, not what it is now."

"What do you mean?" I take out vacuum-sealed chicken, then rifle through the cabinets. I chop onions and garlic at the kitchen counter while she tells me.

"When I was a little girl, my father was very occupied with business. But it didn't matter to me. None of it. I didn't care back then. I had friends and a beautiful backyard to play in. I liked to read, ride my bike, and go swimming in the lake by my house. Yes, a little part of me knew that my father did things he probably shouldn't. I would overhear things. And when he and my mother fought..." She looks away and doesn't respond at first. I give her space, sliding the chopped onions and garlic into the sizzling hot pan. "He hit her. It wasn't unusual for a man like him, but I hated it when she cried. I hated it when he got angry. And I promised myself that would never be me."

This doesn't surprise me, but I don't like it.

"As a little girl, I knew it was socially acceptable, at least in my father's circles, to treat women as second-class citizens. In Colombia, you don't have to look far for that, even here in America in some places." I nod, understanding her point.

"Things changed when I began to develop. I wasn't a little girl to be pushed out of the way anymore, but someone who would attract attention. That was a problem for my father." She looks away. "My mother wasn't a fool, but she was every bit under my father's thumb and fully expected me to be the same. She didn't like conflict, except when she lost her temper. She wanted me to avoid the brunt of his anger, so she tried to teach me to be quiet and obedient." Her lips twitch, and her beautiful eyes meet mine. "You can imagine how well that went."

I grin, onions and garlic sizzling in the pan. "Probably about as well as telling my own sister to do that."

"She did teach me some things. And I'm grateful I have those skills. I can cook, and I like my space clean, like you, so in that way, we'll get along just fine. But I have a mind of my own, Lev."

"I know."

For a long moment, the only sound in the kitchen is the sizzling of the vegetables and the low boil of the pasta water. "I tried to cook for my whole family as a surprise. My father was having a bad day," she says with a rueful smile. "That's what my mother used to say. *Your father is having a bad day.* As if somehow that gave him free rein to act like a child. Anyway, I did what I thought I had seen done before, but the pan I used was too small, and oil splashed onto the flame. I caused a small kitchen fire. My mother found out before my father did, and she took the blame for it."

Her voice trails off. She doesn't like her mother, or maybe she hasn't forgiven her for past sins. I don't know, but she doesn't like telling these stories. I don't like hearing them, but I need to. I need to know every thread that weaves the fabric of who she is today because this is no passing relationship. This woman is my wife.

"When he saw the fire, he screamed and raged at her. He didn't hit her, but he broke things." She looks away. When she looks back at me, her eyes are shining. "I hated that she was taking the blame for me, so I told him the truth. That's when he hit her... for lying."

I season the chicken and lay it in the frying pan and scowl at it. "My father also wasn't a nice man. I understand."

I don't offer details on my own because this is her story, not mine, but apparently, she wants to know.

"Tell me. What was Stanislav Romanov really like?"

Of course, she knows his full name. She's researched my family. "It was his way or the highway... typical." I don't look at her while I stir the pot of pasta because I don't like to talk about this.

"Lev," she prompts, pouring herself a glass of wine. "This is a two-way street, *mi querido jefe.*"

Now that I know what that actually means, it holds a different kind of weight.

"He had his own way of dealing with us. He got physical."

"I didn't ask how he treated everyone," she says in that way of hers that cuts right to the heart of the matter. "I asked how he treated *you*."

There's no harm in telling her, so I don't know why I hesitated to begin with. "You know my brothers and Polina were adopted. My father did that on purpose, believing there were advantages to taking in people who were mistreated and then treating them well."

She nods, understanding. "It's one of the most basic rules of management," she says with a smile. "*El perro es fiel a la mano que lo alimenta*. A dog is loyal to the hand that feeds it."

"I honestly don't remember much before being adopted. My family was poor, and I was orphaned. I had no siblings, just my mother. When she died of illness in Moscow, the Romanovs took me in. But I was the youngest, and much was expected of me, more than I could manage as a child. At least, that's what my mother tells me."

Her eyes soften as she listens, but thankfully, she offers no sympathy. She just takes another sip of wine in that elegant, beautiful way that makes my heart ache a little.

"As I grew older, nothing I did was good enough. He assigned ulterior motives to everything I did and took things personally."

She shakes her head. "What is it with these narcissistic parents?" she says.

I laugh, but she's spot on. There's nothing funny about it. "Yeah. I don't really like to label things, but I guess that's accurate."

I flip the chicken and move it around the pan, appreciating the aromas in the kitchen. My stomach growls. "Wine?" she asks.

"Yeah." I take a glass and sip it. "For a long time, my older brothers treated me the way my father taught them to. Viktor was the one to be feared—too big for my father to handle—so he gave him over to Kolya. Mikhail was the oldest, and we had to obey him." I don't know why I say "had to." We still do. "Mikhail was in charge. Ollie always kept to himself, and Nikko was older but an ally. When I was a teenager, Nikko taught me to shoot. At fifteen, I made my first kill."

She doesn't even flinch, just listens to me as if I'm talking about fishing. It's only then that I appreciate being with a woman who understands. She's not horrified by my reality because hers is so similar. The details differ, but the end result is the same.

"I felt like I had to prove myself for a very long time. Prove that I was loyal, that I was strong."

"How did that assault a few years back affect you?" she asks. *Fuck.* Of course she knows about the assault. She's done her homework. She knows I was overtaken, beaten, hospitalized. We long since got our revenge for that, but I still bear the scars.

"Honestly? This might be hard to understand, but I'm grateful it happened."

She shakes her head. "It's not hard to understand at all. For a man like you, it was a defining moment, no?"

God. She understands more than I gave her credit for.

I look at her and nod. Maybe it hasn't been that long since we've known each other, so why does it feel like we've known each other our whole lives? Maybe humans are more alike than I thought.

"Exactly. It was exactly that. I had two choices: nurse my wounds, let the trauma hold me back..." My voice is choked, and I'm uncharacteristically emotional.

She completes the sentence for me. "Or let it shape you into who you are today. Determined that no one will ever do that to anyone you love again."

The pan is smoking. I shut it off and pull it off the heat, scooping the chicken onto a plate. I toss the pan in the sink and run water on it, steam filling the room.

"Looks delicious," she says. "I've always wanted to try black-ened chicken."

I snort.

I scoop the pasta onto a plate, add some butter and parmesan, and open the fridge to take out a premade salad.

We dig in.

"Why do you shove the greens down your throat like that?" she asks curiously, taking a delicate bite of pasta.

"Because I fucking hate them."

Her mouth drops open. "You don't like lettuce?"

I shake my head and chase the salad with a large swig of wine. "Fucking hate vegetables."

"What are you, ten?"

I smirk at her. "I just made your dinner. I don't have to like my vegetables; I just have to eat them."

"Why? You're an adult."

I flex my bicep and shrug. That's why.

She leans forward, her voice growing low and seductive as she squeezes my bicep. "Because you like to get laid."

"I do."

She grins, one of those smiles that lights up her whole face. "Fortunately for you, so do I."

I'm glad we didn't dwell on the conversation we had. We don't need to. She understands, and so do I.

After a while, the bottle of wine is empty. She sighs.

"My brother will not stop, Lev. There is only one way for us to stop him."

"I know." I lean forward, reaching to tuck a stray lock of hair behind her ear. "Are you sure about this?"

She nods. "I've never been so sure of anything in my whole life."

# CHAPTER FIFTEEN

*Isabella*

IT ISN'T JUST about revenge. It isn't just about establishing myself as the head of the Los Sangre Dorada. It runs so much deeper than that.

I stand and take our dishes to the sink. "I've got them," he says. "Sit."

"I'm supposed to walk on this, aren't I?" I ask, uncertain.

"No, you're supposed to rest it. Let the swelling go down. You're strong and healthy. You'll be fine tomorrow. But for now, let me handle this."

"All right, if you insist." For now, I'll let him have this.

"When do you think they're coming to get us?" I ask.

"In two days," he tells me. "I'm needed back in New York."

"What's happened?"

He shakes his head. "It's not so much what happened; it's what might happen next that's the trouble. You said it best—your brother isn't going to let this slide."

I swallow hard. "Definitely not. Has Javier done anything?"

"Not yet, but the threat is imminent, and we all know it."

"If you'd let me see the communication and what you found, I can decipher it for you."

He doesn't trust me yet. I can tell by the look in his eyes. He wants to. I want him to. But he still suspects that my allegiance to Colombia and Los Sangre Dorada runs deep. I need to convince him that trusting me is the right thing to do.

"Lev, this is what we need to do. By being together, we have the potential to unify our families."

"But not with your brother in power."

"He will see me as a threat, and he will try to kill me. He's going to assume that I'm telling you his family secrets. And I fully intend to do that. He is not wrong."

"Mikhail told me to find out everything I can from you."

"You won't have to try hard," I tell him, my heart pounding with what I'm about to reveal. "But I will only tell you under the condition that we do this together. I want you to know my plan."

He picks me up, and we move to the bedroom. The space is luxurious, with high ceilings, silk sheets, and a stunning view of the ocean. We strip, lying naked in comfortable silence. He entwines his fingers with mine before I continue.

"This is what I'd like to do. First, we solidify our alliance." He nods, tracing his finger over my shoulder, down the length of my body. I shiver, relishing the feel of his touch.

"How do you propose to do that? Be specific."

"I will tell you everything I know."

If I didn't have a plan in place, if I didn't know that everything would be okay, I would feel as if I were betraying my family. But I am not the one who betrayed my family. My brother learned from the best, and he does not have the people of my country in mind.

"Once we solidify our alliance, we take down Javier. I know exactly how to do it, but this is one thing I will admit I cannot do alone."

He nods. "Yes. But so far, it sounds like your brother is going to make this easy."

I give him a smile. "That's what he would have you believe. But it isn't true. He probably has many more people hiding around you than you think. Have you been in touch with your mole?"

"I can't talk to you about that."

I blow out an angry breath. "You expect me to tell you everything, and you can't tell me anything? How is that going to work?"

He considers this, thinking it over. I know the problem is that this is not his decision alone. He runs the risk of disloyalty to his family, and unlike me, that means something to him.

"Suffice to say that we have. And he says there are quite a few of your brother's men in our city, which is why we need to get back."

I slide up next to him, lean over and cradle his cock in my hand. I stroke him lazily until his length stiffens in my palm.

"Yes, so this is the plan. I will tell you everything I know. I have a few methods of infiltrating that my brother doesn't know about. Friends on the inside. I'll have to be discreet." I swallow. "Carlos's sister will be one of them. But her life is in grave danger, and I cannot use her intel until I know she is safe."

He reaches over and thumbs my hardened nipple. Arousal surges through me.

"Yes. Of course."

"Your brother Ollie. He's in charge of international rela-tions. Has he spent time in Colombia?" I bend down and lick the tip of his flat nipple. He hisses in a breath and nods.

I bite. "You'll have to send him back."

He catches his breath. "Tell me the entire plan first." He lifts me to straddle him. I love the feel of his warm, strong legs beneath my body. He rests his hands on my hips.

I swallow hard. "I will tell you everything I know about my family, but you must promise me. The *first* thing we do is end the trafficking. Lev, I'll give you the keys to the king-dom. Once Javier is gone, I know exactly how to make the rest of them follow me. I'm confident I can do this." I slide my hot, wet pussy across his flank.

He nods, his body melting into mine. "Go on."

"After we have solidified our alliance and taken down Javier, we will dismantle the trafficking operation. I will make grand promises to the rest of the men in the cartel. You have to understand they are not loyal to you. They are cutthroats. I will only keep those who will be loyal to me."

He stares at me, understanding dawning in his eyes. I slide his cock into me.

"And then..." My heart beats faster, like the relentless beating of a drum. He thrusts. I gasp, "...our families become one."

I lean over, trailing my finger down the length of his chest. We make love, our bodies moving together in a dance of passion and power, sealing our alliance with each touch, each kiss.

He thrusts so hard my head falls back on a scream. My voice is choked when I practically beg him, "And we will rule together?"

"Together," he says, and I throw my head back, feeling his strength, his commitment. This is where it begins.

"Together, we'll rule." My climax overpowers me as he spills inside me. He groans, holding my gaze in his. Our bodies ignite. I watch his mouth fall open as my own ecstasy washes through me.

"Together, we'll rule," he whispers back. It feels more powerful than when we took our vows.

But I'm too jaded to believe it's that simple.

Who and what will get in our way?

"I'M GOING to miss this place," I say. "It's so beautiful here."

The pilot reaches for my hand to help me board the plane but quickly retracts it when Lev glares. *No one* touches his wife.

*I love that.*

We leave the island reluctantly but fired up with the knowledge that we have work to do.

"Me too. It's beautiful at home, though, too." He kisses my cheek.

Upon our return, we dive right into it. Every day, we fall into a new normal. Work out, sweat, shower, and have breakfast.

Work.

He gives me two days to find out everything I can about Javier's plans. Everything I told him corroborated what his brothers had said. I'm grateful for my family's decided lack of loyalty, or I couldn't live with myself.

I have to do this, though.

On our way to headquarters in The Cove, I sip my iced coffee, made how I always make it—dark, no sugar, heavy on the ice, a splash of oat milk. I tap my fingers on the dashboard, reflecting on what I found out about Javier.

"Hey, I have a question for you," I tell him. I've been

thinking about this. It's time. "I've told you many things about my family. Now I need to know more about yours."

"I thought you knew everything about my family?"

"I don't mean your brothers, Lev. I mean your future family. What do you want? What are your dreams? I've told you mine in detail. You know exactly what I want. I don't know the first thing about what you do."

He frowns. "It's the first time anybody has actually ever asked me. It's definitely not the first time I've ever asked myself."

"Oh? Let's hear it." I sip my coffee.

"I've always wanted a family. I always wanted to settle down. It's why I bought a home right here in The Cove. You know my family means everything to me."

I nod. "I do."

"I want peace. I want to go to bed at night knowing that my wife is safe and that my children are happy. I want to go to bed every night knowing that I did the best I could."

I squeeze his hand.

"Despite what happened in the past. None of that matters anymore," I say.

He is not someone who opens up easily. We spent days on the island, talking about my hopes and dreams, my past, and the ordeals I've been through. But I had to drag his story out of him. And now that I know... I want to give him what he desires.

"Lev, you know I'm not the kind of woman to sit around home and raise kids. I am going to be the head of LSD."

"I know that," he says quietly. "But you're not going to rule alone."

Understanding dawns on me. My hopes and dreams, when meshed with his, could actually work. This just might work.

Asking him about his hopes and dreams is the first time I've allowed myself to think ahead like this. All my life, ever since I knew I was going to take over from my brother, I knew I was going to end him and bring freedom to my people. But I never thought beyond that. I imagined myself as the leader, the one everyone else had to obey. I imagined the end of Javier's reign of terror. But I never allowed myself the luxury of seeing anything beyond that moment. And then I knew...

"What is it?" he asks. "You get all quiet and serious when you're deep in thought. What are you thinking about?"

I shake my head, not trusting myself to speak. There is a lump in my throat the size of a boulder. If I talk...

"Isabella, what is it?" he asks sharply.

And then I need to tell him. For some reason, I need to tell Lev exactly what I'm realizing for the first time.

"I've always been prepared to die for my people. I never imagined myself getting any further than that. I never imagined I'd be... here. *Not* dead."

It's not that I don't want children *ever*. It's not that I don't want to be a mother and raise my kids with a man I could love. And I do wonder if I could fall in love with a man like Lev. I know it's already happening.

But I've never allowed myself to dream beyond the immediate goal. I've never allowed myself to think beyond survival. And now that I can...

"That's the truest sign of loyalty," he says quietly. "You told me your family wasn't loyal."

"Until me, it hasn't been." I think about Carlos's sister, about the little girl with braids skipping rocks in the creek by my home, looking for a bit of freedom. I think about my cousin Rosella, taken from her home. Javier wouldn't rescue her, even though he had the means to do so, because he hated her brother. Allowing her to die was his greatest act of vengeance.

I think about my mother. I don't even know if she loved me, but I know now that her lack of love was a protection mechanism.

I've had it with women being seen as less than. The Romanov family is far from perfect, but the Romanovs are the only ones even close to our circles who value women. Yes, they are no charity, but here, in the Romanov family, they rule with their talents and intelligence. Aria is the best hacker in the world. Aleks's wife, Harper, can out-shoot anyone. I don't know Lydia's sister Vera, but Lydia is a force to be reckoned with.

Here, the Romanov family is the only one that can help me realize my dreams.

I'm not alone anymore. That is both a blessing and a curse.

"Let me ask you a question," Lev says, reaching for my hand. His hand is so much stronger than mine. "My family is yours now. Are you still willing to die for your family?"

"I will die defending what matters most to me. I took my vows to you, not out of love but duty. And duty trumps everything."

"That's a good answer, Isabella. It is an honest one, and that is all I ask for. I will do my best to give you everything. That is my duty to you. My obligation."

Lev is stoic and reserved. But beneath that surface, he has so much more to offer. Others might see the youngest in the family as somehow less than, but I know better. He hasn't been handed anything. He has had to fight for all of it—honor, courage, respect.

We pull up to his family home, and just like my time with him, it feels as if another year has passed. Weren't we just married?

"Today, you will meet Kolya."

"Your mentor. What is his story?"

"My father saved his life in the war, and out of duty and obligation, he came home with us. You could say he helped raise us, though he's more like an older brother than a father figure. He taught us discipline and how to fight."

"He's strong, then."

Lev laughs. "You could say that."

For some reason, I feel a little uncertain. I never feel this way, but I suppose I thought I knew my place in the

Romanov family. Every time I meet another of them, I question it all over again.

"What does he think about me?" I try to keep my tone nonchalant, but I fail. My voice wobbles a little.

"What does it matter?"

I don't care what people think about me. So why did I ask that question? "I want to know where I stand."

"You're my wife, and that's all that matters."

Lev's warm hand covers mine again. We park outside the home, and no one is outside. It's a beautiful, uncharacteristically warm fall day. The leaves are burnt orange and crunchy, a dark, vivid reminder of the change of seasons. Lev and I are on the brink of something monumental, and we both know it.

"I want to know what to expect. Is he antagonistic? Angry?"

"None of those things," he says. "He is as steady as a rock. Nothing fazes him. His mastery of stoicism made me who I am today. But it's much more important that you know the truth, Isabella."

I look over at him. I didn't realize how emotional all of this made me until now.

"What's that?" I ask. The adrenaline of my duty fueled me to get to where I am now, but now that I am actually about to betray my family, I am gripped with fear.

"You're my wife. I took vows to you. I have never been more serious about anything in my life. I love my brothers and Kolya and my family with all my heart. But you are the one

I took vows with. No one will hurt you. No one will disrespect you. Is that clear?"

My voice is little more than a whisper when I respond, "Crystal clear, *mi querido jefe*. Let's go inside." I blow out a breath. "I have a few things to tell you guys."

The dimly lit room buzzes with tension as Lev and I walk in, hand in hand. Lev's brothers sit around the large oak table, their expressions a mix of curiosity and skepticism. Kolya leans against the wall, arms crossed and eyes narrowed, his silver-lined hair giving him a look of maturity, though his eyes make him look younger.

I take a deep breath, meeting each pair of eyes steadily.

"Isabella, meet Kolya," Lev introduces. "Kolya, my wife, Isabella."

He nods silently.

"Thank you for meeting with us," I begin, my voice steady. "I have crucial information for you that can help us take down Javier's human trafficking ring and secure his drug operation for us."

Aleks arches an eyebrow. "And why should we trust anything you say?"

Lev's grip on my hand tightens, a silent warning. I nod, acknowledging the skepticism. "I understand your doubts, but please withhold judgement until you hear what I have to say first. Like all cartels, Javier's operation relies on specific routes and schedules. For instance, the next shipment is due next week through the northern port. His safe houses are located here, here, and here," I say, pointing to spots on the map spread across the table.

Nikko leans forward, his interest piqued despite his wariness. "How do you know this?"

"I've spent years collecting information on his network," I reply. "I also have knowledge of his financials. He uses these banks to launder money, and these accountants are complicit." I slide a list across the table. "With this information, we can hit him where it hurts."

Kolya steps away from the wall, his expression hardening. "That's a lot of detailed information. Almost too detailed. How do we know you're not leading us into a trap?"

Lev's jaw tightens. "Kolya, she's with us now. Her interests align with ours."

But he wasn't done. "Or she's playing the long game, Lev, and setting us up to fall right into Javier's hands... or hers."

Mikhail nods. "He's right, Lev. How can we trust her? She's been on the other side for far too long."

Lev explodes, slamming his fist on the table. "She's risking everything to help us! She's my wife and part of this family now. Show some respect."

Mikhail stands up, his face inches from Lev's. "And what if you're wrong, little brother? What if she's lying to all of us?"

The room crackles with tension as Lev and Mikhail glare at each other, ready to fight. Nikko rises, ready to intervene, but Mikhail's voice cuts through the chaos.

"Enough!" His command is sharp, brooking no argument. "We will consider this information carefully. But Lev, you must understand our caution in this matter. We cannot afford to be blindsided."

Lev's chest heaves with anger, but he steps back, taking a deep breath. I place a calming hand on his arm.

Mikhail continues, "There's one more thing." He signals to a screen. It flashes on. "This is Dmitri, the man whose life is in jeopardy because of her. He's our mole in Javier's operation. He will corroborate or refute Isabella's claims."

He nods and glances nervously at the camera. He shoots furtive looks over his shoulder. "Everything she's said... It's true, all of it. It appears she knows Javier's operation inside and out."

The room falls silent as Lev's brothers digest the ramifications. Kolya is the first to speak, his tone grudging. "Alright, Isabella. You've convinced us for now. But I solemnly warn you, if anything goes wrong, it's on you... and Lev."

Lev growls. "Are you threatening her?"

Kolya stands silent, looking at Mikhail grimly.

I nod, my resolve firm. "I understand. But believe me, I want Javier destroyed just as much as you do."

Lev's grip on my hand eases slightly, a silent show of support. "Then we move forward with her plan," he declares, looking each of his brothers in the eye. "We hit Javier where it hurts, and we take control of his operations."

Kolya eyes me, his suspicion still evident but now tempered with contemplation. "If you're telling the truth, then you're more valuable than we thought."

Mikhail's gaze softens, but his wariness doesn't entirely dissipate. "Fine. We'll take this information and act on it.

But if this goes south, I agree with Koyla, you will suffer the consequences Lev."

Lev nods curtly, his protective stance unwavering. "Understood, pakhan. But know this, all of you: Isabella is under my protection. Any threat to her is a threat to *me*, I will defend her no matter who tries to hurt her."

Mikhail turns to the screen. "Fine. Tell us more about Javier's weaknesses. What else is there to exploit?"

Dmitri clears his throat, glancing nervously at me before speaking. "Javier's organization currently is crumbling from the inside. Morale is at an all-time low. There's constant dissent and in-fighting among his lieutenants about what parts of the business are more important, particularly between Carlos and Mateo. They're both vying for greater positions of power in LSD, and that division is something we can use to our advantage."

I nod, my expression resolute. "Carlos is more interested in expanding the drug operations, while Mateo is all about growing the human trafficking business... he's also more loyal to Javier but lacks his ruthlessness. If we can turn Carlos against Mateo, it would wreak chaos within Javier's ranks."

Aleks strokes his chin thoughtfully. "A power struggle could work nicely in our favor. But what could we do to ignite a conflict like that?"

"I know how we can do it," I say firmly. "There's a shipment coming next week. If we intercept it, I can help you make it look like an inside job. Carlos will blame Mateo, and vice versa."

Kolya interjects, still cautious. "And what's your role in all this?"

"I'll help coordinate the attack and ensure that the right evidence points to Carlos," I explain. "I have the skills and the knowledge to circumvent their security. As I said before, I want Javier's downfall as much as you do."

Lev looks around the room, his brothers' expressions a mix of skepticism and reluctant agreement. "Trust her. I do."

As they prepare to leave the room, Aleks approaches Lev, his voice low. "I hope you know what you're doing, little brother. Our family's future depends on it."

Lev meets his gaze, determination blazing in his eyes. "I know exactly what I'm doing. And I believe in Isabella. She's proven herself to me."

The room begins to empty, but Kolya lingers, casting one last glance at me. "We'll see if your loyalty is true. Don't give us any reason to doubt you."

I stand tall, my chin raised defiantly. "I won't."

With the tension still hanging in the air, Lev and I are left alone in the room. He pulls me into his arms, pressing a kiss to my forehead. "You did great. They'll come around."

I lean into him, my heart racing from the confrontation. "I hope so. We have to take down Javier. Not just for us, but for everyone he's hurt."

Lev nods, his expression fierce. "We will. Together."

I look up at him, feeling both determined and vulnerable. "We must succeed, Lev. It's not just about us. It's about all the lives Javier has destroyed and will destroy if we don't."

He nods, understanding the weight of my words. "We will succeed. *Together*."

I take a deep breath, steeling myself for the days ahead. The battle has begun.

There is no turning back now.

# CHAPTER SIXTEEN

*Lev*

"STAND STRAIGHTER!" Isabella snaps. Harper pulls her shoulders back, and Polina does the same. "Hold your core in. You want to make sure you are in control." The early morning sun casts a golden glow over the patio outside my mother's home, where a group of women is gathered, their faces filled with determination and resilience.

"What's going on here?" I ask.

"I told you," Isabella says, standing on her tiptoes to kiss my cheek as I approach her. "These women need self-defense lessons. I'm the perfect girl for the job."

She looks like a Colombian goddess, dressed in skin-tight clothes and her hair twisted elegantly at her neck. She exudes confidence and strength, skills she's passing on to the women in my family.

"All right, ladies," Isabella says, her voice carrying authority. In front of her stand Polina, dressed in workout clothes—

shorts and a tank top—Alexsandr's Harper, Aria, and, to my surprise, my mother. She looks younger with her hair twisted on the top of her head. I've never seen her in yoga pants and a sweatshirt before.

"From what I've heard, there are going to be more threats to this family," my mother says fiercely. "I'm going to be ready to defend whoever I need to. Including you," she says. Ekaterina Romanova does not suffer fools.

I can't help but tease her. I thrust my hands in my pockets. "So you don't trust us to protect you?

"You can't even protect yourself, buddy," Harper says, giving her a wink. When it comes to shooting someone, she's not wrong. That woman could shoot an apple off the top of the Empire State Building... from here.

"You can protect me, *mi querido jefe*," Isabella says in a patronizing voice. She's going to get her ass smacked for that later. I wink at her, and she blushes. I stifle a grin.

"All right, ladies," Isabella says with authority and confidence, turning back to face them. "Today, you're going to learn some basic self-defense techniques. These skills can help protect you in dangerous situations."

Harper bounces on the balls of her feet, her fingers twitching as if she'd rather have a gun in her hands than air.

Isabella stands straight. "I'm going to demonstrate the first move, a very simple but effective wrist escape. If someone grabs your wrist, aim your arm toward their thumb," she says, gesturing to me. "Can you come here and help me baby, please? I want you to grab my wrist."

"Like this?" I walk to her and watch her closely. "All right. I just don't want you to hurt me." I wink at her. If she hurts me, she's going to get it later, and she knows it.

"You got this," she says.

I grab her wrist, and she executes the move smoothly, freeing her wrist from my grip. The other women mimic her actions, some a little more effectively than others. Isabella moves among them, offering corrections and encouragement. "Good job, Aria. Keep your elbow close to your body. Polina, try to twist your wrist with more force."

She comes up to Harper. "Wrists out. Good. Now twist." Harper follows her instructions, and her wrist slips free. She looks up at Isabella, a look of shock on her face. "Wow. That actually works!"

Isabella grins at her. "See? I knew you could do it."

I take a step back and watch from the background as they move on to learning how to break a chokehold. Isabella explains and shows the technique and, thankfully, doesn't ask me to demonstrate this time.

I'd like to choke her out in a *good way* in the privacy of our bedroom, not in front of my mother, thank you very much. "Aim for the eyes, throat, or groin—the sensitive areas that can give you a chance to escape."

The women practice with renewed confidence, and the patio buzzes with their laughter, comments, and Isabella's sharp directives.

*My wife.* She belongs here in this crowd of women, and she seems to feel the same way I do—the camaraderie, the power. Finally, she calls for a break.

She leans against my shoulder, and I wrap an arm around her waist. "They need to know they can defend themselves. It's important."

"Don't you girls trust us to take care of you?" I'm teasing her. I know she wants to be able to protect herself, and I feel a hell of a lot better knowing that she can.

"Of course," she says. "But did you forget that jellyfish sting?"

"Jellyfish?" I scoff. "I want to see your brother in a shallow grave. What about you? Are you ready to defend yourself when the time comes?" I ask her.

She meets my gaze and nods. "I am. And I'm ready to defend our family, too."

*Our family.*

It's the first time she's used that phrase with me. I lean forward and kiss her forehead. "I know you are."

She follows me inside. "What are you doing?"

"I have to meet with Kolya. You stay here, and I'll catch up with you for dinner. Sound good? We can check out that Indian place you wanted to try."

"Sounds great."

The meeting with Kolya runs longer than I had planned. We go over every detail, and in the end, I go looking for her.

"Mom, have you seen Isabella?" I ask her. My text to her goes unanswered.

"I think she went back outside," my mom says. "She said something about wanting some fresh air."

Isabella doesn't like being inside for long periods of time and often walks outside to clear her head.

At first, I don't see her. It takes a while to locate her, but then I hear her voice. I walk down the steps toward a little paved area where my mother has some garden furniture. Isabella stands in a secluded corner of the garden, speaking quietly on her phone. I can't make out the words, but she's hunched over, speaking in a hushed voice.

What the fuck? I'm on guard right away. Who is she talking to? Why is she hiding here? If she wanted to talk someone, why couldn't she have this conversation in front of me?

I know I have trust issues. After years of being who I am, they flare up from time to time. It feels like everything is beginning to crumble. The warnings from Kolya and my brothers didn't help. I've taken an extreme risk marrying her, and even she knows it.

"Isabella?" She spins around and stares at me with a classic deer-in-the-headlights look. Her eyes are wide, her mouth parted. She says something in Spanish on the phone and then shoves it in her pocket.

I stare at her. "Who the hell are you talking to?" I ask, trying to tamp down my anger.

"It's nothing."

Oh no, she doesn't.

"It's not nothing. You obviously needed some privacy, and it seems we have a serious issue here. Who the fuck was that you were talking to?"

"I thought you trusted me," she snaps.

My jaw tightens. "I do trust you."

"Then trust me that I was talking to somebody I had to speak with. I promise everything I've told you is the truth."

Why does she even say that? I wasn't questioning whether she told me the truth. I assume she did. "Then tell me who you were talking to."

She looks away and shakes her head. "I had to speak to Carlos's sister. We're friends."

"You can't be loyal to your family and mine at the same time," I snap.

"Excuse me?" she snaps back. "Who said that I was being disloyal to anyone? You know what my intentions are. You know what it took for me to give you that information about LSD. I put a death sentence on my head the second I told you everything, Lev."

I look away. "I know." I shake my head. "I'm sorry. It's just that when you act evasive like this..."

"Is it my fault?" she says, incredulous.

"Yes. You were sneaky. You didn't tell me who you were talking to. What the hell do you expect me to think?"

"She's talking to someone she can't speak to openly, but she's promised to tell me everything so I will trust her. Look, I just wanted to keep this conversation private."

I clench my jaw. Pushing isn't going to get me anywhere with her. I know her too well.

"Fine, Isabella. Let's go." I want to ask her to show me the phone; to pull up the person she was talking to so she can prove it, but that feels like a dick move right now. I promised my brothers that I would watch out for her. I promised that I wouldn't let her betray us.

But in the back of my mind... I can't help but ask myself.

*Can I really trust her?*

# CHAPTER SEVENTEEN

*Isabella*

EVER SINCE HE saw me on the phone, Lev has been acting strangely distant. It is hard for me to reconcile the fact that he's the same tender, passionate lover who took care of me on the beach—who *wants* to take care of me when our nights are filled with passion and our days are filled with planning, training, and preparation for what I know will be a monumental confrontation.

It's building. I know it is, and we can both feel the tension, like the climbing clicks of a roller coaster before it reaches the top, revealing the unknown ahead. I can only hope we don't hurtle to our deaths.

I tried to get him to talk to me, but he won't, which is totally in line with his character. I suppose I can't blame him. It looked suspicious. I'm protective of my friend, though, and it matters to me that she trusts me, too.

We are days out before the planned attack on Javier, and Lev has barely been home. I shoot him a text, hoping he can feel my simmering anger.

> Are you coming home for dinner?

I don't get a response for an hour.

> Maybe.

I slam my phone on the couch and anchor my hands on my hips.

It feels like we are an old, married couple trying to navigate a new season of life, but in reality, we're just trying to figure out who we are—on the brink of something new and life changing.

One moment, I feel as if I can fully trust him. I believe he has my best interest at heart, and the two of us will rule together. Next, I am catching my breath, waiting for the other shoe to drop.

Part of me knows that I have to prove my allegiance to him, but goddamn, I need him to prove his allegiance to *me*, too.

What*ever*.

I pick up my phone and send him another text.

> I want an answer. Are you coming home or not?

I don't bother to hide the anger in my tone. I'm still his wife, at the end of the day, whether he trusts me or not, he should answer my texts.

Don't give me shit.

I will give him more than shit. I don't respond.

When seven o'clock rolls around, I stomp off to the fridge. I spent four hours training today, and I swear I feel every muscle in my body. My calves ache, my back throbs, but I am getting stronger with every day that passes. Javier won't see what hit him. Every time my body wants to give out, every time I want to give up, I think about those women back at home. I think about what it will mean when I take my rightful position as head of LSD.

I grab some leftovers, toss them onto a plate, and throw it in the microwave. It beeps a moment later, and I eat without tasting it.

I want this over with. And I want Lev and me on the same page again, goddammit.

Of course, at the back of my mind, a little voice says, *Were we ever?*

It felt like it on the island. It felt like it when we were cooking together, sharing our hopes and dreams.

Then why the distance now?

I toss the dish into the sink.

"You're just gonna throw it in the sink? You're not gonna put it in the dishwasher?"

I spin on my heel, angrier that he came into the room without me knowing than I am about his admonishing me for a stupid dirty dish. "Yeah, I do my fair share of dishes around here. It's one fucking dish. When did you get here?"

"Just now. What did you eat for dinner?"

I shrug. "I have no idea."

He looks puzzled. My heart twists at the adorable furrow between his brows and his downturned lips. The shadow of stubble on his chin and the rumble of his voice.

He scratches his belly, and it's unnervingly boyish.

Damn it all to hell. I am *mad* for this infuriating man.

"Seriously, how do you not know what you ate?"

"Because I like everything in that fridge. I trained for hours, and I was starving. I was looking for food in my belly, not a delicacy." I huff and toss my hair. "Sue me."

We haven't had sex in four days and I'm feeling a little ornery.

"Jesus, woman. You're grumpy as fuck. Do I need to fuck this out of you? It's like you're hormonal and shit."

He's lucky all I have is a glass of water in my hand and not a gun. I toss the water straight into his handsome, arrogant face.

His jaw drops, water coursing down his cheeks in rivulets. I wish it felt more vindictive, but I only feel like a child who didn't get her way.

"What the *fuck?*"

He stalks over to me, but I stand my ground. "Only a complete *dick* blames a woman's attitude on her period."

His eyes narrow on me. "I didn't say period. I said hormones."

"Same thing!"

He throws his hands up in the air. "When the fuck did I give you the impression I was a good guy?"

When did he tell me? He didn't need to.

When he carried me back after a jellyfish stung me. When he made me dinner. When he listened with sympathy when I told him about the bullshit my family put me through. When he defended me to his brothers. Me, Isabella Morales —Romanova.

No one's ever defended me in my entire life.

"You're right, Isabella. Honeymoon *over*."

The shift hurts. The intimate moments we shared, the tentative plans for our future together. It's vanished overnight. I want to reach out to him. I want to cling to the closeness we had before.

He stops short a few feet from me, glares at me and grabs a dishtowel, running it over his face. I deflate a little. I wanted more of a fight from him.

"You piss me off so much. Jesus, woman." He turns away. I can see the restraint it takes for him not to lash out. His muscles strain. "I've got a lot on my mind, and you're acting evasive as shit. I can't help wondering what the hell you're hiding. Jesus, Isabella. Don't fucking push me."

"I didn't share *one* conversation with you, and you decide to question every interaction we've had? Every word I've spoken? You think I'm manipulating you? What are you playing at?"

His jaw clenches, and he doesn't respond. "You think *I'm* playing *you*?"

My throat catches. I'm on the brink of losing everything. Fucking *everything*. What are we even fighting about?

"I need to know you're still loyal to us and not the LSD," he snaps.

"What else can I do to prove it to you? Hmm? *What else do you want?* Blood?"

I want to shake him until his teeth rattle. I want to scream until I'm hoarse. I feel helpless and angry, caught between one family that hates me and another that doesn't trust me.

"You were on a burner phone. That's not your regular phone."

I throw my hands up in the air, my temper boiling over. I half wish someone would douse *me* with water. "Of course I was. If anyone knew I was talking to Renata, they could trace me. But you don't care, Lev. You're too blinded by your trust issues to hear reason." My voice catches. It infuriates me. Tears blur my vision, which makes me even angrier. "I've been trying to find a way to protect us both. I've done nothing wrong. But you won't hear me."

It feels like the clouds have shifted, and darkness is creeping in, heralding a storm. Proving my loyalty to him will be a monumental task, but I'm determined to try. I'm all in with the Romanovs. I am all in with the plans he and I made to rule together.

"My trust issues?" He scoffs. "*My* trust issues?"

I throw my hands up. "What the hell?"

"If you trusted me, you would've had that conversation with Renata in front of me."

I blow out a breath. "Unbelievable." I roll my eyes. "What next? You want me to show you every text I send? You want to approve of who I can talk to and who I can't?"

His eyes narrow on me. Without a word, he turns and walks away.

"Hey! We're not done here."

"*I* am."

I watch his retreating back. My heart hurts. I want to be on the same team again. "I am *not!*"

"I'm not arguing over this anymore. For God's sake, yes. *Yes.* You have to prove your loyalty. But based on what Aleks just told me, you'll have your chance much sooner than later."

I swallow. A shiver of cold runs down my back. "What is that supposed to mean?"

He looks over his shoulder, his expression dark. "Javier's on the move."

I'm at the top of that roller coaster, and the path before me looks fucking fraught. I can't see where it goes. What if I run straight off the tracks?

He stalks into his office and goes to shut the door, but I jam my foot in front of it. The room is luxurious and intimidating, with dark wooden furniture, rich leather chairs, maps, monitors, and a huge, imposing desk. He frowns at me from his desk but doesn't respond. He leans over and fires up his laptop. I watch as water from his face drips onto a map.

I normally love this room because it's an extension of *him*.

"Jesus, Isabella. Leave it."

"I want answers. What do you mean Javier's on the move?"

He walks away from me and paces back and forth, his expression dark and troubled.

"Our guy doesn't know where he is. No one does."

It feels like someone tossed ice down my back. I shiver. "No one?" Javier is a snake, crawling on his belly toward us, and no one can see him.

He shakes his head. "No one. We can only assume he's coming here and is ready to strike."

*Fuck.*

Of course he is.

My mind races. "Renata could find out."

Lev pauses, his eyes conflicted. His tee is still soaked with the water, his hair hanging down like he's a surfer who just came up for air. He frowns. "I've been hearing things. We suspect Javier's behind several attacks on our operations."

"What? He wouldn't risk open war."

Lev's voice tightens, filled with suspicion. "Are you sure about that? Or are you just saying what you think I want to hear? How well do you know him?"

I stand, staring at him. "I'm telling you the truth. Do you think I'd lie to you after everything we've been through?"

He turns away, running a hand through his damp hair. "I

don't know anymore. Your brother will stop at nothing to end us." His voice trails off.

I step closer to him. "And what do you see when you look at me, Lev? The woman who's risked everything to be with you? The woman who's fought by your side? Or someone who was sent to tear you apart?"

He doesn't meet my eyes. "I don't know who to trust."

My voice trembles. I hate that it does. "If we let them tear us apart, they've already won before the battle even starts."

"Then you can't keep secrets from me," he snaps.

"I haven't!" I know I haven't.

"According to Aleks, you have three burner phones, a wig, plus the knife I found in the bedside table."

I stare. I blink. "The phones were to call my connections in Colombia without bringing suspicion down on the Romanovs. The knife is for basic protection, and I certainly have no plans on using it. And the wig... my God, sue me if I thought it would be fun to do a little role play." My cheeks flame to think Aleks saw that. "You've been spying on me."

"It's my job."

I narrow my eyes on him. "Oh, really?" I clench my teeth. "How long, Lev? What will it take for you to trust me?"

"I don't know," he says, shaking his head, and for the first time, it looks like he's warring with his own doubt. He anchors his hands on his hips. "Come here."

"I'm not playing—"

He reaches for me and grabs my wrist, yanking me against his chest. I slam against his hard muscles. His familiar scent makes me want to cry.

"What are you doing?"

"There's only one way to get the truth out of you."

Oh, no, if he thinks—

His lips crash against mine. Our tongues meet. His dominance and my desire clash. I stifle a moan, instantly wet.

He pulls away and holds my gaze. "I must know if your loyalty is truly to my family alone."

Frustration and hurt well in my chest. "I've told you, Lev. I'm with you! But you keep doubting me, pushing me away. How can we ever move forward if you don't trust me?"

"How can I trust you when you keep hiding things that point to your guilt? It's like you're here, but your heart is still in Colombia."

My emotions threaten to choke me. "That's not fair! What more do you want from me?"

He blows out a breath and touches my shoulder. "I want to believe you, Isabella. But every time I let my guard down..."

"You don't have to prove yourself to me. You can trust me. I never betrayed you. Stop treating me like I did."

Lev's eyes flash with a mix of anger and vulnerability. He grabs my arm, our breaths mingling in the heated air.

I will try again. "Show me who you are behind this armor. Let me in."

He crushes his lips against mine, the kiss rough and demanding. He tears at my clothes, the room filling with the sounds of our desperate need. It's been days. It feels like an eternity.

He pushes me against the wall, his hands roaming over my body as if seeking silent reassurance. He cups my ass, and I wrap my legs around his waist, pulling him closer. Our movements are frantic, driven by a need to prove something to ourselves. To each other.

He buries his face in my neck. I shiver, imbibing his scent. I lick his neck, relishing the salty taste of his hot skin, and he groans. "Sometimes I wish this wasn't who we are. Sometimes I wish we were normal people who had normal jobs and worried about shit like, should we get a dog, and when's the next fucking soccer game?"

I make a sound of disgust. "That sounds so basic and boring as *fuck*." I kiss the underside of his jaw, heat rising in my belly, primal need clawing at my chest. I want him inside me so badly I could cry.

"Maybe normal is underrated," he whispers in my ear.

"Let's get through this," I whisper back. "And then we'll give it a go, *mi querido jefe*."

"Deal, *mi reina*." My heart surges in my chest. *My queen.*

"Are you hitting the Duolingo again?" I grin against his neck, and he slaps my ass. I close my eyes and moan.

"Aleks has a new housekeeper who speaks Spanish. I've been quizzing her."

That's so fucking adorable. I push back on his chest and frown at him. "Is she young and hot?"

He holds me with one hand while he yanks my top off with the other. I reach for his tee and pull it up and over his head. I stare at the breadth of his shoulders, the corded muscles at his neck and back. I kiss the tats on his arms.

"No," he snorts. "She's like a sixty-year-old grandma."

I kiss him. My tongue meets his. He utters a low, male sound of approval that does delicious things to me.

"Oh good, maybe she can make me *tres leches.*"

He bends my head back and kisses my neck, and I moan. "Thought you didn't eat cake."

I swallow, the rough, hot feel of his tongue making me crazy. "For *tres leches*, I make an exception."

He grins. I swoon. Christ, my husband is a fucking god. Wordlessly, he lifts me onto his desk, pushing papers and maps aside. Pens bounce off the floor and something inside me thrills at his carelessness. *He wants me.*

With one hand gripping my thigh, he uses the other to open the huge window behind me, letting in the cool night air and the distant sound of the city. I thrill at the exposure, the knowledge that a whole city is right outside. I catch a glimpse of us in one of his huge monitors and grin.

He tears my clothes away and growls into my ear. "You're mine, Isabella. Do you understand?"

I moan, my nails digging into the tats on his back. "Yes, Lev. I'm yours. Only yours."

Gripping me with one hand, he unzips his fly with the other. I hold my breath at the sight of his thick, throbbing cock. I want him *in me.* I can't fucking breathe until he's in me.

My head falls back when he shoves my thighs apart. I'm gripping his shoulders, but my hands are slick with sweat. I'm slipping. I fall, and he catches me in his strong, capable hands.

Our bodies move together in a fierce rhythm, the world outside disappearing as we lose ourselves in each other.

His phone rings over and over again.

"I have to take that," he says in my ear. I open my mouth to protest. "Don't say a fucking word, or I'll punish you."

I bite my tongue and grin as he stabs his phone and hits the speaker.

"Yeah?"

He shoves into me so hard a spasm rushes through me. I close my eyes. Someone talks to him in Russian, and he answers in grunts. I bend my mouth to his chest and lick his nipple. He hisses in a breath and yanks my hair.

How did I not know how sexy it was to hear him growl in Russian? He thrusts into me, again and again, taking the call, growling into the phone, and finally slamming it off, never losing his pace.

As he ends the call, his control snaps. He shoves everything aside and gives me the full heat of his focus. My head falls back, and I scream my release as he roars and spills inside me.

I'm drowning in bliss, blind to everything but the feel of his hot body against mine, the flood of ecstasy in my limbs, his hot seed lashing into me. I come again, a second climax on the cusp of the first. I scream until I'm hoarse. I slump against him, hot, wet, and utterly boneless. I can't *move*. The hounds of hell could be at my back, and I'd collapse in front of them.

Our breathing is heavy, our hearts beating as one in a rapid tempo. He wraps his arms around me. I vaguely wonder how he's still standing.

"Thought you had questions for me," I tease, my eyes closed and a smile on my lips. "I thought you were going to interrogate me with your cock."

"You were the one who had to go and bewitch me," he rasps in my ear. "Got anything to tell me?"

I pause. I know what I want to tell him, but it's too soon.

Isn't it?

*I love you, Lev Romanov.*

*I can't breathe when you're not here.*

*You make me ache in all the best ways.*

*I love you.*

I nestle against his chest, feeling the rapid beating of his heart.

"No," I whisper. "Got anything you need to ask?"

He sighs. "No. I don't want to lose you, Isabella."

"We're going to make this work."

He nods, stroking his fingers lazily through my tangled hair. "I have to go. That call was urgent. I need to meet one of my men."

"Javier?" I ask.

"Yeah."

I swallow. "Can I go?"

Shaking his head, he holds me to his chest. "I wish you could. You're safer here for now."

*For now.*

I don't want to see him go.

I can't explain it, but it feels like if I let him go out that door... he'll never come back.

# CHAPTER EIGHTEEN

_Lev_

FUCK IT. He can wait until the morning.

I don't want to leave her. Not like this.

I fall asleep with Isabella in my arms. I dream we're back on the island, just the two of us. I roll over, and she turns to me, her hand on her belly.

_"I have good news," she tells me._

_"You're having a baby?"_

_She nods. "I don't want to fear this anymore. I don't want to fear us. I am ready for the next step."_

_A sudden explosion shatters our peace. The glass in the window flies into the room. She screams and falls to the floor. I cover her with my body._

I wake in a cold sweat. Isabella's beside me, wide awake. "Lev? What happened? Are you alright?"

Fuck, it was just a dream. *Just a dream.*

I am not alright.

I reach for the water on the bedside table and take a sip as she lies beside me and falls back asleep. I look at her flat belly.

She isn't pregnant.

Where has my mind gone? God, we need to get rid of Javier. The road before us is so fucking fraught.

I stare at the ceiling, unable to fall back asleep, when my phone buzzes. I glance at the screen.

Dmitri Petrov... our mole within Javier's LSD.

What time do we meet?

You with Isabella?

Yeah

You need to make sure she doesn't overhear us. Meet me at headquarters?

now?

Yeah?

I glance at the time. It's three a.m.

On my way.

I get out of bed and pull the covers over her.

I want everything in me to know I can trust her. I want us to be exactly what she said she wanted—a team. Inseparable.

That means putting this bullshit behind us.

That means facing whatever happens next.

I get to headquarters in record time. Dmitri sits outside on a bench. It's cold tonight, a chill in the air. My breath hangs in the air in front of me.

We nod to each other in silence.

"Hey, boss."

I nod to him and sit next to him on the bench. "Hey. When did you get back?"

"Javier sent me here a few days ago."

"He still has no idea who you are?"

He shakes his head. "None. You have no idea how divided they are. He only trusts himself."

I nod. That corroborates what Isabella has said as well. "And what has he instructed you to do?"

"I've been sent here to make sure nothing goes wrong with the shipment that's coming in tomorrow night."

I blow out a breath and laugh mirthlessly. "What could possibly go wrong?"

He huffs out a laugh of his own. "Seriously, though. But before we make any moves... I gotta show you something."

I know before he shows me what I'm going to see. I don't know if I can trust it, but there's only one reason he called me here in the middle of the night where my wife can't hear us.

I take the packet he hands me silently.

I curse under my breath as I look over the transcript, the communication, the texts.

"They know she's here..."

"They don't just know she's here, boss. They sent her here. She's been working with Carlos Cabrera since before you met her. Do you have any evidence of her contacting him?"

A cold shiver runs down the length of my body. This can't be happening.

"No, but..." My voice trails off.

Dmitri waits patiently.

"She's been in touch with his sister."

"I knew that."

"But have you listened to what they said?"

I feel sick to my stomach.

"Her presence here is part of a larger tactical maneuver."

I shake my head. "None of this implicates her. You're making assumptions."

With a frown, Dmitri shows me the record of a phone call. "Look, boss. This is a record of her phone call with Carlos."

I look at the time stamp. The exact time I caught her hiding with her burner phone.

She said she was talking with Renata. She lied to me.

I nod. "Thank you. Have you told anyone else this yet?"

"No, sir."

"Keep it that way."

A shadow crosses his face, but he nods. "I am sorry to be the bearer of bad news."

"You did your job."

I leave.

# CHAPTER NINETEEN

*Isabella*

I WAKE UP NAUSEOUS. I look around the room and pat the bed next to me as if to confirm what I already know —he's gone.

While it isn't outside the ordinary for me to wake up alone, after last night...

"Lev?" I ask, holding my breath while I wait for him to answer. My heart sinks. I look to where he normally plugs his phone in, but it's gone.

My God, I was so tired last night. I sit up and sip from the cup beside me. It doesn't help. I have a sour taste in my mouth, and my belly clenches.

"Lev?" I ask again, even though I know he isn't here. I don't know why I feel so alone. It's so vast here, so empty and vacant. I rub my belly and, for the first time in my life, consider what it would be like if I *did* get pregnant.

*Could* I be? Birth control fails sometimes. I frown, wondering, as I head to the bathroom. But a few minutes later, after I've brushed my teeth and washed my face, I feel right as rain. Strange.

I bet it's nerves.

I pick up my phone and text him.

> Where r u

There's no response. My gut tells me something is off. I'm staring at my phone, hoping for a response from him, when a notification of another text pops up.

> Renata: Isabella, are you home?

I frown at my phone.

> Yes. Why?

Home. This is home.

> Carlos is gone. Javier is making his move. They are coming to you as planned. Do you trust Lev?

I hate that I have to think before I answer.

> Yes.

But after last night... I am not so sure.

> Do you know where he is right now?

I scowl at the phone. What is she doing? Renata is my best friend on the planet, but what the hell is she even doing right now?

No, why?

The little dots indicating she's responding flick across the screen. They disappear. They come back, and I'm growing impatient.

What the hell is going on?

My sources tell me he's with another woman. I know he is just a figurehead and a means to work with the Romanovs, but I wanted you to know. Be careful about trusting him.

Just a figurehead?

Just a means to work with the Romanovs?

He made love to me last night. He made me scream in ecstasy and marked my body with his teeth and hands. I've memorized the details of his body, the way his eyes grow stormy or hopeful, depending on his mood. I know exactly where he has the faintest glimmer of a dimple in his right cheek, a hint of a cleft in his chin, and how long his stubble gets when he doesn't shave for a day.

I know the sound of his voice when he's amused or angry or curious, or when he's just at ease. I know the way he sleeps, with his arm tucked under his head and a gun on the bedside table because even in rest, he's willing and able to defend me.

I know how he under-salts his food and over-butters his bread. I know how he tracks every penny that comes in and out of his bank account, even though he's independently wealthy like all the Romanov men. He trusts no one and is always on alert.

I know what he wants. What he hopes. What he dreams, and how, most of all, he wants the normalcy of a family to come home to.

Just a figurehead?

Are we both being used by our families?

What woman?

I have no idea. Look into it.

Oh, I totally fucking will.

Okay, I will. Thank you. Are you alright?

I don't know… Carlos is getting suspicious. He was wary last night. I spent the night at Gia's.

I clench my jaw. If my best friend gets hurt because of this bullshit—

Stay safe.

I glance at the time. I have an hour before I'm supposed to be teaching another self-defense class at the Romanov family headquarters.

I might as well go early and do some investigative work. Ask some questions.

*Woman.*

He's in touch with another woman?

*My God,* I will fucking castrate him with a steak knife.

I make coffee and pour it into a cup. When I open the door, I'm not surprised to find three guards standing like a barrier in my path.

"You can't pass, Mrs. Romanova."

*Of course* they'll tell me this.

I make a sound of disgust. "First, my *God,* I'm no *Mrs. Romanova.* There are plenty of those to go around. I'm Isabella, thank you, though you can call me Miss." I look down my nose, gathering up all the authority I can and funneling it into one withering look. "Have you seen my husband?"

"Not since last night, ma'am," a tall, beefy guy with a shaved head says. "He said to keep you safe."

Keep me safe, or keep me *here?* After what Renata said, I don't know what the truth is.

I text him again, but it goes unanswered.

I told the girls I would give them their second class today, so whether he's here or not is irrelevant. I'm going to keep my promise.

"Move," I snap at the guard.

"No, ma'am."

"My God, there's a difference between *miss* and *ma'am.* I am hardly an old lady." He gives me a once-over. "If my husband saw the way you just looked at me, you'd lose those fucking eyes."

He whips his head away from me as quickly as he can. I'm not bluffing, though. Lev would kill him.

Would he?

Or has this all been part of an act?

Lev doesn't act, though. That's not part of his character. His bold honesty is one of the things I love best about him.

*Love.*

If he's cheating on me, I'm going to kill him.

"Move," I snap to the guard. "You do not want to block me right now."

"If you go, I'll have to tell Mr. Romanov."

"Go! Do it. Maybe he'll actually show his fucking face, then."

I shove past the guard. He reaches for me, but I stop him by swiveling my camera on and capturing him on video. "Go ahead. Touch me again. Let's see what my husband says when he sees this video I'll send him."

The guard tosses his hands in the air.

I stalk past him toward the small, silver Lexus Lev gave me when we came home after our honeymoon and head straight for the Romanovs.

I glance at my phone.

No response.

If he's still alive, I might kill him.

When I arrive, my mother-in-law, Ekaterina, stands on the front step, waving to me adorably. Something catches in my throat, and I have to look away. I don't want anyone to see me cry. I've never had anyone be so glad to see me before.

I quickly get myself together and exit.

"Morning!" she says. "I have pastry and coffee for everyone, but most of the girls are ready to dive right in. Did you want to grab something to eat?"

"Mom." Polina steps outside wearing her workout leggings and a tank. "*Look* at the woman. Does she look like the type that eats pastry for breakfast?"

Her mother laughs out loud. "Definitely not." She winks at me. "You and Lev are absolutely a match made in heaven. Do you two make protein shakes together?"

I can't help but snort at that. "You have no idea."

Match made in heaven? I stifle a sigh. We could be.

"Alright, girls," I tell them all as we're lined up outside. "Last time, we went over how to disengage a wrist grab. We also discussed how to gain leverage by hitting the most vulnerable points. Most men are larger and stronger than most women, so relying on brute force or fighting in most cases won't be helpful. Let's continue to go over techniques that might be."

I move to the center of the room, my eyes scanning over the eager faces of the women gathered in front of me. Polina, slender and willowy and eager to learn. Aria, glasses perched on her nose, alert and ready. Harper, with her thick brown hair tied up in a ponytail, a gun in a holster by her side. Even Viktor's Lydia has joined us.

"Today, we'll learn how to escape a bear hug from behind. This is a common technique in a hostage situation, so it's important to know how to react effectively."

I motion for Polina to step forward, demonstrating how to position her hands. "If someone grabs you from behind in a bear hug, the first thing you want to do is drop your center of gravity. Bend your knees slightly and shift your hips down. This makes it harder for the attacker to lift you."

She watches as I continue. "Next, create space. Use your elbows to strike backward into the attacker's ribs or stomach so they loosen their grip. You can also stomp on a foot or use your heel to strike a shin."

I step back. "Now pair up and practice."

I walk between them, offering suggestions and encouragement. "Good. Remember to keep your movements quick and forceful. You want to create pain and surprise so they release you. Always keep your head on straight so you have the advantage. Men will often rely on brute force when taking or hurting a woman. Be smarter."

I watch them grow confident, their movements more fluid. I can't help but feel a sense of pride alongside a growing sense of doom.

What will happen next? Are we prepared?

Where the hell is Lev? I have so many damn questions for him.

"Good job, ladies." My heart thunders in my chest. I hold my breath, unable to look over my shoulder. I know that voice.

I don't know what to think.

I turn and stare at Lev. He holds my gaze. A well of questions rises, bubbling to the surface. I have so much I need to ask him. So much I need to know.

Will he answer my questions?

I swallow hard and stare ahead, trying to control the shaking of my limbs.

"Good morning, beautiful," he says, heading to me. My heart warms in spite of myself.

Maybe Renata was wrong. Maybe...

I hear the whistling sound at the same time he does. We stare at each other in a split second of recognition before he screams, "Go for cover!"

An explosion shatters the quiet. Screams erupt all around us as the stone bench in the garden explodes. Smoke billows in and clouds all around us. I fall to the ground, and it takes me a second to realize he's on top of me, sheltering me beneath his heavy frame. I can't see what's happening.

"Stay down!" he thunders, not just to me but all of us. "We're under attack."

Smoke keeps coming and coming, and it finally dawns on me. "Lev, it was a detonation to distract, but the rest are smoke bombs. They're coming. Let me up!"

He leaps off me, and we both grab our guns. I choke on the smoke all around us but keep my head like I told the girls. I fall to the ground so I can breathe better and swivel my gaze all around.

"Make sure everyone's safe!" I scream. "Your mother, your sister!"

"Where is everyone?" Lev yells.

"Harper!"

"Here!"

"Lydia!"

"Here!"

I breathe out a sigh of relief.

"Mom?" Lev shouts.

"Here!"

"Polina?" No answer. "Polina!"

*Shit.*

I crawl around us, looking for anything that will give me a clue when I see through the fog and smoke a pair of guy's legs and a woman clad in workout leggings.

"Let her go, or I'll shoot!" I scream. I barrel-roll through the fog and slide right into his legs. He falls on top of me and elbows my neck. I scream when he grabs my wrist but quickly out-maneuver him so he cannot hold me down.

There's a sudden scream and thud, and my husband appears as if transported magically, the look on his face through the cloud of smoke terrifying.

"That's my wife," he says before he cocks his gun, points it at our assailant's head, and pulls the trigger.

"Um, and sister," Polina mutters as we stare down at the dead body of her would-be kidnapper.

"Sorry," I tell her, my hand on her shoulder.

"Meh, you can keep him," she says with a wink, but Lev doesn't hear us. He's already on to the next one.

We work as a team. I shoot down a man in a tactical vest while Lev slices his knife through a man who goes after his mother. I watch with pride as Aria perfectly orchestrates sliding out of a chokehold before she draws her gun and pulls the trigger. Ekaterina holds her own, sliding her wrist out of a grab before she slips a knife out of a boot holster and slices him.

Lev screams for backup into his phone, and the Romanov men pour into the backyard. For long moments, there's nothing but the deafening sound of gunshots, terrified screams, the clash of weapons, and the moans and pleas of our assailants. I'm panting over the body of a man who's vaguely familiar—my brother's friend, I'd guess—when the dust begins to settle.

Mikhail glares into the crowd. "Is everyone accounted for?" I see the shadow of someone behind him. He doesn't see, and there's no time to warn him. I roll onto my right shoulder, take my position, and pull the trigger, but when my bullet hits its mark, another shot rings out, followed by another and another.

*Jesus.* Harper's fucking amazing with a gun. She's at the other end of the patio and still hit him straight between the eyes.

"Jesus," Mikhail mutters.

We gather everyone up. "You're injured," I say to Lev. He has a gash across his cheek, and there's blood dripping from a cut on his forehead.

"I'm fine," he snaps. "Are you?"

*No, I'm not fine. I'm nauseous and feel weird, and we were just attacked, and were you with another woman?*

I shake my head. We're wounded and reeling after this attack. The Romanov men are yelling at each other in Russian. Lev curses.

"Fuck," he mutters. "What do you know about Javier's tactics?"

"He's a sneaky motherfucker," I snap. "Renata told me this morning that his men were here. An outright attack like this is consistent with his usual, but..." My voice trails off.

"But what?" Lev is growing impatient.

"He'll be sneakier." I turn to Mikhail. "Is everyone accounted for?"

"Yes." He blows out a breath. "But Javier's not finished, is he?"

I shake my head. "Not a chance. That was a warning. He wants to keep us guessing."

"Son of a bitch," Lev growls.

"We could send them to a safe house," Ollie says quietly, his arms crossed over his chest behind Mikhail. "I had them prepared."

"I am not going…" a powerful wave of nausea suddenly washes over me, unbalancing me abruptly, I almost pass out. With sheer willpower alone, I force myself to regain my composure, stand straight and start again, "I am *not* going to the safe house," I snap.

Lev's jaw clenches.

"Polina." He jerks his head at his sister.

"Mmm?"

"Test her."

 Polina stares. "Lev, I—"

"Do it," he snaps.

I stare at him, my jaw unhinged. "Test me for… what?" The others are staring at us. Lev doesn't meet my eyes. Heat flares across my chest as they begin to disperse.

"Everyone in the dining room," Mikhail orders. He lowers his voice. "We'll leave you two alone."

What the hell is going on here?

Lev's jaw clenches and unclenches. The smoke from the bomb has dissipated, and we're left reeling, covered in blood but otherwise unharmed. I stare at him.

"Talk to me."

He rifles a hand through his hair. Why does he look so guilty?

"I took it every day on the island."

He swallows hard. "You didn't, though."

"Yes, I did. You said I wouldn't need it anymore, but I still took it, because—"

My voice trails off when his face grows grim.

"It wasn't birth control. I got rid of that shit. You haven't been on birth control since then."

I stare at him, hardly believing what he's telling me. "You fucked around with my birth control?" My voice is a low whisper. I feel like I'm choking. I shake my head from side to side, not believing he'd stoop so low. "And I know what you did behind my back, too."

I watch his brow furrow. "What the fuck are you talking about?"

"You left in the middle of the night. You think I don't have spies, too? How did I know anything about Javier, hmm? What the fuck, Lev? I thought you liked being with me."

He walks over to me and brushes his hand across his face as a medic rushes over to us. "Sir, sit, please. We'll tend to you both."

Lev has a hushed conversation with them.

"Excuse me! I'm sitting right here. What the hell?"

But they don't respond.

I watch as they clean Lev. I watch as Polina leaves and comes back a few moments later, her eyes wide and her face pale.

"You need to pee in this," she says in my ear, handing me a

small paper bag with a cup in it. Thank God she's got a medical background because I would literally die.

This can't be happening.

"I've got this." I take the bag from her. I've never taken one of these tests before, but I need to know.

First.

Lev pulls me aside and runs a hand through his hair. He's paled, and his eyes look haunted. "You need to know. I fucked around with your birth control. Now that I know you... now that I know who you are, I wouldn't do something like that. Now that I... know that I love you."

I stare at him. He's speaking a language I know yet it seems like I can't understand. I blink.

"I told you I would find a way to shackle you to me. The vows were only the beginning."

"And yet you cheated on me," I whisper, shaking my head.

His face contorts, and he shakes his head. "Never, Isabella. That's utter bullshit. I never cheated on you! I wouldn't. I fucked with your birth control because I wanted you to have my baby. I wanted to bind you to me in a way you couldn't dissolve." He shakes his head.

"How did you fuck with it?"

He looks away. "I replaced your pills."

He...*what?*

I glare and narrow my eyes at him. "Your brother put you up to this, didn't he?" When he doesn't respond, I have my answer. I stare in disbelief, too stunned even to be angry.

Yet.

"I told you I didn't want a baby. You said you agreed that children weren't commodities."

And he told me how important it was to him to have children, to be a father. If he wants them, are they really commodities?

But it's *my body*.

I push past him and make my way to a bathroom. I do the whole pee-on-a-stick thing.

I watch the two pink lines show up.

I stare, disbelieving.

*Pregnant.*

# CHAPTER TWENTY

*Lev*

THOSE WERE NOT my finest moments.

She's gonna fucking kill me.

But cheating? Where the fuck did that come from?

Isabella stands in front of me, her fists clenched by her sides, but she looks as if she's going through a whirlwind of emotions. "Pregnant!" she screams before she cups her belly. "Is the baby alright?" she whispers. "How could you do this to me?" she rages before she shakes her head and swallows hard. "I need to check on the baby. Oh my *God*. I swear to God, if I find out you did cheat on me, I'm going to murder you, bury you, bring you back to life and kill you again, and then I'm going to take all your fucking money for good measure because you fucking owe me, you fucking son of a bitch!"

Okay, alright. Clearly, she's not in her right mind at the moment.

"Listen. Kill me later. I'll fucking bare my neck for you. But first, we need to figure out what the hell you're talking about."

"Who were you with last night?" She snaps. "Hmm?"

I anchor my hands on my hips and glare at her. "You first. Who did you talk to, and what the hell are you thinking?"

"*You* first!"

"Fine! I was with Dmitri. He had a lot of shit to tell me about what you've been up to."

"Me?" She shakes her head in disbelief. "And *I* talked to someone who told me you cheated on me," she says, a warning glint in her eyes telling me she's about to do something drastic. I could restrain her but she's a master of getting out of restraints.

"Who told you that? It's a lie."

"Of course, you'd say that," she scoffs. "This coming from a man who fucked with my *birth control*."

"Ah, very nice. That's ripe coming from someone who's in contact with Carlos Cabrera."

She stares. "*What?*"

"You heard me."

Isabella gets to her feet and paces. Stewing. "We are going to forget about the baby for a moment because I know my brother, and he's going to come soon." She stabs a finger in my direction. "Though you are still fucking *toast*. You *asshole*."

I growl at her. "Go on."

"This is what he does. This is exactly what my family does. They pit everyone against each other. Javier lacks the ability to really take down the Romanovs, with all your alliances and strength. What he'll do is pit us against each other."

I frown. It makes sense, but it's probably exactly what she'd say if she were guilty. Still, I need her to clarify. "Alright. Go on."

"So, someone told you I was in touch with Carlos. For what purpose? Where's the proof? For God's sake, do you think Carlos lets Renata have a phone under her own name? Of course my contact with her will look like contact with him." She frowns at me. "Have you *seen* Carlos? Skinny, ugly motherfucker. I wouldn't let him breathe the same air I do, much less let him *touch* me." She shivers as if she had a brush with another jellyfish. "*Gross.*"

Fuck. Good point. Still... "I read a transcript. They said you were sent here by your brother."

She laughs mirthlessly. "Leave it to Javier to save face. Of course he made you believe that." She rolls her eyes. "Do you think if Javier sent me here, he would have me hide in your warehouse dressed like a man and then *marry* you?"

She's right. Of course he wouldn't.

"Lev," she says gently. "Don't you see what they are doing? Your man told you I was disloyal. My contact told me *you* were. How can either one of those things be true? This is exactly what they want us to think." She frowns. "Wait. Is the pregnancy thing true?"

I cringe. God, I'm an asshole, and I want to believe her. "Yeah."

She draws a breath in through her nose. "I'm getting another test, and I will fucking kill you, later. But first we will work through this. Want to know how we make them show their faces? Come out of hiding?"

"How?"

She leans in. "We give them what they want. We break up publicly. Let them think they won." I nod. It makes sense. "Let's pretend they won. Even if it were true—you cheated on me, and I..." Her voice cracks. She swallows. "And I betrayed you. Even if this were true, you and I would still break up."

We're fucking playacting, and it still feels like someone's driving a knife in my rib cage. "Yeah," I whisper. "Right."

I want to hold her to me. I want to kiss her. I want to prove that Dmitri's evidence is wrong, that we were set up.

I want to show her that having my baby won't destroy her, destroy *us*.

I want her to know that I didn't do it just because my brother wanted me to but because I *want* a baby with her.

I want to make it all up to her, too, because, goddamn, I'm a fucking asshole.

The only way forward, then... is apart.

"I love you," I mouth as I take a step away from her. She blinks, and a fat tear rolls down her cheek.

Maybe not all is lost.

She whispers. "And I love *you* even though I will never forgive you for knocking me up, like fucking *ever*."

"I'll make it up to you," I promise. "Now. It's go time."

Isabella draws in a breath. Her nostrils flare, and she clenches her hands into fists by her side. "You liar!" she screams. "How could you? I thought I loved you. I thought I could trust you, you fucking piece of shit!"

Her voice catches at the end. Either she's a really good actress, or she's putting more of her real feelings into this than I anticipated.

*Fuck.*

This sucks.

She's good.

"You aren't leaving," I tell her. "You're having my baby now."

That isn't far from the truth. Jesus fucking *Christ,* I feel like a douchebag now.

The thought of her walking away from me forever is like a knife through my heart. I know we made this decision together, that I deserve for her to leave. I never should've messed with her birth control.

I should've told my brother no. It doesn't matter that he's my older brother and *pakhan*; it doesn't fucking matter.

My feelings for her have grown well beyond duty and protection, and something tells me that she feels the same way.

I have a job to do, and I'm gonna fucking do it right.

"Don't you dare walk away from me!" I say, and I don't need

to act. I am begging her not to walk away, even though I know that's exactly what we both must do.

She storms past me and gives me the middle finger. I'm not so sure that's part of her act.

Nikko stands in the doorway, his lips thinned. "What happened?" he asks after Isabella storms past him. He shuts the door with a click.

I blow out a breath and shake my head. "I fucked with her birth control. She's pregnant. She didn't want to be."

His brows rise, but he doesn't judge. "Oh. Wow. Yeah, that'll do it."

Still, he knows who we are. "I hope you have a nice couch you don't mind sleeping on."

"Yeah, well, it isn't just me who fucked up. I can't trust her either." I turn around, making sure everyone hears me and sees me. I sigh. "I'm going home."

Nikko shakes his head. "Brother, you need to have that head looked at."

I need my head looked at, all right, but not for the reasons he thinks. "I'll take care of it. It's just superficial. Keep an eye on her. I know she's safe here."

I know she's not fucking safe here, and if anybody thinks I'm really leaving, they're out of their fucking minds. That's what they need to believe, though.

I walk to where my car is parked, lean in, and talk to my guard. "You're gonna take my T-shirt. Put it on. Wear this ball cap. Peel out of this driveway and head home. Pretend that you're me. Do anything that I would do. Got it?"

He nods. We quickly exchange clothes. His are too tight on me, but it'll do. "You want me to be a decoy. You're staying back?"

"Exactly."

I stand in the shadow of an overgrown hedge and watch him drive away, then slink down behind the one area of the house that has no cameras trained on it. Even Aria's drones won't see me.

I go down the back door to my mother's basement, where I'll hide out until Javier strikes. And I know it's gonna be soon.

I can't text her. I can't talk to her. I can't reach out to her. I can't even see her on any of the surveillance cameras. Fuck it, I hate this. I need to know she's alright.

I need to know that my new baby is alright.

My phone buzzes with a text from Mikhail.

> Where are you?

> Driving back to my place. Is everything alright?

> They're coming.

# CHAPTER TWENTY-ONE



I PACE back and forth in the Romanov's study, the weight of everything pressing heavily on me.

*I'm pregnant.*

*Javier is using us against each other.*

*Lev and I have broken up publicly.*

*He loves me*

*I'm pregnant.*

The decision to break up with him was a calculated and necessary move... But still, pain lingers a bit, like a fresh wound that only deepens my resolve to face the threat against us.

I will not be held back. *I am Isabella Morales Romanova, and no one will hold me back.*

"Let's get you something to eat," Polina says. "And you need to be doctored up. Are you alright?"

I nod, wiping away tears on my cheeks. I don't have to feign heartbreak because I *am* heartbroken.

Maybe it's the pregnancy hormones. I want Lev. I want to be right with him again. I want him not to be a jerk who fucks shit up on me.

I want my husband.

Meanwhile, my mind is working relentlessly to find any clue that could turn the tide in our favor. I'm working through every possibility in my mind.

What is Javier's plan of attack? He's coming here, that I know. He'll attack the Romanovs and likely come straight for me. They're his enemies, but I betrayed him. There is no greater crime one could commit.

I feel like the knowledge of how to stay ahead of him is right at my fingertips. Right beyond my reach. I know there's more here than meets the eye... but what?

I can't think beyond the strange mix of nausea and hunger that's affecting my concentration.

Polina brings me some food but doesn't ask questions or push. She knows what her brothers are like.

I take a nap, half expecting that I'm not going to be able to fall asleep, but I guess pregnancy takes more out of you than you'd think. It's warm and comfortable here in the guest room. I close my eyes.

Something happens during my nap as if my brain waves fire, and disparate thoughts knit themselves together while I'm sleeping. Because I wake up with an answer to a question, I wasn't sure I had.

It's the map.

*The map.*

When we were in his office making love, the maps crinkled beneath us. There were places marked where Javier struck. Lev's been poring over it.

*That map.* I need to look at that map again.

I call Aria. She answers on the first ring.

"What's up? Are you okay?"

"I'm fine, I need to see into Lev's office. Do you have cameras in there?"

"Honey, you do not put cameras in the Romanov boys' offices. Are you kidding? They'd murder me."

"Okay, alright, fine. Is there a way you *can* get in?"

She laughs. It's a little evil, and I love it. "Of course."

I blow out a breath. "There's a map on the desk... I need to see it."

"Alright. Give me ten. But this did *not* happen."

A few minutes later, my phone rings. "Got it. Open your phone and tap the white triangle."

I do what she says, and crystal-clear footage pops up on my phone. "There." I tap the screen and stare at the map, pointing to a series of what look like random markings. Renata told me there was a map, but I didn't know what she was talking about. It seemed random, trivial, but it isn't.

This is a map of The Cove. When I first saw it, I thought it had something to do with Lev's plan, but now, I know it has to do with Javier's. "These symbols," I tell Aria. "Do they look familiar?"

"Yeah," she says, getting excited. "They look like coordinates. Maybe a code."

"We need to decipher this code. It could lead us to the heart of their operation. I can't see it very clearly here, though."

"This is as close as I can get," Aria says with a sigh.

"Alright. I need to get back to our home."

I'm still calling it *our home*. It isn't *Lev's place* anymore. In my heart, I know... this is where I belong. With him. Together.

"Listen, Isabella. We can't afford any mistakes. This is our chance to strike back."

"I know," I whisper. Javier is on the move; I know that now. "I need to talk to Lev."

*Where is he?*

I pace the room, my stomach growling with nausea laced with anxiety. I want this over with. I know what cruelty Javier is capable of, and I won't allow the Romanovs, *any* of them, to be hurt on my watch.

"I've got Lev on a secure network," Aria says. "No one knows you're talking."

The air crackles between us. "Lev?"

"Are you okay?" he whispers.

"Yeah," I whisper back.

"He's coming. That's all we know, though. We don't know where or when."

My heart pounds. "I think I do. There was a map in your office, and I think it's a code. We know the shipment's coming in. Our plan is to intercept it and make it look like an inside job, right? So Carlos and Javier will suspect each other."

"Yes, but they changed where the shipment's coming, and our sources have dried up. Dmitri has no idea. He says Javier's in a rage and doesn't trust anyone."

I shake my head. It's the exact type of thing my father would've done.

"Yeah," I whisper. "He's a prime candidate for thinking one of his men betrayed him. Listen, that map in your office... I need to see it again."

"Why?"

"It's just a hunch. Listen, you're the one who knows how to decode information and strategize. Let's look at this together."

"That map was only the first one. A draft. The more detailed one is back in the warehouse." In the warehouse. Where we first met. Where he kidnapped me and took me back to his home.

"The warehouse?"

"Yeah," he says softly. "Should we go?"

I nod. "But tell no one. Remember, we hate each other." I frown. "What the hell are you wearing?"

He looks down at his too-tight T-shirt and shakes his head. "Don't ask. Let's get to the warehouse. First, you go outside and say something to my mother to make her believe we're not together anymore."

"My God, your poor mom."

"She'll be fine. I'm arranging for us to switch transport on the way to the warehouse."

Still...

He makes a series of calls, peppered with a good deal of angry cursing in Russian. I don't know what he's saying, but I know we've kept our ruse. Everyone thinks we've broken up.

It's time.

I walk downstairs, clomping the whole way to attract attention. He's long gone, going through back rooms and staircases in his borrowed clothing so no one suspects it's him.

I march out the front door.

"Isabella?" Ekaterina stands on the front step, her gaze world-weary and tired. "Where are you going, love? Lev wouldn't want you to leave."

I shake my head. "I can't stay. I'll be fine. I... It's complicated, Ekaterina." My voice cracks. I don't have to act much at all. It *is* complicated.

Her gaze meets mine, and in that moment, understanding passes between us. "Stay safe," she says quietly. "You are strong. You are resilient. No one can ever take that away from you."

I reach for her hand. "Thank you," I whisper and lean in. "I'll be back." She squeezes my hand wordlessly. I walk toward the car that waits.

I know they're watching. All of them. The Romanovs. My brother's people.

My friends.

My husband.

I slide into the car and pinch the bridge of my nose. I'm trembling. So much is at stake. Everything, *everything* that matters depends on what happens next.

I look out the window when I notice a familiar scent. My skin prickles with awareness. I look around the interior of the car. Why do I smell a familiar scent that... reminds me of my brother? The cloying scent of *Zegna Intenso*, my brother's signature cologne, fills my nostrils. Ice pulses through my veins when I meet the gaze of my driver in the rearview mirror.

"Going somewhere, *Princesa loca*?" Javier says, his look murderous. "Maybe the... warehouse? Yes? Yes! Let's go. I need to introduce myself to your new husband."

# CHAPTER TWENTY-TWO

*Lev*

THE CAR IS SUPPOSED to meet us at coordinates on the east side of the city so Isabella can make a quick transfer.

But it never arrives.

*Fuck.*

I wait five minutes.

Ten.

Where the fuck is she? I pace a groove in the ground outside my car when a text comes in from an unknown number.

*Fuck!*

> Warehouse, Mr. Romanov. We are waiting.
> Come alone or she dies.

My blood boils.

Isabella can hold her own; I know that. She's hardly a helpless female tied to train tracks waiting for me to rescue her.

But she's my *wife*. And she's pregnant.

I'll fucking kill them.

I get into the car, knowing I'm driving straight into a trap. I could call my brothers, but my wife is in danger. If they suspect I called anyone, they'll fuck her over.

If they hurt her... if they harm one single hair on her head...

I get there in record time, park the car, and check my weapons. I've got two semi-automatics pistols, fully loaded, and a knife in my boot. I slam the door.

"Javier!" I scream. "Come out and face me, or are you going to be a fucking pussy?" Rage boils in my veins as I stomp toward the front of the warehouse. The last time I was here, I met my wife, and I dragged her home as a traitor. This time, I'll kill the bastards who threaten her safety and bring her home as my queen.

Together, we'll rule.

The door flies open and Javier Morales himself stands with narrowed eyes, staring at me.

"How nice of you to stop by, Lev. We have a lot of catching up to do, brother-in-law."

"Yeah," I say genially. "We do." I want to see who he's brought with him. I glance around and see no one. "You bring company?"

"No!" Isabella yells from behind him. "He's alone because Carlos betrayed him, Lev."

"Shut up, bitch," he snarls at my wife. It's at that point I stop thinking with my brain.

I close the distance between us in an instant and hit him so fast and so hard, his head snaps back. He comes up, rage in his eyes, lunging at me, but I duck and evade his punch. I come back swinging. "You don't talk that way to my wife," I growl, landing the first satisfying punch to his gut. I hit him again and again. Blood pours from his nose.

I throw Isabella a knife, and she catches the handle mid-air. Pride surges through me. He gets me good, a hard jab to my abdomen. I'm doubled over, trying to catch my breath, when he snarls at me. "You were the one that turned Carlos against me."

I stare at him, too stunned to speak. "Me? I've never even met the guy."

He grits his teeth. "It's your fault. You came to visit your brother in Colombia. He works with my enemies and they promised Carlos more money and attention." He spits on the ground. "If not for you, I would've been the most powerful cartel in the entire world."

Wow. Isabella's right. This asshole *is* a completely delusional prick.

"Your family might," I snap, my gaze locked on his. "But with your sister in power, *not* you." I hit him so hard the nerves in my hand vibrate.

The man staggers back, clutching his stomach, but I don't give him a moment to recover. I reach for a metal pipe and swing it with all my might, the dull thud of the impact reverberating through the warehouse. He drops to his knees, blood dripping from a gash on his temple.

"You made a big mistake coming here," I snarl, lifting the pipe again.

Isabella slashes at the rope that binds her wrists. She comes up behind him, her eyes blazing with a mix of fear and determination. Javier tries to crawl away, but I kick him hard in the ribs, sending him sprawling.

"That's for hurting her." I lift him off the floor, only to throw him down again, hard. "No mercy," I growl, and Isabella nods, understanding the gravity of our situation. Together, we are a force of nature, brutal and unstoppable.

Javier tries to get up again, but Isabella is quicker. She slashes his arm, and he screams in pain, blood spraying from the wound. He swings wildly, catching her across the face with a backhand, but I'm already there. I bring the pipe down on his shoulder with a sickening crack, and he howls in agony.

"You don't hit my wife!" I roar.

Isabella, her cheek already swelling from the blow, moves in with cold precision. She plunges the knife into his thigh, twisting it viciously. His scream is a high-pitched wail of pure agony, and I almost feel pity for him. Almost.

"You think you can hit my wife, disrespect her, and get away with it?" I hiss, leaning close to his ear. "You think you're stronger than we are? That you've won by lying about who we are and what we've done? You're dead wrong."

He gurgles something unintelligible, blood bubbling from

his lips. I grab his hair, yanking his head back and exposing his throat. "Do it," I command Isabella.

"You ruled with terror," she hisses. "Your reign is over, Javier."

Javier's body shakes furiously back and forth with the realization of what is about to happen.

Without hesitation, Isabella draws her blade across his throat in a swift, practiced motion. Blood gushes out, and his eyes widen in shock and horror. He collapses to the ground, twitching, his life draining away in a growing pool of crimson.

We stand there, panting, covered in blood, the echoes of the brutal fight still ringing in our ears. Isabella kneels in front of him. "You will die with the knowledge that *I* am the new head of Los Sangre Dorada. You have lost, Javier. And so has our father."

She looks at me, her face hard but her eyes softening.

"Let's get that damn map and call your brothers," she says quietly. "Before anyone else comes."

I nod, tossing the pipe aside.

We work side by side. Isabella's nimble, blood-stained fingers dance over the map, tracing paths and uncovering hidden messages while my mind maps out the strategic implications of each discovery.

Minutes pass, every second crucial. We're exhausted, but we push through. We've ended the first part of Javier's reign of terror. We have to finish it off completely.

Exhaustion tugs at our edges, but we continue, driven by the glimmer of hope our combined efforts have reignited. Finally, a breakthrough comes.

Isabella's eyes widen as she deciphers the final piece of the code. "Lev, this is it. These coordinates lead to a hidden compound. It's where they're holding prisoners and planning their next move." She shakes her head. "It was under our noses the whole time."

My eyes narrow with fierce determination. "We have to move quickly. We'll gather our forces and strike before they have a chance to retaliate."

I call Mikhail. Isabella places a hand on my arm and whispers, "We can do this. Together."

I bend and kiss her while Mikhail answers the call. I hold her gaze.

"Javier is dead. Carlos is heading to the location I'll send you."

I tap on my phone and send him the coordinates.

"Aria was close," he says with pride. "We've got our men two blocks away. Hang on, they're closing in."

My heart is beating too fast. I don't want to let her go. I came so close to losing her. If only Javier hadn't wanted me to feel the pain of her death, I would have.

In the midst of the chaos and urgency, I find strength in her. Forged by fire, through pain, I feel as if we're invincible. Together, we'll face any storm, and in the aftermath, we'll create our future together.

We leave the lifeless body of our enemy behind, stepping over the blood-soaked floor.

"We're there," Mikhail says. "Stand by." Isabella closes her eyes. We're close. So fucking close. She leans her head on my shoulder, and I slide my arm around her slender back.

"They've got Carlos in sight. Ollie and Nikko are there, and Viktor's not far behind. He has a blonde woman with him..."

Isabella's eyes fly open. "Renata! Oh my God! Be careful with her!"

Mikhail curses. The telltale sounds of a gunfight breaks out, muted by the phone, but Isabella's eyes are filled with terror. She covers her mouth with her hands and whispers a prayer in Spanish. My heart beats along with hers.

I want to give her peace. Quiet. Safety.

*The keys to her kingdom.*

"I've got him!" someone shouts in the background.

"That's Carlos," Isabella whispers. She closes her eyes, and a tear rolls down her cheek. "But what about Renata? My God, how could he bring her?"

He brought her because she was the last bargaining chip, I'd guess. I clench my jaw.

"And the woman?" I ask Mikhail. My heart beats faster alongside Isabella's.

No answer.

"Renata?" Isabella says, her voice choked. "Do you have her?" She cries freely now. Isabella puts on such a brave face, but when she loves, she loves deeply. She's been through so much, my brave, beautiful woman.

She holds her breath, and I hold mine along with hers. I grip her to my chest. Her breathing is ragged, but her heart beats as hard as ever.

Finally, a voice comes on the line.

"I've got her."

It's Ollie.

"You have Renata? Put her on the phone!" Isabella demands.

There's a series of rustles and low voices before a weak female voice comes on the line. "Isabella?"

"Renata! Are you alright?"

"*Sí, estoy bien, no te preocupes por mí. ¿Se fue? El tipo grande mató a Carlos. Gracias a Dios. Diles, Isabella.*"

Isabella's eyes shine with relief and determination.

"Goddamn it, woman. What is she saying?" I demand, my voice impatient.

Isabella lets out a ragged breath. "She said she's fine. She asked if Javier was gone. She said 'the big guy' killed Carlos, thank God. That would be Viktor." She swallows hard. "And then she said to tell them…"

"Tell us what?"

Isabella shakes her head, her eyes pained but victorious. "Tell the Los Sangre Dorado their leaders are dead. Tell them they owe their allegiance to me and you now."

In the dim light of the warehouse, she flips on her camera and flashes a triumphant grin.

"I am Isabella Morales Romanova," she declares. "And this is my husband, Lev Romanov. Javier Morales is dead. Today marks the end of an era. Tomorrow, a new one begins. I want all those loyal to the Los Sangre Dorada cartel to report to me immediately. We will convene this evening."

The message sent, she lowers the camera, her expression fierce and resolute.

"Lev. Take me home."

# CHAPTER TWENTY-THREE



*Isabella*

AS SHE LOWERS THE CAMERA, I see the tension in her shoulders ease. We're not out of the woods yet after Javier's death, but she's accomplished what she set out to do. Determination is etched in the lines of her face, and I know she's ready to face whatever comes next.

She can do this.

*We* can do this.

The silence in the room is almost deafening, the air thick with the weight of our actions. I glance at her, wary yet relieved.

"No remorse for your brother?" I ask, studying her face.

"None," she replies without hesitation. "Lingering doubt? Remorse for my brother?" She scoffs, tossing her head. "It's like you don't know me at all. This was an end to an era that needed ending. My brother was a terrible human who deserved none of the power or accolades he garnered." Her eyes are cold, resolute. "I hated what I had to do, but he would only hurt more people." She shakes her head. "It had to be done."

"I understand," I say softly. "I'm sorry it came to that, but I'm proud of you. Do you think he had any loyal followers left?"

"Time will tell, but I suspect not," she says. "He was the type of leader others wanted dead."

She looks exhausted, and I can see the weight of everything starting to bear down on her. "Now, Lev," she says with a heavy sigh. "Take me home. Please."

I hold her gaze, feeling a surge of protectiveness. "Which home, beautiful?" I ask, pressing a kiss to her forehead.

Her eyes flutter closed at the kiss. "The one here in America first. We'll have to travel to Colombia next."

I nod, wrapping an arm around her protectively. "The clean-up crew is coming. Any special requests for the body?"

She casts one last lingering glance at her brother's lifeless form. "Make sure he is buried. My mother would want that."

We head towards the exit, stepping over the remnants of the battle. In the end, he was just flesh and bone, no longer holding any power over her—or anyone.

And as we step into the night, I know we've crossed a line there's no coming back from. But together, we'll face whatever comes next.

As we approach the exit, my phone rings. *Viktor.*

"Everything secure?" I ask him.

"All clear, Lev. No signs of any more threats."

I blow out a breath. My wife was right. They destroyed themselves internally first. We only dealt the final blow.

Still, tonight's meeting should be interesting.

We step out into the dark of late night, a convoy of black SUVs waiting, engines idling.

Good. It's about damn time somebody else recognizes my wife is royalty.

I help Isabella into the nearest vehicle, sliding in beside her.

The ride back to our house is silent, each of us lost in our thoughts. Isabella leans her head against my shoulder, and I can feel the tension slowly leaving her body. I check to see if she's still awake. Barely, but she's holding her own. She's strong, but even the strongest need a moment to breathe.

As we pull up to our house, the moon is beginning to rise. Our men quickly secure the perimeter, and we make our way inside. On instinct, I check to see if we're safe, but no one's followed us.

There's no one left who would.

Once inside, I lead Isabella to our room. She sits on the edge of the bed, her eyes distant. I kneel in front of her, taking her hands in mine.

"You did great, Isabella," I say softly. "You did great."

She nods, a small, tired smile playing on her lips. "We're not done yet, Lev. Tonight, we must face them. But for now..." Her voice trails off. "I just need a moment. A little rest."

I brush a strand of hair from her face and kiss her forehead. "Rest. I'll be right here."

She lies back on the bed, and I sit beside her, watching as her breathing evens out and she drifts into a much-needed nap. I stay vigilant, my mind already strategizing for the evening meeting. I have Aria send us a list of all men loyal to the LSD.

An hour later, Isabella stirs. She sits up, looking more determined than ever. "Is it time?"

"It's time, beautiful. Hungry? Thirsty?"

"Mmm."

"Let me."

I make her some buttered toast and a cup of hot tea, two of her favorites.

We prepare ourselves for the meeting. She sets us up in the office and starts the video conference call. We patch Mikhail and Aleks in as well.

The atmosphere is charged with anticipation. The members of the Los Sangre Dorada Cartel stare in silence.

Isabella takes a deep breath and steps forward. "As of today, everything changes," she announces. "We are no longer bound by the old ways. Under my leadership, we will rise stronger. Those who wish to continue under my leadership may present their case to me. I will determine who will and who will not continue with me after a series of interviews and tests."

Oh. Smooth move. She will only take men she determines are loyal.

I stand beside her, my presence reinforcing her words. Together, we lay out a vision for the future where loyalty and strength will lead us to unprecedented power.

By the end of the meeting, it feels like the room is filled with a renewed sense of purpose.

"Tomorrow, I will be in contact with each of you. As you are aware, my marriage to Lev Romanov puts us in a unique position of leadership across countries. Do *not* consider any type of retaliation. The Romanovs are willing and able to defend. Those loyal to my brother are disloyal to me."

Some of them pay homage to her, and others leave quietly. All on the roster are accounted for. She isn't worried.

"Before I left Colombia, I established strong relationships with every one of them. Loyal dogs don't bite the hand that feeds them, you know."

I stare at her in disbelief. "How did you do that?"

She shrugs. "I had some money. My father didn't leave me penniless. I paid off gambling debts. Medical bills. I had a few mortgages taken care of and erased the history of some of those on my brother's shit list. It took time, but it was worth it. Did you sense any open hostility among them?"

I shake my head. "No, and I couldn't puzzle why not. I see now." I thought they were just better at hiding it. We end all calls and collapse together back in our bedroom.

Isabella grips my hand tightly. "We've done it, Lev," she whispers. "This is just the beginning."

I nod, feeling the weight of what we've accomplished and what still lies ahead.

"We did. *Together.*"

# CHAPTER TWENTY-FOUR

*Isabella*

THAT NIGHT, I dream fitfully. The greatest threat against us may be gone—for now—but I know as well as anyone that the battle ahead is what really matters.

I wake up every few hours. I place my hand on the flat of my belly and sip from the glass of water that Lev put on my bedside table. I rustle in bed and feel the weight of his hand on my side.

I should be angry with him—should be fucking furious. And maybe I am, somewhere deep down below the surface. I'll give myself space to feel, to process, and to deal with whatever happens. At least I didn't expect this to be all sunshine and roses. But right now, all I feel is... relief.

Javier is gone.

And while he might have some who are still loyal to him—and we *will* weed every last one of them out—he has no power over me anymore. Over any of us.

I hold my belly. It's too new, and I'm not far enough along yet to make it feel real. But I have to admit... I don't feel the way I thought I would.

I told him I didn't want any children. I told him I didn't want to be a mother. But now that it's happening, I'm surprised to find it doesn't feel like the death sentence I thought it would.

A baby. Children. Maybe a little girl who has her daddy's eyes and my spirit. Perhaps a little boy with that dimple in his cheek. Here, in the Romanov family, my children will have people who love them. Aunts and uncles, a grandmother and cousins... a father who actually wants them and a mother who will do anything for them.

I swipe at my cheeks.

I can run the Los Sangre Dorada and have a family, too.

Right?

"What are you thinking?" Lev's voice is rough and husky in the early morning quiet. He gives my ass a playful swat. "You should be sleeping, woman."

"So should you," I retort. I sigh and close my eyes. Nestle my ass closer to him. He groans and hugs me tighter. A shiver of pleasure washes through me at the warmth and weight of his arm over me. I don't *need* a man to protect me, but damn, does it feel good having one who will.

"Sleep, beautiful," he says softly. "We have a ton of shit to do tomorrow."

And the day after, and the day after.

I close my eyes. Wordlessly, he runs his fingers through my hair. Tension seeps out of my body with every gentle stroke. I missed him. I want him.

I'm totally madly in love with him. I focus on my breathing. My rapid heartbeat gradually begins to slow. I close my eyes, and I fall back asleep.

When I wake hours later, the bright light outside my window tells me it's well past sunrise. The smell of bacon and coffee wakes me up. I stretch my arms overhead and sit up in bed, waiting for a wave of nausea. Thankfully, I feel mildly queasy, but that bacon smells like heaven.

I stretch and put my feet on the hardwood floor, the memory of what happened the night before plaguing me.

I should feel more remorse for killing my brother. It was brutal, it was savage... and it had to happen. I knew it did. I'd practiced for that moment for years, and when the time came, I did not hesitate.

But that doesn't mean I liked it.

The door to the bedroom creaks open. Lev stands there, shadowed in the doorway, a silhouette against the frame.

"Morning," he says in that deep rumble of a voice that makes me shiver.

"Morning." I stifle a yawn.

"Coffee?"

"You know it."

A beat passes where the silence hangs between us, and

neither of us moves. We have so much to say that it seems words fail us.

Then both of us talk at once.

"I should be pissed at you—"

"I fucked up—" His voice is choked. Repentant.

"I know why you did it, but you shouldn't have—"

"I did what I thought I had to, but—"

"Maybe having a baby isn't the worst thing—"

"I love you."

Well. That does it.

I stare at him, dumbfounded. "Guess you just pulled the ace. Dealer takes all."

The corner of his lip quirks up, but then he sobers. "I promise you. I'll be the best husband and father I can."

I swallow the lump in my throat. I can't speak above a whisper. "You already are."

I reach for him as he crosses the room with his big strides, invading my space and pushing me back. I welcome the weight of his body on mine. I cherish the taste of his lips. I sigh, sinking into this one stolen moment of peace and forgiveness, such rarities in families like ours.

He tangles his fingers in my hair and gathers my wrists in his strong, rough hands.

"I've missed you," I murmur, my body waking up as if he waved a magic wand in front of me. My pussy tightens, and a low hum of need vibrates through me.

"I've been right here."

I reach for him and pull him over to me. We roll over together. Slowly, our clothes fall to the floor in a heap until we're stripped. I revel in the hard planes of his abs and the broad expanse of his shoulders. The way he looks at me as if I'm the most precious person in the world.

The heat of his gaze, dark and intense, never leaves mine as he lowers himself on me. The warmth of his skin sears mine, every touch a promise. His mouth on mine underscores the way he feels about me and my response acquiescent... to *us*.

My breath catches as his hands roam over my body as if committing every curve and angle to memory. I stifle a moan when his fingers trace the curve of my breasts, my peaked nipples, easing me closer as I arch into him, a silent plea for more.

His hand spans the full length of my back as he holds me to him, and his lips trail a path down my neck. Pausing at my collarbone, he nips the sensitive skin before continuing his journey lower. Every kiss he bestows on me feels like a silent plea for forgiveness. Every sigh I release is a step closer to surrender.

My hands find his back, my fingers digging into the firmness of his tattooed muscles, pulling him closer. The tattered remains of my resistance fall away like ash, gone with the hint of a breeze. Here, it's just us, lost to the world. Lost to the differences that divide us and the friction between us. Here, we become one.

When his mouth fastens on my nipple, I gasp, and my hips rise, crying for more. I relish the dark, utterly masculine sound of his chuckle against my skin.

"Not yet," he rasps, the low reverberation of his voice trailing down my spine.

I stifle a moan as my nerves light up under his touch. I'm trapped in a whirlwind of contradictions—I want this to last forever, and I want him in me *now*. I want to fight and feel him overpower me, and I want to submit and melt into him.

He spreads my legs with a knee, the hard length of his erection pressed into me, a reminder that he sees all of me and he fucking loves what he sees.

That makes two of us.

He rises on one elbow and slides his free hand through my wetness, finding my clit and circling it slowly while his mouth closes on my nipple. I arch and moan. "Lev," I beg, need choking me. He slides through my core, his thumb pressed to my throbbing clit.

"Patience," he growls.

I bite my lip to stifle a whimper.

I've never surrendered to a man in my life.

I've never wanted to.

But in that moment, it takes all the strength I have to calm my frantic need to be filled by him and reunited, and instead, melt into the rising well of arousal and desire.

I slide my hands up the length of his powerful body. He positions himself above me and holds my gaze for a long moment before he enters me in one swift, perfect, satisfying thrust. I cry out, lost in pleasure. We move together as one, united and unafraid, the only people left on earth. Every thrust binds us, every breath we draw a fusion.

As my pleasure builds, he quickens his pace, pushing us both to the edge. I rake my nails down the length of his back, clinging to him, lost to sensation, worshiping his body and giving him mine. I love the way he grips my hips as if I'm not close enough and he needs me closer.

The seconds before climax are heaven. With a final, claiming thrust, we both fly into ecstasy. I scream out his name, waves of pleasure crashing through me. He groans in pleasure as he spills into me.

My hands flatten on his back, and he holds me to him. We lie there, still reeling from the enormity of mutual surrender and shared bliss.

I run a lazy finger over his shoulders, now damp with the effort. He buries his face in my hair and inhales.

As we slowly come back to reality, our duty lingering before us, he presses his lips to my temple. "I love you."

I swallow the lump in my throat and nod. "I know."

He laughs out loud and shakes his head. "You never fail to surprise me."

I ruffle his hair and pull him to me, kissing the rough stubble of his cheek. "Good. You need a little more excitement in your life." I sigh. "And I love you, too. But I really, *really* need to eat something and use the bathroom, and I'm worried about what happened while I was sleeping."

It's time to go to Colombia.

# CHAPTER TWENTY-FIVE

*Isabella*

COLOMBIA IS ONLY one hour behind us this time of year, but I know the cartel, and I know they are moving quickly.

"Let's get ready," Lev says. "We need to fly to Colombia, Isabella. We'll talk over breakfast." I stifle a whimper at the loss of his weight on me when he gets to his feet. "Let's find what you can eat."

I blink. I knew it had to happen, but the reality of it all is giving me a bit of a shock. Yeah, it's gonna be interesting heading up a cartel while being married to the king of the jungle.

But I suppose that will keep things interesting.

Turns out, I can eat anything. He's made bacon and eggs, potatoes and toast. I slather butter on a crispy piece of toasted sourdough and hum approvingly at the rich, tangy taste. I chase that with a few slices of crispy, salty bacon, scrambled eggs, and golden potatoes. I definitely earned this appetite.

"Oh my *God,* this is the best food I've ever eaten in my life."

Lev pours me another cup of coffee. "Have you ever had coffee made in front of a campfire? Bacon still sizzling from the cast iron before the sun rises over the mountain? Eat that shit after a ten-mile hike the day before, and you'll think you died and went to heaven."

"Hmm," I say, buttering another piece of toast. "Can't say that I have, but I'm game to travel. But only if there's running water. And maybe WiFi. Air-conditioning in the summer and heat in the winter. After, like... maybe the baby can walk."

I don't miss the way he cringes when I say *baby.*

"About that," he begins, scratching at his bicep. I stare at the ink beneath his fingers, the dark script that reads *Memento Mori.*

"What does that mean?" I interrupt.

He looks down at the scroll thoughtfully. "'Remember that you will die.' I remind myself every day."

I blink. "That's not morbid at all."

"It isn't," he says, shaking his head. "It just means, appreciate being alive. Today. Today could be the last day you have."

I think of Javier's lifeless eyes. The gravestones in Colombia with my parents' names on them.

I think of the burgeoning life within me and wonder if it doesn't all just make sense.

"I interrupted you. You were going to say something about the baby?" I'm still working on this food. It's delicious, and I'm regaining my strength.

Lev nods soberly, his warm eyes meeting mine. "We need to be careful, Isabella. The life we're stepping into isn't just dangerous for us but for anyone we bring into it. If we're going to have a family... we need to be sure."

I pause mid-bite, the weight of his words settling over me. "You mean, if we're going to have more children."

He nods, his expression serious. "I want them to be safe. I want *you* to be safe."

I put down my fork and reach across the table, taking his hand in mine. "Lev, I know the risks. And I know that our world isn't perfect. But we're building something new, something better. Together. And we'll protect our family with everything we have."

He squeezes my hand, his eyes softening. "I know we will. But it's going to take time. We have to be smart about this."

I nod, understanding the gravity of our situation. "Agreed. We take it one step at a time. For now, we focus on taking control and making the changes we need to. The rest will come when it's right."

Lev's lips curve into a small smile. "You're indomitable, aren't you?"

I grin, picking up my coffee cup. "That's why you married me, isn't it?"

"Among other reasons," he says with a shrug. "It had something to do with you spying on us, if I recall correctly." He winks.

It feels fitting that we met in the warehouse, and we ended Javier in the exact same place. A bookend of sorts. And now, what we needed, what I hoped for—it all lies before us.

I have to keep my head on straight and lean heavily into the strength of my new allies. "Let's talk about our plans."

We finish our breakfast, the conversation shifting to our plans for the day. We discuss our strategy for Colombia, the allies we need to contact, and the changes we'll implement. Despite the challenges ahead, I feel a sense of excitement and purpose.

I like that.

After breakfast, Lev and I pack our bags quickly, preparing for our trip. As I fold my clothes and place them in the suitcase, I can't help but feel a bit of anticipation and nervousness. This trip to Colombia is the first step in solidifying our power and ensuring the future we want, merging our families.

But first, we end the human trafficking.

God, I can't fucking wait.

I look over what I packed. Anything else we need, we can find in my homeland.

*My homeland.*

A wave of nostalgia hits me when I think about going back to where I grew up, where I was raised... my people. I'll never forget the lush, vibrant landscapes, the rolling hills, and the beauty of the Andes. The freedom and peace I felt when I rode my horse in the countryside. The wind in my hair.

The music and dancing during our traditional festivals, the sense of pride and joy I got from celebrating my heritage as if partaking in an ancient dance in which I was only a visitor.

My memories bring both comfort and pain, reminders of what I've forged and what I've lost.

But what lies ahead still thrills me.

"Are you alright?" Lev asks, his hand on my lower back. "Do you need crackers or lemonade or something?"

I smile at him. "How did you know those things can help?"

He shrugs. "I have a sister, a mother, and the internet." I smile at him, but he forgot one thing—an interest in my wellbeing. I know that now.

"I'm good. There's just so much that's happened, and I have mixed feelings about going home to Colombia."

He nods. "Makes sense."

Leaning in, he gives me a quick peck on the cheek, but it's all I need. I draw in a breath and square my shoulders, ready to go. We finish packing in record time.

Lev wraps his arms around me from behind, resting his chin on my shoulder. "Are you ready for this?"

"Yeah, but I need to know. Where is Renata?"

"She's with Ollie," he says, opening the car door for me and gesturing for me to get inside.

"With Ollie," I repeat, but he doesn't offer any more details.

"She's fine," he says. "Promise."

She's my best friend in the hands of men who were rival mafia this time last month. But he's right—I must trust him.

"Can I talk to her?"

"Soon."

I slide into the seat. It's a cool day in autumn, but the seat is warm. "Did you heat the car up?"

"Seat warmer." I didn't know until now how much I needed this in my life.

I lean back and nod, drawing strength from his presence. "Let's do this."

He fields calls on his phone while I watch the world wake up around us. It's a new day, a new beginning. And with Lev by my side, I feel almost invincible.

I wordlessly place my hand on my belly. The thought of having a baby with him... it isn't as bad as I thought.

We make it to the plane in record time. He isn't fooling around—no helicopters or commercial flights. It's a private plane he secured just this morning.

We board the plane, and as it takes off, I gaze out the window at the shrinking landscape below.

Lev takes my hand, squeezing it gently. "To our future," he says, his voice filled with determination.

"To our future," I echo, smiling at him.

As the plane soars into the sky, I close my eyes and steel myself for what lies ahead.

I need to prepare. I need to know everything. My eyes still closed; I ask about the aftermath of last night.

"Was anyone injured?"

"Viktor shot Carlos several times and left him for dead. He then called in to update us; when he returned to collect him, his body was gone; he was found crawling through the woods a while later, it's unclear if he'll survive. Javier is confirmed dead. The clean-up crew took care of him."

"Where are they taking Carlos?"

I open one eye in time to note a shadow crossing his features. With our shift in allegiance, it's time for him to tell me confidential information. It will take time to build a comfortable place of trust. But we're learning. Step by step, little by little.

"A safe house north of The Cove."

My heart surges. He trusts me. He's leaning into this as hard as I am.

I nod. I could ask for coordinates and details. I could ask that he patch me in to talk to whoever's holding him.

Or I could trust that he will operate as he wishes within the confines of his family as I will mine.

Wordlessly, he reaches for my hand and gives it a squeeze. "Thank you for trusting me," he says quietly.

I nod. "Thank you for doing the same." I give him a sidelong look. "Does this mean we're calling a truce?"

He looks back at me, a brow quirked as his lips curve downward. I shiver. I love Stern Lev. "For now. Don't think I'm not gonna whip your ass for what you pulled."

My jaw drops open even as a wave of excitement zaps my nerves. "What? *Me? You* were the one that fucked with my birth control."

He grunts. "I know. I thought we made peace with that..."

"Excuse me, sir, I believe I can bring that up for at least nine more months."

He pretends to be thinking it over. "Fair." He shrugs. "You're still going over my knee."

I swallow hard. But the way his eyes are twinkling tells me everything I need to know. He knows I like this. He knows I crave this. And we both know what we need to do.

We'll get there.

"Is everyone at home alright?"

"At home?" he repeats as if he needs to clarify which *home* I'm referring to. That's where the merging of two families might get a little tricky.

"Yeah. Your mom's place," I say in a whisper.

"Yes," he says. "Everyone's fine. It's you they're worried about."

I stare out the window at the thinning clouds and pale blue sky, so he doesn't see my eyes water. I want to stay strong, but even I can't completely ignore these damn pregnancy hormones. I swipe at my eyes.

"Oh?" I ask.

I fail at hiding my emotions. Wordlessly, his arm snakes around my shoulders, and he pulls me closer to him. He runs a hand down the back of my neck and kisses my forehead.

"Yeah," he whispers. "I told them you were great. I told them you're brave. And I promised them I'd take very good care of you."

I smile but shake my head. "The girls better not think this little jaunt to Colombia gets them out of our next practice."

"Mmm," he nods soberly. "Of course not." His lips still twitch.

I smack his chest. I know he's giving me shit. "I'm serious!"

"I know you are. We'll be back in time."

I lean back against him. "Polina was a fucking beast when they attacked."

He huffs out a breath that's a half laugh and half groan. "You girls are going to make the rest of us obsolete."

I stifle a snort. "Hardly, though I fully intend on using Aria's prowess in support of my plan for world domination."

"I'm sure she would love that." He squeezes my shoulder.

"But will Mikhail?"

"You've demonstrated your leadership abilities and your honesty. I'm sorry any of us ever questioned it. Don't worry about Mikhail. We're allies now."

The power of the Romanov Bratva and the talent of the Los Sangre Dorada will be dynamite. We'll have to exercise caution and use fool-proof methods of communication, for starters. But the potential for what our families could do together is damn near mind-blowing.

"I'll want to coordinate our efforts to rebuild and heal," I tell him.

"And we'll want to do the same."

We all will—our families. Our rival factions.

Me and Lev.

Five hours later, after a few more snacks and naps and establishing our plans, we land in Colombia in the early afternoon.

"Do you have friends here? Allies? Relatives?" Lev asks another question as we gather our bags.

I nod. "Of course, but I'm not here for them. This won't be a time of visiting friends and relatives but securing my men. It's time to assert my authority and make it clear human trafficking is no longer part of our operations. We'll have to squash any dissent."

"Absolutely. And you anticipate some?"

I sigh. "It's inevitable. The key is to bring it to the surface and end it, rather than letting it simmer and cause division."

"And then what?"

I nod. I'm not here on some sort of mercenary rescue mission. I'm here to solidify the newly hatched Los Sangre Dorada and make it my own.

"We will start there. After I see who remains loyal, I'll be better equipped to make our next move."

Lev leans over and kisses me again. "You're going to make an excellent leader."

I wink at him. "So will you."

I step out of the plane into the bright, warm light of my homeland and feel a little wistful. It's so different here, so beautiful, though I think I'll grow to learn to love The Cove in my own way.

Unfortunately, I can't trust everyone here. Not now, not after Javier's death. Though we'll keep my involvement confidential, unrest always follows the fall of a leader. I must settle my family home and put our affairs in order, but first things first—we drive to the cartel's headquarters.

I need to quickly assert my dominance. Calling together the leaders and most powerful members of Los Sangre Dorada, I organize a meeting at my family home. Later today, I have a meeting with a lawyer to manage the property and assets I now control as the sole remaining survivor of the Morales family—the one responsible for carrying on our legacy. It will not be the legacy my father wanted.

Twenty-two men arrive. Two have gone rogue, but I did not come into this position blindly. Juan-Carlo, an older man who took me under his wing when I was just a little girl, has kept me informed. The two who have gone rogue were stealing from Javier and expect blowback. I'll deal with them later.

"Thank you for coming," I tell the men assembled before me. Lev sits beside me, his back ramrod straight. I don't miss the way the men stare at him with a mixture of respect and fear—his reputation, and the reputation of the Romanov Bratva, has preceded him.

Lucky me. There's something about knowing this man who they fear, this man who is mine, that makes my heart beat faster. I squeeze his hand under the table. He runs his thumb over the top of mine. I swallow and clear my throat.

I begin, my voice commanding. "In the wake of my brother's death, I will assume the position as head of Los Sangre Dorada. Effective immediately, all human trafficking operations end. We will be completely disassociated from any tasks or connections. Anyone caught defying this order will answer directly to me." I look at Lev. "To both of us."

I will not wait one more second to end this reprehensible work.

I let the weight of my words settle. "We have many other lucrative avenues of revenue to pursue." Murmurs ripple through the room, some nodding in agreement, others looking uncertain.

Lev stands, his presence a silent promise of support. When his deep voice rings with authority, the men sit up straighter. "Isabella and I are united in this decision. We expect loyalty and commitment to these new directives. Anyone who disagrees is free to leave—but understand that opposition will not be tolerated."

It's crucial they know that Lev and I will rule together. They might try to defy me alone, though usurping my place of position would be difficult since none of them have Morales blood. But *none* dare defy me with the power of the Romanov Bratva at my back.

I look into Lev's eyes with my next words. "I have secured an alliance with the Romanov Bratva. The combined forces of our families will forge us into a powerhouse."

We hold hands in front of everyone. I stand straighter. "Any questions?"

I field a handful of questions, but thankfully, these men were loyal to me, and few were to my brother, the dictator. It's honestly going better than I anticipated.

Over the next few days, we work tirelessly. I do my best to be firm but fair with Lev by my side. Slowly, I begrudgingly earn the respect of the remaining few who were initially skeptical, those I hadn't won over before Javier's demise. With Lev's strategic mind and unyielding support, the transition is smoother than I had hoped.

Within a few days, our trafficking ring crumbles like a rickety old bridge. I take pleasure in watching those held captive set free while simultaneously working our other income streams. Solidifying the cartel's new normal will take time, but the initial days are promising.

With the amount of work that we need to do, we stay a bit longer than planned. It doesn't take long for us to hit our first wrinkle. I'm honestly relieved because there's no possible way we'd skate through this transition without opposition. I'd rather bring the toxins to the surface now and cleanse them for good.

"A small faction is resisting our new direction," Juan-Carlo tells me, scrubbing a hand across his leathery face. His warm brown eyes are wary. "Address them directly and publicly. They are too cowardly to continue."

I nod and call a meeting.

When everyone is assembled, I take my place as their leader. I stand and address them.

"It's come to my attention that some of you are unhappy with my decision to end what my brother began." I sip on a glass of lemon water, hoping my nausea subsides. I need to stay strong in the face of adversity, no matter what it takes. No one here needs to know I'm pregnant yet. They might see it as a vulnerability they can exploit, and I have yet to determine who's loyal.

Damn it, though, I'm craving a good, hearty plate of golden empanadas and an afternoon nap, but duty calls.

One of the dissenters stands, his voice laced with defiance when he addresses me. I know exactly who he is—Luis Esperanto. "You are ruining us! Your plan eliminates forty percent of our income." He spits on the floor, eyes flashing. I open my mouth to speak when Lev gets to his feet, his hands clenched.

I put a steadying hand on his shoulder.

"Ruining us?" I scoff, my voice cutting through the tension. "Esperanto, what's truly ruining us is clinging to the filthy, reprehensible business of human trafficking. It's a stain on our legacy, a legacy that I will *not* allow to be tarnished any further. If you're so concerned about our income, perhaps you should focus on expanding the countless other ventures we have instead of whining like a coward." I meet his gaze squarely. He isn't the type to take direction or a dressing down from a woman, but I give him no choice. I place both of my hands on the table in front of me.

"And let me make one thing perfectly clear," I continue, my eyes boring into his. I put the full weight of my power as leader of the Los Sangre Dorada behind my glare. "This organization will evolve, with or without you. Adapt or get left behind. If you can't see the value in forging a more honorable path, not to mention the potential of far more lucrative means ahead when we eliminate distractions and harness the power of our resources, then you're not just a hindrance—you're a liability. And liabilities, Luis, have no place in my operation."

"Are you threatening me?" he snaps.

Lev vibrates beside me, holding himself back with concerted effort.

"Oh, love," I say, my voice laced with condescension. "You are hardly a threat. You are so much more expendable than the women you parade so casually." I cock my head to the side. "When was the last time *you* gave birth to an heir?" Some of the men snicker.

I pause, letting my words sink in. "So, I suggest you either get on board with the new direction or find yourself a new line of work. Because trust me, I won't lose a wink of sleep over cutting dead weight."

He opens his mouth and closes it again, finally sitting down with a huff of anger.

Lev stands beside me. I nod.

"Talk to my wife like that again, and I'll make you regret it... you'll beg for death before the end." Lev's voice is a low, dangerous growl, radiating anger in palpable waves. The men shift uneasily, murmurs rippling through the crowd. His eyes, cold and lethal, lock onto the dissenter, promising pain and retribution.

I nod my thanks to him and continue, my tone icy. I will not put up with this bullshit.

"Let me be clear. I will not tolerate dissent, not from any of you. Those of you before me now are here as an act of mercy from me."

The man's lip curls in a sneer, but before he can respond, Lev speaks up again. "This is the new order. Adapt or I'm happy to escort you out."

The look on his face says what he doesn't say out loud—he would be more than happy to escort him.

"Some resist change," I say, my voice loud and clear. "But change is necessary for us to grow. And grow we will."

No one speaks for long moments. "What will it be?" Lev asks, his tone grim and his gaze steely. Realizing the futility of resistance, the man nods his head, grumbling.

"You'll watch for any dissent among them," I say quietly to Juan-Carlo. "And report directly back to me."

But with each day that passes, as we prove with the data we've collected that the power of the Romanov Bratva alliance will make us thrive, dissent dwindles. The men here have longed to be part of something greater. My brother did me a favor, sowing dissension and rivalry among his men. Now that I've given them this opportunity, they're grateful.

Being a member of the strongest cartel in Colombia with the ability to influence North America is an opportunity none here would ever take lightly.

In all of this, my respect for Lev and his for me grows. We have weathered the storm of resistance and come out stronger on the other side.

One evening, after a particularly grueling day of dealing with cartel business, he pulls me close, his eyes softening as he looks at me.

"You've done it," he murmurs, his voice filled with admiration and a hint of pride. "The transformation is happening. I got off the phone with Mikhail earlier, and he's fucking *thrilled* with what's unfolding down here."

I smile. Good. And we've only just started. *"We've* done it," I tell him. "And we have a lot of work yet to do, but we can do it."

Life isn't a fairy tale. We both know that, but neither of us were fairy-tale people to begin with.

The road ahead is littered with challenges, and we are already facing many of them. But there is a strength in our union that makes the fight worthwhile.

I sigh, feeling the weight of the day's battles lift slightly as I place my hand on my belly, a symbol of the new life we are nurturing together. I lay my head on his shoulder, finding solace in his unwavering support.

"Transformations *are* happening," I say with a smile. "And out of all that's happened and will... ours is my favorite."

# EPILOGUE

*Lev*

"I REALLY THINK I want to do...*neutrals*. Something calming. You know? White, ivory, beige..." Isabella waves her hand around the room and places her hand on her belly. She tips her head to the side and turns to look at me. "What do you think, Daddy?"

Isabella struts around the room, a spring in her step that speaks volumes about her new role as the reigning queen of the LSD. Her heels click on the hardwood floors.

"Wow, that didn't take you long."

"Long?" she asks, her gaze curious. I love when she looks at me like that.

"I expected you to be a lot more focused on the Colombian contingent of our kingdom," I say teasingly. I lean down and kiss her cheek. Even with those death-defying heels on, she's still so much smaller than I am. Not that it holds her back in the least.

"Did you think running a cartel would take all day? Please, Lev. I have standards. Efficiency is everything."

I smile at her. "How did the meeting with the council go?"

"Let's just say they won't be questioning my authority anytime soon," she replies with a wink. "They learned the hard way that underestimating a woman is a very bad idea. Now, back to more important business. *Neutrals,* or color? What do you think?" She leans back and puts her hand on her abdomen with a flourish. "For the baby."

"What do I think? I think you're funny, laying your hand on your belly like that, as if you're nine months along and ready to burst." It's only two weeks after we've come back to The Cove from Colombia, and she's in full-on mama-to-be and queen-of-the-kingdom mode.

"I have a bump!" she protests, though her warm, dark eyes twinkle at me. "Honestly, Lev. You act as if it's normal for me to have a belly like this."

I brace my hands on either side of her slender frame and bend down to kiss her tiny belly. "You look like you had a burrito and maybe have a bit of indigestion."

She bats me away but can't help the grin that spreads across her face. "But I wasn't even asking about my belly. *Yet,*" she amends. "What do you think about doing a nice, calm, neutral aesthetic?"

"Have you been talking to Polina again?"

"Of course," she says with a sniff. "I never had a sister. I have years to make up for." I was unprepared for how it would make me feel, seeing Isabella with my sister and mother. In some ways, I've taken it for granted, having a family like mine, something she never had. After all I've done to her, offering her the comfort of family and home seems like the least I could do.

I shrug. "I think you should do whatever the hell you want. I don't care. You want to do rainbow-stripes or an underwater sea adventure or those cute little elephants, have at it."

She snorts and purses her lips. "Cute little *elephants?*"

"You know," I say, shrugging. "Those little cartoon ones they put on all the baby gift bags and shit."

"Once again, we've hit another weirdly American thing. We don't really do these elaborate theme things."

I nod and shove my hands in my pocket. "Neutral it is. Do you have any Colombian traditions I *do* need to know about?"

She rests her hand on my arm. "I love that you're asking."

"I need to know these things. I mean, I could Google, but..."

"Much better to ask your wife. I like that theme."

We walk out of the room hand in hand. I've learned that in some respects, it is better to ask my wife. The push and pull between us is something that thrills me. I never want to lose that spark, that fire. But Isabella knows her mind and I love that about her.

"Let's see," she says thoughtfully, as we walk toward the kitchen. "Baptism, of course. It's a very significant event in my country. We have the ceremony and follow it with a large reception."

I nod. "Done." I pull out food and arrange it on the counter while she chops up lettuce.

"We do have baby showers."

"Of course." I take down plates and fill two glasses with water.

"In Colombia, we select the godparents fifteen days before the baby is born. We'll have to talk about that, though, Lev."

I put out silverware and nod. "You want Renata to be the godmother?"

She slides the chopped lettuce into a bowl and takes it to the sink to wash. "I do."

Renata is still being held in captivity by Ollie. Though Isabella has said she trusts her, she didn't argue when we told her we'd have to vet her thoroughly. That tells me she wants to be sure her best friend isn't compromised either.

"Fair. I can make that happen."

She takes out a container of rice and beans and begins to heat it up. I've gotten used to rice and beans around here, a staple of her diet and a nod to her heritage. "I'd like traditional foods at the baby shower. Empanadas, tamales, and arepas, please. And I'd like to help prepare them."

"Makes sense. It's important you help me understand what and how you want to celebrate your family's traditions."

She plates rice and beans for both of us. "Of course." Reaching across the table, she squeezes my hand. "Thank you. I guess I must forgive you, hmm? Your groveling really is quite touching, *mi querido jefe.*"

I take my hand away and roll my eyes. "Is that so?" She's not wrong. A man does not screw around with a woman's birth control, knock her up, and go about his day like he didn't majorly fuck up.

We've made peace with it all, though. We fought long and hard to get to where we are and we will still, but we've made it this far. She's pregnant, and no longer furious at me for putting her in this position. She talks about the baby's coming with excitement. She'll be such a good mama to our baby.

We've united our two families. And while we still have a long way to go when it comes to outing all our enemies and putting an end to the threats against us, we both know this: we'll always have to be vigilant. There will always be another threat, another danger. But with our families joined together, we're so much stronger than we've ever been before.

"Any drama?" she asks, taking an ample bite of her lunch.

"Always. Ollie and Renata are like a powder keg, waiting to explode. He still doesn't trust her."

Isabella frowns. "I'll have to have a talk with her. But you know..." she taps her chin thoughtfully. "There's potential there."

I stare at her, unblinking. "You're kidding, right? You thought *we* were like oil and water? They're like gasoline and a lit match, Isabella."

She shrugs and takes a sip of her water. "Meh. It's not like I didn't expect that. We Colombian women like to spit fire.

And a little drama is just part and parcel." She smiles sweetly.

I shake my head. "I won't argue with that. Expansion is a good thing, though. Clearly."

Isabella nods, her eyes sparking with excitement.

Uh oh.

"Speaking of which, how do you feel about expanding our little empire? I'm thinking some place tropical. I hear Hawaii is just ripe for a little business."

"Hawaii."

"Mmm," she says thoughtfully. "There's so much *potential*."

"I'll give you potential." I shake my head.

She wiggles her brows at me and slowly pushes up from the table. Apparently even with her nonexistent baby bump, the woman can still *run*.

I don't care, though. She can run all she wants. She can even hide.

I will always chase her.

I thrill at the capture.

Isabella Morales *Romanova* is mine and always will be.

*THE END*

# CHAPTER ONE

*Ollie*

There are two types of people in this world: those who lie well and those who are shit at it.

Santiago Morales is the latter.

The goddamn pussy kneels on the rain-soaked ground, a thin trail of blood trickling from a wound in his forehead. His cheeks are hollowed, his dark brown eyes haunted and gaunt. Isabella Morales's first cousin is a walking skeleton, haunted with terror of the devil he serves, in the custody of the devil he fears.

Sucks to be him.

But Jesus. Even I would feed the men who worked for me. The guy looks like he's subsisted on bread, water, and a steady diet of waterboarding. Carlos Carrero is a fucking narcissistic tyrant.

"Please," he begs in broken English. "I don't know."

The shifting storm clouds over the late afternoon sky reveal his terrified eyes. I fucking hate the way he trembles. He knows where Renata is, and he deserves to die.

Renata Carrero is *mine*.

I walk in a circle around Santiago as his bloodshot, widened eyes track me. He licks his dry, cracked lips and swallows, as if trying to gather up his courage.

"You have to understand," I tell Santiago in a deceptively calm voice. "The entirety of our operation hinges on finding Renata. If we don't find her, we're at an impasse. She has information on us that's incredibly time sensitive." I lean over and pat his cheek. He flinches as if I'm wielding a whip. "Doesn't that make sense to you? Hmm?"

At eight o'clock this morning, back in The Cove, our men holding Renata in custody were found dead with bullets between their eyes.

Just as well, really. I would have had to kill them for letting her go.

"I don't know. I swear to God, I don't know!" he sobs. I clench my jaw and glare at him. Jesus motherfucking Christ, let me go out of this world with my balls intact, no matter the circumstances.

I narrow my eyes and stand in front of him, my arms crossed. Emotions like this never move me. Some people think I'm the quiet one because "still waters run deep" or some poetic shit like that.

I keep quiet because I don't give a fuck about playing Mr. Nice Guy. It's just easier to shut the fuck up. Makes people wonder.

"You can kill me," the pussy says, looking away. Bluffing his fucking mouth off. "Do whatever you want to me, I swear I don't care! But you have to believe me, I don't know."

I sigh and shake my head.

A dog barks and an angry woman screams something unintelligible at the market behind us. Worked out well the marketplace was in full swing today because the muffled sounds of the people behind us mask our job. Even if they did see us, they'd keep walking. No one in this neighborhood gives a fuck about us and knows better to go anywhere near business involving the cartel.

I stare at him and shake my head.

I don't care that he's covered in blood. I don't care that I'll instruct my men to make an example out of him, to bury him and spread the news of his death far and wide. All I care is that I'm looking for answers, and I'm going to find her no matter what.

In the distance, a siren wails, momentarily blocking out the chatter of the market.

I let out a belabored sigh and shake my head. "It doesn't have to be like this, Santiago." The two men I brought with me stand stoically behind me. Loyal to the Morales cartel they're now loyal to the Romanov Bratva by association since my brother's marriage to Isabella.

The one to my left has short gray hair and a neatly-trimmed beard. His clothes are pressed, and the ink on his upper right arm indicates his affiliation with Fuerzas Militares de Colombia — the Colombian military.

The guy beside him is younger but larger, his muscles flexing when he clenches his fists. He reminds me of my brother Viktor — bulky, muscular, fearless. Both of these men hate traitors, and I don't fucking blame them.

One speaks in rapid Spanish to the other, and they both shake their heads. I speak Spanish but poorly, so I only catch the gist. They said something about this taking too long. They would be happy to help me.

There was a time when the man bleeding out in the rain, begging for his life, considered these two his brothers. They would've died for Santiago and his family.

They want justice.

They don't care where she is. All they care about is making an example of this asshole so no one else gets the wrong idea again.

"If you tell me what I need to know, I'll make it worth your while." Now I'm the one lying. He's getting a bullet between his eyes no matter what he does.

*"¡Por favor, señor! No puedo decirle nada. Carlos fue el que me lo dijo. ¡Él es el que la persigue, es a él a quien debe encontrar!"*

Carlos? Even though I know Spanish, I shake my head. This doesn't make sense. "Carlos Carerro is dead."

Carlos Carrero was found dead before I came down here. Confirmed. We buried him beside Javier.

He realizes his mistake and quickly shakes his head. He jabbers on in Spanish so broken and rapid I don't quite get everything. It doesn't help I'm fixated on what he said either.

*Carlos.*

*Carlos fucking Carrero.*

Renata Carrero's brother. Our mortal enemy. If Carlos is alive, we've got bigger problems than we realized.

I take a step toward him and grip his hair. "You mean to tell me Carlos is still alive?" He's made a big fucking mistake telling me this.

The two men look at each other in wide-eyed terror. I can see the whites of both of their eyes. One of them whispers a rushed prayer, as if on instinct. If Carlos is alive, they're fucking dead.

I don't want a sliver of misunderstanding between us, so I speak to them in their native language. My voice booms in the narrow alleyway so loudly they both jump. "*¿Alguno de ustedes sabe algo sobre esto!*"

*Do either of you know anything about this?*

"*No, señor,*" they say in unison.

Santiago cries to himself. I turn and stare in his eyes. "You're lying. I know you are." I speak softly, almost gently, making sure he hears every damn word I say. "Carlos Carrero is dead. And you know exactly where she is and who took her."

He shakes his head, his full body trembling. "I don't!"

Jesus he's stubborn. I glare at him. "Show him," I snap at the men.

In seconds, they pull up screenshots from Santiago's phone showing Renata's arrival. "We've been watching. We know," the older man says, his voice cold and unwavering. Renata's beautiful face is evident despite the grainy resolution. "This was taken today."

Santiago pales, now that the evidence of his betrayal is undeniable. He turns his head, as if looking away will make this all go away. The coward.

I *hate* cowards.

"You thought you could hide her and get away with it. You thought you could be a pawn for those who wish to betray us." I lean in closely. "You thought you could lie and survive."

He sobs, shaking his head from side to side.

"Do you know what happens to those who betray us?"

"No! No!" the whites of his eyes remind me of a rabid animal. I shake my head and stand up straighter.

I'm done. If Carlos is out there, we've got to fucking *move*. We're goddamn sitting ducks.

I nod to the men behind me. The gray-haired one pulls out a gun and hands it to me. I love the heft and weight of it and how easy it is to pull the trigger. I love the feel of the cold metal in my palm and barely restrain myself from caressing it.

I aim the gun at Santiago's head. He babbles on and on in

Spanish and then begins to plead in broken English. "No! No, please, I have family. You can't—"

I spit on the ground. "They're better off with you dead than knowing you're a traitor."

"I didn't — I'm not—"

The gunshot echoes through the alley. Santiago falls to the ground. His head hits the pavement with a sickening thud, blood splattering his gaunt face.

Maybe this is the part where I should feel something. Remorse, perhaps? Regret? Something that makes me human and not a robot conditioned to react and never feel... but no. I'm only mildly relieved one more traitor's gone and definitely pissed off we didn't get more from him.

I want Renata Carrero for myself.

Frowning, I turn to leave.

"Clean this up. Make sure they all know what happens to traitors."

"Si, señor. Should we speak to Isabella first?"

"Yes. Ask her the best way to communicate this message and do not take all fucking day doing it."

"Si, señor, si."

I walk into the shadows as the sun sets, rain beating down on Santiago's pathetic, lifeless body behind me.

It's all fucking behind me.

She's here. I know she is. I can fucking feel her here. And when I find her, *she'll* find out what happens to traitors, too.

Pre-Order your copy of 'Savage: A Dark Bratva Arranged Marriage Romance' by scanning the QR code below (Available September 27, 2024):

Fueled by dark chocolate and even darker coffee, USA Today bestselling author Jane Henry writes what she loves to read – character-driven, unputdownable romance featuring dominant alpha males and the powerful heroines who bring them to their knees. She's believed in the power of love and romance since Belle won over the beast, and finally decided to write love stories of her own.

Scan the QR Code below to receive Jane's Newsletter & be notified of upcoming new releases & special offers!

Be sure to visit me at www.janehenryromance.com, too!

www.ingramcontent.com/pod-product-compliance
Lightning Source LLC
Chambersburg PA
CBHW070410310726
48977CB00003B/628